ANOTHER SON

Cover design by Linda Kosarin/The Art Department
Typeset by Raymond Luczak
Cover photo copyright of the author

For more information, please contact:

Web: www.kurtisbell.com
Email: anotherson@kurtisbell.com

Published by Isabell Fromme Publishing.

Paperback: 978-0-9995823-0-5
Hardcover: 978-0-9995823-1-2
Ebook: 978-0-9995823-2-9
Kindle: 978-0-9995823-3-6

Distributed by Ingram Content Group
Printed in the United States

First edition 2018

ANOTHER SON

The Story of a New Teacher
for the Modern Age

KURTIS BELL

Isabell Fromme Publishing

CONTENTS

AUTHOR'S NOTE

As this is the book of a new teacher, his lessons and dialogue are in standard print and without quotation marks.

The narrator's dialogue is in italic to make it easier to differentiate.

I am the author of this book. I am not the teacher nor the narrator. The story contained within this manuscript is fiction but the teachings in this book are non-fiction. The lessons are based on scientific knowledge and religious beliefs combined to make sense of the seemingly incomprehensible.

Life and living are not fictional or fantasy, life and living are very real and raw. To deny the reality of the true nature of life is to escape truth.

INTRODUCTION

I am of no importance. This is the story of my friend. A person I've come to admire, believe, and understand. Though he often confused me, I found that I truly loved him, as I have never loved anyone or anything else, ever. Deeply, profoundly, beyond all reason why. He is someone I cannot even attempt to explain to you. I feel strongly, however, that he is someone that I need to introduce to you in order to keep him alive in spirit and memory. To keep his teachings and lessons viable and current.

He told me, I must try to share any knowledge that I have that will help another person. Sharing of knowledge is the most precious ability that human beings possess over all other animals.

This is the story of a man that made a lot of sense of the world around me. What he had to say also helped me to understand the people around me, and myself as well. He was a good man. He knew and felt things that I have always known and felt but never really thought about or really understood.

He was a dangerous man to many in this world. He was a bright light to others. He was human like me and you, but he was something more. He just knew things that he shouldn't, unless he was crazy or mystic, but he was neither crazy nor mystic. He was kind; he was helpful in a way that would last for a lifetime. He was the most normal yet abnormal person I'd ever known. When he talked, I'd listen because there was so much more to what he said than the words alone would convey. He understood things; not just knowing about something. He understood things like from personal experience; that is why he seemed to understand far more profoundly than just simply knowing. In other words, he had wisdom. He understood: humor as well as sorrow, pleasure as well as pain, desire and fear. He could horrify you and at the same time he could comfort you. When he talked with people, you knew he understood them and accepted them as he did himself. He did not judge or prejudge. He praised and was joyful.

His was the culmination of a person's life experience and the knowledge obtained in that lifetime as relayed to me over three years. I met and lived with many people during those three years but all seem very vague to me now in the light of that one person.

My friend had a simple way of looking at the complex world around him and life in general. He rendered a simple lesson and delivered an all too familiar message. He was a human being of the modern world with a seemingly innate and personal awareness of all of history, almost as if he had actually lived it. He just had a way of saying things that made everything appear much clearer. He made abstract concepts, events, and other people in this world make sense; especially the concepts, events, and other people that just don't make sense to most of us, or are just too horrible to fathom.

Long-standing mind sets and beliefs take time to modify and over the course of much time it became easy for me to see the obvious logic in his credo. As with any great teacher, he said much more in his actions than in his words.

His teachings were, at times, seemingly very repetitive and verbose. But I understood why after a while. Every human being is extremely different and the way they see and understand the world is immensely diverse. The knowledge that he was trying to relay had to be done in various ways to be understandable to the huge variety of people that he met so his teachings did not have to be interpreted by others for individuals to comprehend, as it is for so many teachers and prophets of the past. He knew from history that when lessons were interpreted by others then the meanings could become manipulated to serve the interpreter's purpose and lose the true intention.

The one thing he taught me was the most important thing in the universe and that is we live only in the present. Now I understand; I can choose to look at my curses or look at my blessings, I can choose to make a change in my life or let things be as there are, and I can cherish and appreciate this moment or let it slip by unnoticed. The present is the key to all things past and future. It is the fulcrum upon which all things balance. The present is the point where I build or I destroy. It is the instant that changes my eternity. It is the handle on which my hand rests that pulls my future in one direction or the other. It is the point where everything affects everything. Now I truly understand why he said that the most important thing in the universe was this instantaneous moment of the present because it is now, and no other time, that you live. This is life; and life and living is simply only the present.

Who or what God is, and what the afterlife is or what it is about, or if either even exists, is really not important. People have obsessed over these concepts since the beginning of the species but they are really not essential. How humans treat other humans and all living things is what is important. If that is done well then everything else will be pleased and pleasing. What is crucial is how you live and consider all other living things.

I would venture to say with the utmost conviction that after hearing his teachings, you will have a vastly increased understanding of yourself, and the world. "Give a man a fish and you feed him for a day, but teach him how to fish and you feed him for life." What he taught me did not give me knowledge; it gave me knowledge of knowledge. He gave me understanding.

MY STORY

My story starts from the first time I met this man. For me that was the beginning.

I am an ordinary person without a strong or notable family history. My father was a working man like his father before him and so on. My mother, too, was an ordinary person, special to me of course, she was my mother and I loved her. But she, at the time, was considered a housewife because she stayed home and took care of the house, my two brothers, and me. Her lineage was the same as my father's. I am the same as my mother and father, just an ordinary working person trying to take care of myself and enjoy a reasonably good life doing the things I like to do. I was married when I was younger, and now I'm divorced, without children and on my own.

A little over three years ago I was in the process of moving to a bigger city with the hope of exploring my opportunities of a better job and to meet more and different people. I essentially dropped everything, packed some bags, and left. I wanted to expand my horizons. I was driving a vehicle that had served me well for several years but now seemed to have an issue with staying running for more than a kilometer before it wanted to stop and die. I had my head under the open hood looking at all the different components. I was trying to figure out if there was something that I could do to keep it going long enough to get to someone who hopefully knew more about the problem than I did and would fix it without emptying my bank account. I heard a vehicle slow down and pull in front of my car behind me. I turned around to see a bus, like an old converted school bus and a couple of people get out. One came toward me. I was a little apprehensive as the road I was on was somewhat deserted and there seemed to be many more of them than just my meager, little lonesome self here and I felt kind of isolated and vulnerable.

A man came up to me slowly which put me in the awkward position of not knowing whether to stand there and stare at him or continue looking under my hood like I was minding my own business. As I contemplated which to do, I kept seeing more and more people emerge, not particularly well-to-do types, which didn't help to alleviate my unease. Oddly, though, I did seem to feel slightly better when I saw a couple of females in the group. In that instant, I thought that rather strange because just the fact that there were females in the group did not necessarily make them any less likely to take advantage of my situation.

While I was in my "don't know what to do" state, the rather tall, well-built man in his mid-thirties, steadily walked up to me and asked, in a deep soothing voice, if he could be of any assistance. I confessed to him that I really didn't know what the problem was but that the car just didn't seem to want to go any farther.

He looked in the engine compartment then up at me with a kind, slight smile and said, "You have any gas in it?"

"Yeah," I answered, "I just filled up a while back."

"Well," he nodded and gazed back at the engine, "at least the simplest question has been taken care of." After a moment, he said, "I have to confess, I'm looking in here because it seems like the thing to do, but I really don't know why because I have no expertise in mechanical things. I don't know what the problem is and I'm probably not going to figure it out by fooling around in here. Give it a try and let's see what she does."

Without paying any attention to what the other people were doing, I hopped back in the car and tried to start it. This time the engine kept turning without any sign of starting and shortly the sound of a battery losing juice, so I stopped. More of a feeling of dread came over me as I knew that I was stranded and now this stranger and his group were aware of it as well.

The man's face appeared from around my hood and looked at me with tight lips, in an expression of; "looks like you're not doing well and I would hate to be in your shoes." But I felt it as compassion for me and not a look of a predator at his prey. I got back out of the car and walked back to the front and looked in at the engine for lack of anything else to do. I had a cell phone that either decided to die or just couldn't get a signal from there, I wasn't sure which and I wasn't in the mood to find out; it just wasn't working, that I knew.

"My name is Billy," he said, holding his hand out. "Unfortunately, none of us have a working cell phone here. Why don't you hop in the van with us and we'll get you up the road where we can get you some help?"

My hesitance and expression must have been obvious as he continued, "I promise we're not going to take advantage of you. We're not a gypsy commune or a party gone wild. We're just a group of travelers heading down this road. Come on and meet everyone."

With that I secured my car and walked with him over to his friends and made introductions all around. Their warm welcome made me feel more and more at ease. Soon I became aware of a man in among the rest that was different. Not that he looked any different from the others, and not that he said anything particularly different, or acted any differently other than being somewhat more reserve; but he just seemed like he took everything in and just had an understanding.

Something about the way his eyes would look around at everything and then look into yours. His expression was soft and reassuring; genuine. I had an odd feeling, not a bad odd, just a different odd feeling, that I somehow knew this person from somewhere; like I knew more about him than I should. It was a comfortable feeling, as if we were friends somehow. Though I knew I had never actually seen this person before, it was a chemistry, I guess, that I felt he knew more about me than he could or should have, and I was okay with that.

Before long though I got the feeling that he had that effect on everyone there. This was a group of people that you really wouldn't expect to be travelling down the same road together, not to mention in the same vehicle. They were all different types of people; different ages, nationalities and energy levels. I got the feeling that at least most of them had been traveling together with him for a little bit of time already.

He was a simple, easy going man of average stature and ordinary features. His body looked a youthful mid-thirties but his calmness made him seem older. The most distinctive thing about this man was just how ordinary he appeared. His heritage appeared to be a mix between the African continent and Europe. Even the tone to his voice wasn't notable in any way. In fact, he didn't seem like he had any real definitive accent of any kind. Oddly, as time went on, the inflictions in his accent seemed to change depending on what he was saying. He could have originated from the middle East, the Far East, Europe, or even the Americas. His dialect was impossible to pin point. Whatever his origin he was worldly and well-travelled.

Before getting on the bus, he had introduced himself as Jos. I wondered if it was short for Joseph, but apparently it wasn't, his name was just Jos. Everyone pronounced his name with the O long like "Joe" with a hiss at the end. The one thing that I noticed about him that was different was that when he spoke people actually wanted to hear what he was saying. That was my first insight into the man that I would come to know as a remarkable person and friend.

He invited me to join them on the bus until we could find someone to help with my car. Soon I was on the bus and heading down the road with a whole bunch of new people. For a long while there were the normal welcoming questions and ice breaking banter that comes when you first come into contact with a new group of people. When there was a lull in the conversation Jos took the opportunity to speak. Everyone immediately directed their attention to him.

Driving Is a Good Way to See Humans Interact With One Another

Driving down the road, especially in traffic, is a great example of how humans treat other humans. It is a good analogy of how we intermingle and get along with other people that we do not know.

Many emotions come into play when we are driving. We can see, and tend to show others, our "status" or "wealth"; to some, that does not matter. We can see how the vehicle is cared for, or if it is cared for. Some people name their vehicle and treat it as a living thing and others do not, and even think the idea is silly.

It is a good way to see how we feel about others and how we want others to see, or not see, us. Are you trying to hide yourself from others or are you right out in the open? Are your windows tinted dark or are you in a convertible?

Driving is regulated by governments, and traffic laws are in place to make driving safer for everyone. But, unless everyone follows all the rules, without exceptions, then the safety that the rules are trying to ensure become less effective. The only rules that everyone will follow all of the time are their own. I tell you this; humans must govern themselves.

When you get a large number of humans together doing anything, you are going to have many different ways of getting anything done. When you get a large number of humans driving together, you are going to have a large difference in driving practices. When you have a large number of differences, you get conflict; and when you get conflict, you tend to get violence.

Driving is the most dangerous thing that most people will ever do, and they do it with complete and reckless abandonment. Because people drive so often and see it so routinely they become complacent and do not give it the respect that they should. Mostly people follow the rules because they still recognize the need for safety.

Here are some interesting statistics that just show how, when people only care about themselves without regard to others, it can be disastrous. The *biggest* killer in most countries is not disease or wars but vehicle drivers. This clearly shows the importance of courtesy to other people and the relationship of driving and how humans treat each other on a daily basis.

When drivers start showing courtesy and respect and tolerance to all other drivers no matter what the other driver does, then you will see a change. When drivers stop thinking only about what they want and start thinking about everyone else, you will see a change. When drivers stop concentrating on what is going on inside their vehicle and start concentrating on what is going on outside their vehicle, you will see a change. When drivers stop bending the rules and traffic laws for their convenience, you will see a change. When drivers start to understand that a little inattention will inhibit your ability to prevent the accident that is coming at you, then you will see a change. A little inattention, or a little alcohol, or a little of anything that inhibits full concentration may not in itself cause an accident, but it always severely diminishes the ability to prevent one.

Just then a car quickly pulled into the lane very close to the front of the bus just in front of us. Ahmed, who was in his mid-twenties and driving, exclaimed loudly, saying some rather unsavory choice words.

Let me guess, first that startled you, then angered you, correct? You are tempted to let them know that, correct?

Almost ashamed, Ahmed nodded. "Hell yeah," he grunted under his breath with obvious adrenaline pumping.

Do not feel bad about that. It is a normal response built into your nature by thousands of years of evolution. The thing to change now is how you actually *do* respond to it; how you change your behavior and your reaction to it.

Here is where a little tolerance is very important. Maybe they were not aware of just how close they were to you; maybe they were doing something else and thought they were well clear of you; maybe they were just trying to be nice to the person behind them and get out of the way as soon as possible without thinking about how it will affect you. The one thing you can be reasonably sure of is that they really did not try to upset you. That was *probably* not their intention. So, if you give them the benefit of a doubt and a little tolerance, you will be much safer; and you will not let it ruin your own day. But, for the sake of argument, let us just say they *were* trying to upset you; are you going to let them manipulate you like that?

Ahmed's head cocked to the side, his shoulders shrugged and he nodded again. You could tell he saw the truth in what Jos was saying.

It is hard to control gut reactions. That "gut reaction" is something that has been programmed into every human being since the species started. That is one of the major problems in the world right now; outdated human programming. Rest assured, Ahmed, that you are not the only one struggling with this. That is why I say that driving in traffic is an excellent way to see the dynamics of human interaction with each other. It is a great learning tool; for learning about other people and learning about yourself.

Free Will Is Your Choice

When someone talks about having free will, it is not necessarily only the ability to do what you want; it is having the willpower not to do what you ordinarily would do. Free will is the ability to control your own will and not simply follow the urges of the flesh, or that "gut reaction," or the influences around you. Look at the world through your eyes and not through the eyes of others. Free will is the test to see if you will exercise your ability to do the right thing that is your truth despite what your body is urging you to do, or other outside influences are urging. Free will is that inner strength that makes you do what your mind tells you is the right thing to do.

That is free will. Everybody wants it. Everyone thinks they have it. But only some know how to exercise it; and fewer still actually do.

"I always thought about free will as having choices, or making your own choices," Ahmed said. *"The freedom, or I should say, the ability to make our own choices. Some people do not have a choice. At least some people feel that they have no choices sometimes."*

Jos questioned Ahmed if he was talking about feeling enslaved somehow. Obviously recovered now from the previous incident, he glanced at Jos and nodded.

Everyone makes his or her own choices in this life. You may have limited options available to you, but you probably have a lot more options to any situation than you think; and generally, people do not consider all the options they really have. With the different options, only you can make a choice, but then you have to live with the consequences. You cannot blame the choice you make on someone else, regardless of the situation. You, *and only you*, made the choice. Everybody can always assign blame but the truth is that every decision you make you make alone. Every action you take you take alone. The responsibility lies with you. Where your life is now is only because of your previous choices and decisions.

Throughout life you are constantly running into situations that require a decision. In fact, almost every moment of every day you are making a decision between something. The decision you make tends to put you right back at another choice. The reason for that is every decision you make at any moment changes the future.

These decisions that you are faced with always have options. If there are no options, then there is not a decision, is there?

Jos paused for a moment with a suspicious grin. He looked around at everybody.

Knowledge and experience are the key to this. Without a doubt the more options you have, and are aware of, the better the decision you are going to make. Do not just stop at the most obvious, or the easiest, or the quickest, think of all the options because you will make a better choice if you do. That is where knowledge really comes in handy; all kinds of knowledge, strange and trivial knowledge, and the stuff that lets you think "outside the box."

Rudy Rashid was a slighter nervous man, about the same age as Ahmed, with eyes that seemed to study things. The seat he was in was actually just behind Jos, but because everyone was sitting sideways in their seats, he was just to his side.
"When I have a difficult decision, I ask God for help," Rudy said.

So, how has that been working out for you? How often have you actually heard a verbal reply? Many people say they ask God to help. I tell you this; ask other people, they have the answer. God resides within every living thing. If you actually want to hear an answer, ask the God that resides in others. You will get better results.

You do not think that you are the first person to be faced with the difficult type of decision that you are currently faced with, do you? It may be different people involved, or different situations that you are confronted with, but many people have gone through similar situations just like you. A lot of history has come before you. They can offer very valid options to your decision making. That is the best way that God answers you anyway.

Reese, another member of the group, was a hulking presence, somewhat older with an unintentionally harsh voice.
"Sometimes the decisions I make are really not my fault," Reese said. "I mean, I do not have a choice. I feel I have to make the decision that I make."

Like it or not, you have to live inside your body. Your body has to live with the decisions you make. A lot of people, when they make a bad choice, want to point a finger or give an excuse for why it was not their fault. The fact still remains they have to live with the results; good or bad.

Whether or not there is a conscious thought directing it, you are responsible for the actions your body takes. It is like the embarrassment you feel, and the emotion you have, when your body farts unexpectedly. You can blame the beans, or the fact that someone made you laugh. You still have to live with the results for the rest of history.

You may get angry at someone and think about hurting them, you may even derive some satisfaction at the thought, but it only depends on your action whether or not you have to live with the consequences of actually hurting them.

You are not just your body. You are your body and your thoughts, your emotions, your feelings, and your memories. There is so much more to you than just your body. That is what gets lost on some people. You, are your body *and* your mind. In this life, it is your actions that are judged.

Jos looked right at me.

As time goes on you will understand more; about yourself as well as life in general. The universe is a strange and very complex *living* thing; very hard to take in all at once. But, when you understand the truth, it is really quite easy to comprehend.

As Jos went on about with more trivial talk to lighten the mood, I realized that as confusing as he was, he struck a chord in me that made me feel like I understood more than just what I was hearing. He did that a lot; he would sound very confusing but at the same time he really made a lot of sense.

We stopped in a small village on the outskirts of a large city, with a garage a block or two from a café. The area was the obviously more run-down side of the city. You could tell that, at one time, this area was a nice place to live; young families, new hopes and dreams. But as time moved on, the area had aged and no longer appealed to the younger or more affluent types. Hence, the price of property had gone down, so now you had the people that had been here for years and the ones that had moved in because of the low cost.

The group went into the café and I walked over to the garage. After talking with the proprietor about my car, I made arrangements for him to go get the car and bring it here to fix. As he was filling out the work order, I had a thought; actually, more like a feeling came over me. I asked the man if he could fix my car, then hang on to it until I came back. He informed me of a storage fee if it was going to be here for long. I accepted the notice and thanked him. I don't really know why, but I walked over to the café with the others having decided to continue on with them.

The first people from the group I saw were Ahmed and Rohm. Rohm was quiet, late twenties, smartly dressed and seemed a little more serious than some of the others, but still very approachable. I felt a little weird with what I was about to ask, but it felt right all the same.

"Hey," I said, "do you think it would be alright if I came along for a while?" To be honest, it had never even crossed my mind that I didn't know anything about these people or even where they were going.

"Sure," Rohm answered. "Had a feeling you'd be joining the group."

Jos, Natashia, and Rudy walked up to us, all with knowing smiles and slight nods.

You've thought about your options and made a decision. You will now have to live with that decision for the rest of eternity. Are you prepared for that?

The way Jos posed the question made me stop and think. 'For the rest of eternity,' that is a long time. I had never really thought about how long eternity really was up to that point, and didn't even then. I wondered why he put it that way. But, even after a moment I knew it was the right thing to do and nodded.

Well, I can guarantee that the decision you have just made will change everything; and not just for you but for everybody you will have anything to do with for the rest of your life.

Natashia, Connie, Jos, and I all sat down at a table in the café; actually, a restaurant that had seen better days. Natashia looked in her early thirties with very strong Slavic roots and an accent to match. Connie Kahn was of Asian descent but was very clear with her language skills, whichever language she was using at the time. She knew more than one.

The rest of the gang sat at other tables close by. Everybody could hear everyone else's conversations, and conversations were exchanged between tables. There was a nervous looking waitress almost hesitating to come over to the group. I got to thinking if she somehow felt intimidated by all these people coming in all at once.

Then she came over with some tattered menus and asked about drink orders. After she got all the orders, she left and Jos started to speak again. When he did, I noticed that everybody suddenly got quiet and started to pay attention to what he was saying.

The Yin and Yang of It

All things have an opposite. That is, the yin and yang of it. For every up, there is a down, for every right, there is a left, for every good, there is a bad, for every pro, there is a con. Now, when it comes to pros and cons, a lot of times that has to do with a particular point of view. For there are many things in this universe that are good, but they all have a bad side depending on how you look at it. What is good for one person is not always good for another. The only true good thing about the yin and yang of anything is trying to get a balance.

If you can find and get to some kind of balance, then that is a win/win situation. *There are always two sides to every story, and the truth lies somewhere in the middle.* Even living things, like the human body, do not have anything that just goes one way. The only thing in the universe that only goes one way and cannot change is time; and even that has a yin and yang; past and future.

If your body only had a sympathetic nervous system, your heart, among other things, would just keep speeding up until it was out of control and could no longer function. On the other hand, if you just had a parasympathetic nervous system, your heart would just keep slowing down until it stopped. Your heart beats just right, provided everything is in good order, because your nervous system has found the right balance.

That is how you have to find your place in the world; you have to find a good balance between many different things. If you find a job that you love but it does not pay enough money for you to live on, then you are off balance and something is going to suffer. On the other hand, if you find a job that pays really well but you just cannot stand to do it, then something else is going to suffer. So, you try to find a balance between what you want to do and what will pay what you need. Then you will be happy with your work because you have found a balance. A marriage is the same way, just like any relationship. Parenting is the same way. Having fun and enjoying life is the same way; you must find the balance between the pros and cons. That is the yin and yang of life.

We continued to wait for our drinks as Jos continued on ...

Cannot Win

Have you ever heard the phrase, "You cannot win if you do not play?" Well, the flip side to that is, "You cannot lose if you do not play." And if you are talking about the lottery, or gambling, there are a lot more losers than winners, so it would be better to just not play; you are much more likely to not be a loser than be a winner. But, now, have you ever heard the phrase, "It is better to have loved and lost than never to have loved at all?"

The whole point here is: you *cannot* succeed if you do not try. You can try and not succeed, but if you do not try you *will not* succeed. Everything in life has its risk to benefit ratio. What are the benefits if you succeed and what are the risks if you do not succeed? To every decision there is a benefit to risk ratio.

We were still waiting for our drinks to come, and at this time, I noticed that I did not see the waitress anywhere around. I wondered where she had gone, but it was only a brief passing thought as Jos continued to talk.

One Nice Thing Theory

When you think about how much suffering there is in the world, it becomes overwhelming. There is no way that one person or even one group of people can change all the suffering that is going on. So, why even try? At least you can fully enjoy your life and help others when you can, right? Well, not really.

Jos paused and took a moment to have eye contact with everyone.

Think if everyone were to do one "nice" thing that they would not normally do each day; and conversely, not do one thing that is "not nice" that they would normally do each day.

Now I am talking about simple "nice" things like: holding a door open for someone; looking at someone when you pass by and giving an acknowledging nod; giving a smile at a nice comment someone extended to someone else; stopping just a moment to let someone else pass; or *just giving someone the benefit of a doubt or a little tolerance*; simple everyday things. And, not doing something "not nice" like: not looking behind you to see if someone else is coming through the door you just let go of; averting your eyes so as not to look at anybody else and therefore not acknowledging them; making some rude or negative grunt, moan, or comment when you are disgruntled; rushing ahead of someone when it really is not going to make any difference anyway; not giving someone else a slight benefit of a doubt and a little tolerance; little things that make living with other people not so enjoyable and that you yourself would not want around you. With some seven billion people in the world just imagine if everyone did just one "nice" thing, and did not do just one "not nice" thing every day. It does not take a really smart person to think of the effects that would have on the entire planet, not just humans.

Do nice, do not do not nice. It is a simple message. Whether you are a Jew, a Christian, a Muslim, a Hindu, a Buddhist, or an Atheist, it all works out the same; the better the world is for one, the better the world is for all.

Now, Jos looked around for the waitress who had mysteriously vanished. He had a curious look on his face. His mind was momentarily pulled away. Then Jos said ... well, more of a mutter to himself ...

There may be an opportunity here.

He left it at that. One more glance around the room and then a shrug of his shoulders. No one else in the gang seemed to be concerned with the absence of the waitress; they were just focusing on Jos.
"You just mentioned the religions. So, do you think there is a God?" Connie Kahn asked. "Do you believe in a God, or gods?"
Jos looked at her with a wry smile ...

Monotheism Versus Polytheism

First, I do not *believe* in God; I *know* of God. As for how many there really are, that is something that has been debated since the beginning of recorded history and it is not over yet.

Monotheism is predominately the religious preference at this time. Pretty much everyone who believes in a God believes that there is only one God. That was not always the case. The pharaoh Akhenaten was the first in history to suggest monotheism; even before Judaism. Prior to Judaism, and for a long time after the beginning of Judaism, polytheism was the predominate practice of most people.

Jos looked around the room at the eleven of us sitting there. A big smile crept across his face as he amused himself with the deep, trivial details of history. To him, history was important. But he knew that to most people it was just that; history.

When it comes to God and the belief of humans, the emotion is very strong; strong enough to kill for.

History has shown that as time moves on, the beliefs of the majority change. Now, in the present time to suggest that there is more than one God would be considered utter lunacy and sacrilegious. Well, except for Hindus.

Now the question is not whether there is one God or many gods, the question is which God of all the current religions is the right God and which of the laws of God are to be followed; along with the major question, if there really is a God to start with.

Atheists Take on the God Question

Atheists, of course, do not believe in a God. For most atheists, life is what it is, and when it is over it is over.

Now there is a difference between an atheist and an agnostic. There is some confusion with these terms. An agnostic is not convinced there is a God; they are not saying there is or is not a God, they just do not have any proof one way or the other and leave an open mind. They are decidedly undecided. Most agnostics that I know have not made a conscious decision about God one way or the other because they just do not think about it much, and/or they just do not really care. Whether there is a God or not, really is not going to change the way they live or the way they want to live so why bother with a question that really is not going to change anything regardless of the answer.

On the other hand, an atheist has made a conscious decision that there is no God, Supreme Being, Master Designer or Great Creator. The atheist has also made the conscious decision that there is no such thing as magic, miracles, spiritualism, or afterlife. They feel that life is a gift and should be cherished for that very reason; that it is all there is, and you do not get another chance and you do not get to live again after you die. There is nothingness after death.

Both the religious person and the non-religious person feel they have undeniable proof of their point of view and cannot understand why the others cannot see it. In fact, the feelings are so strong and profound for some people that killings and wars have been the result. And the interesting point here is that generally it is the religious and the devout that are the ones doing the killing and starting the wars to make their point. It is the religious people that shout out that life is the gift from God and is very precious and should be cherished; yet it is the atheist that generally actually practices that philosophy. And there is the yin and yang of that.

Unfortunately, in this realm of reality, humans will never obtain pure undisputable proof one way or the other. I am here to confirm that. How do you *prove* a thought or a feeling; a consciousness? Many will argue with that statement, because they are that convinced of their own certainty of the answer. This is the result of ages of teachings and written records of beliefs and religions throughout time.

Atheists may be "Godless" but you have never seen an atheist take another life "in the name of God." The sixth of the Ten Commandments was, "Thou shalt not kill." An atheist has never used the excuse that; "but this time God said it was okay."

A lot of people, religious people, vehemently disagree with atheists. They disagree to the point of violence. But atheists are just one group of people. There are many people that belong to that group but that does not define them as to who they are as an individual. Just as being a religious person does not define that person as to who they are as an individual. It just puts people in the "us" or "them" categories. It is another way to divide people up into groups.

Now, some of the others were starting to look around for the waitress. It was really strange how she just seemed to vanish when we showed up. At first, most of us thought she had to take a minute for herself. Then most of us started to think the moment was taking a bit longer than what would be anticipated even for a long personal moment.

It was starting to feel a little like a movie scene. I was starting to think that some big monster gang was going to show up. Jos took a minute also to look around again at the empty restaurant then he shrugged. Everybody looked back at Jos and he looked at everybody. With another quick glance around he continued on with what he was saying ...

The Gang Theory

Here is the story of "us" and "them," and what it really means to us and them. Humans fit themselves into groups. They find the things about themselves that make them similar or different from other groups and tend to associate with others with similarities. You have heard the expression often: "Birds of a feather flock together." Sometimes it is with the families that they are born in. "Blood is thicker than water." Whatever the particular association is at any given time, we feel better when we are with a particular group. "There is safety in numbers." People may even be put into a group by other people, or join a group to produce a product or carry out a task; such as doing a job.

Humans have an innate need to associate. People need to belong to some association, some group, or "gang," for lack of a better term. In fact, I will use that term, "gang," to make the point. Language is such that in order to communicate we have to give labels to all things. Some things that are the same thing have different labels. When we are talking about associations they can be groups, flocks, pacts, mobs, teams, or gangs, just to name a few labels for showing "like similarities."

Some different "gang" associations are race, sex, sexual orientation, religion, ideals, age, interests, the list can go on and on. For some reason people find comfort in a shared experience or similarity with others. Their loyalty to that particular gang can, and often is, extremely strong. In fact, that gang affiliation can be so strong as to be dangerous to the individual themselves. Once in that particular "gang" people can be swayed and coerced beyond their own separate thoughts and feelings. They will take on a "gang mentality" and become "one" with the pack. This is an inherited trait that has kept the human species around. Humans are a symbiotic species.

People belong to a myriad of different gangs at any given time. When someone is described as a twenty-two-year-old, black, gay, man that is a Christian and works as a computer programmer, he has just been put into six different gangs. His age gang, his race, his sexual orientation, his sex, his religious beliefs, and his job title. If he has had a heart transplant, that just added him to yet another gang.

People do not commonly realize just how many gangs they belong to at any given time. Some gang associations are obvious and quickly recognized. The color of your skin, your sex, and your age are generally the first gang associations people make. Then, when you talk, if you have a distinctive accent that will be assigned another gang based on nationality.

However, no gang affiliation truly defines any one individual to any genuine degree.

There are many gangs within gangs. A Christian church will be filled with men gang members, women gang members, young gang members, old gang members, white gang members and black gang members, just to name a few. And if that Christian church is in France, it will be part of the French gang members, and it will be part of the Christian gang members and it will be part of the religious gang members. Again, just to name a few.

It depends on when and where you are that makes the difference as to how you are going to react when it pertains to your "gang"; depending on which gang you are associating with at the time.

You have to pay some sort of "dues" in order to belong to any particular gang. Some dues you pay for, some you have to learn, or some come with time, some you are born with, some you earn and some you inherit. Some gangs you cannot be part of no matter what you do. You cannot *think* you know what it is like to be "in the gang" unless you have actually been there. A black man will never be able to know what it is like to be a white man, just like a white man will never be able to know what it is like to be a black man. They may *think* they can but they cannot. You *have* to be in the gang.

You can *and should* have respect for other gangs, but you can only respect them for their differences, and understand that they may belong to your "gang" at any given time. The white man may not know what it is like to be black, and the black man may not know what it is like to be white, but they both know what it is like to be male and not female. So, at some point they will both be in the male gang; and, hence, of the same gang.

Gangs tend to form and/or merge when attacked. When living things form gangs they tend to be smarter or stronger or more defensible than they are by themselves; or they just share a mutual feeling and understanding that others cannot. An excellent example of this is the event that happened on September 11, 2001. The United States has a myriad of gangs, many battling constantly among themselves; blacks and whites, Jews and Christians and Muslims, gays and straights, Democrats and Republicans all at each other's throats. Until an outside gang attacked them, then they all came together and formed the United States gang and worked alongside each other putting all differences aside for a common good.

Jos stood up for a moment and looked around. Billy stood up also and did the same. Then Jos eased back down and looked around at all of us sitting there silently listening. With raised eyebrows and a slight smirk on his face he said ...

I did see a waitress come to our table; yes? Billy, do you mind terribly looking around to see if we are in a twilight zone or something?

Billy, without looking at Jos nodded and then moved away. He appeared to be just as confused and concerned.

Too Good to Be True

Religion is one type of association. Whether or not you are religious puts you into a "gang." Then, whichever religion you believe in subdivides you into other gangs. Religion, or lack of, is just one of many parts put together that help to define an individual. It is just one gang of so many gangs that one person can belong to.

Some people believe religion was developed to make life livable or at least worth living. When all the hardships in life are taken into account it is necessary for some people to have a deity that can help them out when needed; or have a reason for living when all seems hopeless.

Consider in years past the general hardships of average humans; in many times in history, actually most, some of the population of an area was enslaved, many were "conquered people" and subject to the customs and whims of the victors. For many people, life was a tremendous hardship just to survive. In many cases, when they found something that made life bearable they clung to it.

You have heard the expression "If it sounds too good to be true then it probably is?" Does that not ever make a person wonder about an entity, or deity, they can "pray" to and get results for the most profound and complex problems in existence? Ask for forgiveness and you will be forgiven, pay a penance and receive a favor; an entity that you can bargain and deal with. Something that you can hope will make life better for you somehow. If not make life better now, at least something that will make all things right in the end.

Even in cave drawings of 10,000 years ago, it clearly shows a religious belief. Religions are how human society was able to conduct and govern its interests, long before governments and laws. But that was at the beginning of human society.

THE RESTAURANT

Billy came walking back followed by a heavyset older gentleman in street clothes. He came up to the table that Jos, Natashia, Connie, and I were sitting at. In a heavy breath, he said, "Folks, I'm really sorry, but my cook hasn't showed up yet today. I can make you some sandwiches myself, but I really don't cook anything back there. I'm really sorry."

Natashia said, "That's OK. We can wait for the cook to show up; we're not in real hurry."

Looking rather embarrassed, the gentleman went on to confess, "Well, to be honest, I'm not really sure that he will show up at all."

I looked around the café, and it seemed like at some time in the past it was a nice little restaurant, but times had been as hard on it as it had been on the whole neighborhood. Everything was kind of run down, old, and unkempt. The whole neighborhood that we were in was not particularly crime ridden as such. I mean, it wasn't a particularly scary place and I didn't really feel uneasy or unsafe. It just had seemed to suffer from age. People had simply moved on; and nobody really cared anymore, and it showed.

The gentleman was very much the same way; he must have been here when the place was new and full of promise. Now his widened waistline showed his age, the deep wrinkles in his face showed his wear, and the slouch in his shoulders when he walked showed his resignation.

Jos, on the other hand, was a healer I could see that already. You could just see it. He could not part the sea, he could not walk on water, and he could not move mountains or fly. But what Jos could do was equally miraculous in this day and age; Jos could make you understand. He could make you trust him and believe in him as much as anyone believed in the prophets of old. Jos could explain things in a way that made sense. You could feel the kindness and sincerity in Jos. Jos offered hope.

Jos stood up and put his arm around the guy's shoulders, kind

21

of turned him around, walked a few steps away from the table, and talked to him. The fellow looked at Jos then looked down at the floor as Jos continued to talk. After a few minutes of discussion, the guy looked back into Jos' face and then around the room. They took a couple of steps further with Jos talking and stopped and continued the discussion. Then I saw the guy's shoulders shrug as his head nodded gently. The man then walked into the back with Jos following.

When Jos returned from the back, he informed us that Jack, the owner of this little restaurant, was interested in a proposal that he offered Jack about the restaurant. Now Jos wanted to see just how well the gang had been listening to what he'd been saying as he'd been traveling with them.

The proposal that I offered the owner, Jack, was a chance to sit back and let us make this restaurant a success for him. As you can see, it has fallen into a state of disrepair and lack of soul. That phrase sums up the problem with this place; lack of soul, lost hope, despair. A business, like any living thing, must have certain rules.

I have come to realize that humans have five rules. Simply, rule number one is the drive to survive; rule number two is the drive to procreate, or the sex drive; rule number three is the drive for control; rule number four is the drive to succeed; and rule number five is the drive to understand. Rarely, does anything supersede rule number one, survival, even rule number two. And, rarely does anything supersede rule number two. In fact, many times the sex drive is the reason for rules three, control, and four, success.

When a business loses rule number one, the drive to survive, and rule number four, the drive for success, it is doomed to fail. I propose that we renew the hope and soul of this place to show you what I have been trying to tell you about human beings.

The gang all looked around silently at each other for a moment. Then slowly you started to see half grins, slight shrugs and soft nods. Their attention returned to Jos.

First of all, you have to look at this restaurant as a living thing. The building is the body; the physical presence of the business, the chemical structure that exists in the three-dimensional world. This restaurant has lost all will to survive and Jack has lost all drive to keep it going. He is allowing us full control to do what we can do to bring it back to life. I made a deal with him that if we do good he will reap the benefits, and if we do not he will be compensated. He is willing to extend that trust because he is just so tired of trying.

We will really need to start from scratch. First, it needs a new name; so, we all know what to call it. Let us call it the "Burger Steak" to start with, just so we have something to label it. The name can always be changed later if needed. But the true lifeforce, like any living thing, will be the energy that runs it, that controls it, that inhabits it; and just like any living thing it will be the sum total of everything about it that makes it good or bad, succeed or fail. Let us get started.

Adam, I thought about you when I talked to Jack about doing this. Your background will come in very handy.

Adam was older than all the rest, I would have to place him in his early fifties, just because you could just start to see grey hair in his temples. Later, when I asked him how he came to be with this gang, he just shrugged, looked at me and said, "That's a good question. I was ready for a change in my life, I was at a point to change, so ..." He shrugged again and just let it go. Adam seemed to portray a person with a clear vision and strong point of view. It felt like he had true leadership potential.

Adam nodded agreeing. "I've been working in restaurants since I started working. I've always wanted to try out some recipes. This'll give me a chance."

Good, we have a driving force. Now, I am not going to call Adam the boss, but we do need a leader. He will be the driving force. If everyone became the driving force, then we would all be driving in many different directions and that would be disastrous from the start. Like a human with multiple personalities. What we have to do is get behind him and work together to try and accomplish his goal; whether we get it or not at first.

Everyone nodded.

We are going to be in this thing together. No one person here is the sole beneficiary of the work. We all get to share the profits of the work in certain proportions according to what each of us decides each person's value is to the whole.

I have talked to you before about this, every person has a value and it is different from others. That is just the way life is. Even in the Earth's ecosystem, everything has a value; algae, plants, worms, birds, tigers, and humans. They all contribute different things and they all consume different things, therefore they all obtain a value to the whole of the Earth. One example is kind of like where you sit in the food pyramid. Are you at the top or the bottom? Now just because you are at the top does not mean you are more important.

Everything *needs* the bottom of the food chain or the things on top perish. The top may be a good place to be, but it is the place that is not really needed to survive. Remember, to everything there is a yin and a yang.

The first thing everyone has to do to understand *how to work in harmony* is to give the proper respect to the different values of each individual. If you are not honest with yourself and what your true value is to any given circumstance, you are always going to be mad, sad, or upset with things.

Like when you first walk into a complex manufacturing plant, you are of little value; you are new, you are not experienced at what to do at this location, you do not know the routines, you are easily replaced. Your value is low. But when you are at home with your family, you have great value. You are irreplaceable. Your individual value changes through time and circumstances.

Human Value

You have to be realistic. If I had a pencil puncturing my side into my lungs, do you think a doctor is more valuable than a talent scout? Well, yes. But if I am trying to get a job as an actor on a TV show then do I think that the talent scout has more value than the doctor? Again, the answer would be, yes.

The point is that everybody on Earth has a value whether anyone wants to actually say it or not. That value is based on many different things, some of which are: how many people they affect with each of their actions, or how much time and/or practice does it take to be able to do what they can do, or how much they know and can teach others.

Now, I am not talking about more important; I am talking about a particular "value" with a given circumstance. When it comes to individual "human" importance everyone carries one credit. Every human being experiences one life; no more and no less. Every human being records one point of view. But for that matter, every living thing experiences one lifetime of whatever species it is, for however long it may be. *Every living thing records one point of view and contributes one set of circumstances.* Every living thing has the ability to affect change to the existing universe as long as that thing is alive.

But, for the sake of determining pay, or compensation for work, you have to determine a value. First thing that everyone here has to do is set a value on each other in order to determine what percentage each one will get from the profits. Jack has to be considered also because he has a value to this business even if he is not working here. If it were not for him this place would not be here for us. Then you will have to find the value of the business itself, and therefore how much it has to have. The business has to have a set amount because the cost to run it is pretty much set and cannot be "forgiven" if the business is not there. But it also should get an extra percentage based on productivity, because the more it does the more it is going to need. You know the business itself is just like a person; it needs food like water and electricity and product, it needs new shoes and clothes occasionally like a new paint job or water heater. All of these things need to be taken into account when you start to figure what percentage everyone needs. So, remember to count the business in just like another person, or one of the gang.

Everyone looked at Jos with an incredulous look; the fact that he would even mention that we should put a value on someone else puzzled everyone.
"How can you say something like that?" Adam said.
Jos looked around at everyone, and a sharp grin came across his face.

And what is so odd about saying something like that? Why does that shock you so? Why do all of you seem so stunned?

The truth is that putting value on things is pretty common. You first have to understand what is meant by value. Only humans barter and trade goods and services. Other animals do not ever barter and trade.

Humans started out like any other animal. You will notice with pack animals that they work in groups. They, too, are symbiotic. They work as a team to acquire food, either by killing or by scavenging. When the food is obtained there is generally always some kind of hierarchy as to who gets what and in what order. Human history shows no difference in their development. They were either hunters or gatherers and had the same developed kind of hierarchy when it came to distribution.

The value of another human being is directly related to the benefit that individual can do for the people assessing the value at any given time. If an employee can provide a product or service that others cannot to an employer, then that is a very highly valued person. If an employee provides a product or service that many others can provide as well, then their value is considerably less.

As distasteful as it is all human beings in a complex society of any kind must have some kind of value placed on them. What is any individual worth? Let us just take a very simple example: to a restaurant, what is the difference in value of the chef, to the server, to the cleanup staff, and to the manager? Any product that is made and sold cost a certain amount to make, and then it has to be sold at a particular amount to show a profit. With that amount in hand how much percentage did any individual have in producing that product? What part did they play? How "valuable" would the other parties involved with the production of the product place on any of the other individuals?

Jos could see that the profound implication of what he was saying was becoming distasteful and let the topic stop right there. He could see that they understood what he was getting at. They were starting to process just what each position in the restaurant would be valued.

He took a minute to take in his surroundings and then he changed the subject. It was interesting how he would change a subject. Though, when he would change the subject, it still always seemed to have a bearing on the subject at hand. In this case, he was trying to get us to think simply. Not to overthink the problem or get unnecessarily hampered. Almost laughing, he humorously said ...

The Most Uncommon Thing on Earth

Most people think that the most uncommon thing on this planet is precious metals or gems; like gold or diamonds. Some people think the most uncommon thing on earth is the ability for people to just get along with others. Others might think that the most uncommon thing on the planet is a specific talent for something like singing or art. But, in truth, the most uncommon thing on this planet is basic *common sense.*

When you look around, you find that simple common sense is really rather uncommon. Comedians have made entire careers of pointing out this simple flaw in human characteristics. The ability to just look at something logically and simply is rather uncommon for most human beings. Sometimes they allow their emotions to overpower the process. Sometimes it is their current belief or knowledge that does not allow them to just look at something logically. Prejudices and beliefs cloud seeing things with common logic.

It was said by a few very wise men in the past; it was true then as it is true today: "The intelligent people have doubts, while the ignorant are full of confidence." Also: "You cannot learn what you think you already know."

Humans are very, very reluctant to change, even if the change quite obviously makes more sense. This is probably how it has been done, or what has been thought for years. It has been ingrained in the consciousness of people for so long that any other thought process is looked at as subversive or alien or counterproductive. The end result is that the common sense of something is just simply refused.

When you stop to think about anything from now on, just use some good old common sense and think about it again. If it makes sense, then it just makes sense. Does that not make sense?

Life is far more simple than people make it out to be.

The first thing that anything needs in a beginning is a fresh start. A body needs to be clean and fresh to begin anew. So, with that, let us start taking what we can and start cleaning the cafe up. Adam, if you will take some time, come up with a menu; make it short and simple to start. Just like anything else, you start simple and evolve to a more complex system, or in this case, menu. Once you have a menu we can come up with a theme, then we can set it up accordingly.

On that note, everyone got up and started getting busy. Connie suggested that someone take an inventory of what was in the restaurant and what we had to work with. Mariam was an older lady with a calm, soothing demeanor and a quiet, caring voice. She decided to check the stock of food supplies. Sochin, a dark, serious young man, decided to look at the tables and chairs and the layout of the floor plan to try and get a sense of how to set up seating to be most efficient. Reese started looking around at the building itself to see what needed to be fixed and what just needed to be cleaned. Literally, everyone just jumped in and took control of something that they were good at and just got started bringing the Burger Steak to the delivery room, so to speak, to give it a new birth and beginning.

When someone needed a hand, they asked for it and were never denied. When someone was not busy, they looked around to see where they could help. When someone wanted to go to the bathroom, go outside to smoke, sit down to drink a soda, they just did it, knowing that as soon as they were done they would jump right back into the thick of things. Everyone had a vested interest for the restaurant to do well and to get up and running as soon as possible. When they took a little break, they were not slowing down everyone else; they were slowing down themselves, so as soon as they could, they got back to helping out. It was really nothing I had ever seen before; people really did not have to be told anything. Even Reese, who, through the very short time I had seen him did not really impress me as a real go-getter, was not wasting any time. I realized I had judged too soon. Everyone was really going at it at full steam.

As people were working around the place, I would hear Jos talking occasionally about different things. I always found myself straining to hear what he had to say when he was talking away from me. It might have been just passing banter, but he always seemed to have some point to make. I was cleaning the windows when I heard him working behind me on something and talking to someone ...

The Truth

Truth is simply knowing right from wrong. You do not need a religious leader to tell you the truth. You do not need a law to tell you the truth. You know in your heart right from wrong.

This is the simple truth; *do not harm other things needlessly*. The truth that everyone knows without being told is; "Do not do onto other people that which you do not want done onto you." Muhammad said it that way, Jesus said it the other way around, but they both mean the same thing. Treat every living thing as if *you* are that living thing, because in the end, you are. We are all interrelated. Treat every living thing with compassion, respect, and tolerance. Consider other things as you consider yourself. That is how the Buddha said it.

The New Testament, John 18:37-38 says: "Then Pilate said, 'So you are a king!' Jesus replied, 'You say that I am a king. I have been born and have come into the world for this reason—to testify to the truth. Everyone who belongs to the truth listens to my voice.' Pilate asked, 'What is truth?'"

I heard Jos pause for a long moment, and wondering why, I turned around to see a grin come across his face. Just standing there with a cynical smile, he said ...

Off the subject: I have often wondered how people knew what Jesus actually said to Pilate when it was spoken strictly among themselves; or, for that matter, how do they know what he said to God in the garden of Gethsemane when they were all asleep? I have just always wondered about that.

Then he went back to rubbing the silverware he was cleaning with a cloth and continued ...

Anyway, "the truth," has been debated, commented on, changed around, and used in so many ways. Many people have interpreted the meaning of "truth" for millennium. What is *meant* by the "truth"?

When Jesus said, "I have been born and have come into the world for this reason—to testify to the truth. Everyone who belongs to the truth listens to my voice." He was talking about just simply knowing right from wrong.

Now, knowing what "truth" is, it is pretty easy to understand what he was saying, is it not?

After Adam had come up with a menu, the whole gang sat down to discuss a concept. Adam did what Jos had suggested; he made a simple menu that would be easy to work with and relatively cheap but would still be somewhat sophisticated. The idea was to make essentially different hamburgers and put them into meals. They would be hamburger patties, big ones, but instead of hamburgers on a bun, they would be hamburger patties on a plate with a sauce. He'd take hamburger meat and in one kind add cheese and bacon chips, in another he'd add spices like sage and pepper, and he'd have a turkey burger, and one with a lot of pork added with spices. He then decided to have a choice of potatoes: buttery mashed, loaded baked, crispy hash balls, and cheesy scallops. Then a choice of side dishes. He thought about making the burgers rectangle in shape and then slicing them; you know, to make the plate look nice.

Adam asked if anyone knew anything about baking; pies or muffins or cakes. Natashia spoke up and suggested that not only could she make dessert plates for the restaurant guests but that she could make extra to sell on the side for a little extra boost. Billy stepped in at that point and asked if he could help Natashia do the baking, as it was always something that he wanted to learn, which brought a smile from Natashia. Billy looked like a man that could really handle the taste testing aspect, as I said, he was rather tall and essentially build like a weight-lifter. Plus, I could not be sure but I think Billy really liked Natashia; well, humans are human.

Now it came time to assign everyone a position. Adam looked to Sochin and Connie and started asking about what kind of design they thought would really bring the place to life with that kind of menu, and what would be most efficient in this space. Sochin said, Adam's menu made him think of a nice, comfortable sit-down dinner with friends or a little romantic night out, but for the average guy or girl that wasn't too pricy or pretentious; just something nice for some plain meat and vegetable people.

Reese piped in that the food had to be good, that was important, but what would be more important would be the way people were treated; the ambience, the atmosphere would be the real selling point. Ahmed added that the quicker we got them in and got them out, the more money we'd make.

That sort of started a little rift going. Reese thought it was important for guests to feel comfortable and at home and want to stay awhile; at the same time, Ahmed thought it more important to turn the tables quickly to make the business more profitable.

Jos was just sitting back letting everyone talk, and yes, bicker a little. I watched as his face never changed expression. He neither looked concerned nor reassured. He was, however, watching intently, listening to every word. It was like watching someone working things out in his head. Soon, as Ahmed and Reese talked about it, almost everybody took a side and started to argue their gang's point. This was not a heated argument, there was no loud voices and oddly seemed like no hard feelings toward anybody there; it was surprisingly business-like. But the two sides were vehement about their position.

Jos continued listening intently to everyone. When both sides became silent, Jos spoke. He had not been sitting there taking a side or determining the merit of either point. He just expanded on a previous idea he was trying to relay. At this point I guess he felt it was a good opportunity to demonstrate the point he was trying to make earlier more clearly.

Even something like a "point of view" can bring together a gang of like-minded people that actually have nothing else in common; just a simple idea or point of view. That is why before when talking about gangs, I was trying to show that even though every gang has its own group, there are always times when gangs need to ban together with different gangs in order to work together for the betterment of the larger gang.

Now here, however, you see the true nature of human beings and individuality. Everyone sees things from different points of view. The old adage that if you put three people in a room and ask for an opinion you are going to get at least two different answers.

This is where you are all going to have to come to a mutual decision or compromise that works the best for both views; a balance. Respect and flexibility with tolerance will go a long way here. If humans can figure out how to put people on the moon and bring them back, then I have no doubt that you can work together to figure this out.

The gang went back to going on about having a nice place to hang out on one hand and turning customers over quick on the other. Both Ahmed and Reese were right. Like Jos had said before, however, everything has a yin and a yang; there are two sides to every story and the truth lies somewhere in the middle. Everybody will be the happiest when a balance can be found. Sochin seemed to come in and break the tie; or better said, he came in and tied them together.

Looking at Jos, Sochin admitted both Ahmed and Reese were correct. They needed to make a nice place to come to, a comfortable place to be at, but at the same time, the business had to produce, and therefore had to have a turnover in order to be successful; and if it wasn't successful, what was the point. Then Sochin glanced at Adam and indicated that he agreed, they should make it a really nice place to be, very inviting. But then we would have to move very fast to get the meals out quickly, turn over the tables quickly, and be ready for the next guests quickly. We would have to develop a very gentle way of letting the patrons know that if they really like the place they needed to help us keep things moving. Why not let the guests be part of the solution also?

With that Jos shrugged and nodded approvingly.

Then Connie suggested that we come up with a place that the guests could go after they eat and continue the enjoyment of the place but free up the table space. It could even be a place for people to wait if the gang ever got that busy. Curtis was the last in the gang that I noticed, because he was always in the background, never really stood out. He was in his forties but seemed more modern than the younger people. Mostly, I guess, because he was always fooling around with some new gadget. Curtis suggested a bar, but that was quickly decided against because Jack didn't have a liquor license for his place and that would be too advanced of a step for a little baby café to attempt this early in life. Maybe when it got a little older, everyone agreed.

"How about a soda bar or a candy bar," Curtis said without realizing the humor in it. Everyone else got it and laughed, breaking the stalemate and tension. But then they stopped laughing and still smiling looked at each other with a "Not a bad idea" expression and the conversation took off again.

With Sochin now taking charge, they started to figure out where to put the tables and chairs for the maximum seating without crowding. They took two small tables big enough only for two guests and put them in the back somewhat secluded for a more intimate area. Mariam, forever the romantic, suggested getting some large plastic plant decorations to act as separators. The gang really started to brainstorm like a well-oiled machine and working together came up with really good arrangements.

Then Adam told everyone what they would need as far as people handling certain duties. He then started asking everyone what they felt comfortable doing. Adam was going to be the head chef and needed two sous chefs to help; Sochin and Rohm thought they could handle that. We had nine four-person tables and two two-person tables, so he decided that we would need four waiters or waitresses. They decided to call them "table captains," because they would be in complete charge of the table. Mariam, Natashia, Connie, and Rudy agreed to take on that task. Someone had to be responsible for the cleanup detail and decided to call them "hygiene officers"; Ahmed, Curtis, and Billy volunteered to do that. Someone would have to be in charge of keeping the records and ordering supplies; that was something that Reese was familiar with so he acquired that task. Adam said that we would really need someone at the door to greet and direct the guest and it was decided that person would be called the "gate keeper"; I took on that role. And everyone agreed that Jos should just play backup assistant for anything and everything. Now that everyone had their place, they went about learning how to do their job in unison with all the rest.

The Most Precious Thing in the Universe

As the gang was going about doing things in the restaurant, Connie looked up at Jos and smiled. "This is so cool," she said. "This place is going to be so precious; the most precious thing ever!"
Wiping off a table, Jos smiled that frequent big grin on his face.

I like the word "precious." It sounds so … well, precious. People think that diamonds are the most precious things on Earth. Some people think life itself is the most precious thing on Earth. But there are huge amounts of these untold riches in the universe.

I tell you this, the most precious thing in the universe is *knowledge*; the ability to think and create. The knowledge that is obtained by experience and time; the passing on of that experience, the sharing of ideas, that is what is so precious. It is the human ability to conceive of an idea or a concept and to share the thought with another and to let it expand and grow; that is *precious*.

In the billions of years that Earth has been in existence, there is finally only one species, one living thing, that has the ability to think creatively enough to conceive of things that are not possible in the natural universe. With everything that is available in the universe how sublime is a single, creative, imaginative thought? How precious is that?

Your experience, even right here and right now, is different than everyone else's experience right here and right now. Your thoughts and feelings create a different knowledge and experience, individual to you alone. That is the most precious thing ever.

Knowledge, it is the only thing that the rich and powerful and famous cannot have more of than you can. But you have to work for it just like anyone else.

Learning and Teaching

Do you go to school to be taught or to learn?

The reply was mixed. To everyone in the room, the question was confusing; to be taught and to learn are the same thing. As the confusion became apparent, the remarks slowed to a silence.

A teacher can teach, but the student will not learn unless they want to. You go to school to learn. Regardless of what the teacher is teaching, you will only learn from them if you want to. And you only listen if you are interested. You teach yourself all that you know, sometimes you use the knowledge that others give you and sometimes you seek out that knowledge on your own. A teacher can help you think about things, but only *you* learn for yourself.

This is why I say: be careful when you "teach" something to somebody. Be very cognizant of your motives and actions. The pupil may not go down the desired path. Offering guidance is generally a much better way to *teach* another individual something than outright instruction. Offer knowledge and then provide guidance to obtain the goal; but let the individual teach the desired lesson to themselves.

It is unadvisable to try to beat a lesson into someone, either metaphorically or literally. You generally create undesirable effects.

Ever heard that it is better to get someone to do something when you make it their idea to do it? If you can transmit the desire for the other individual to learn something, then they will actually learn it for themselves, and you can just provide guidance when solicited. The lesson will be much better learned and remembered. You also give yourself a chance to learn as well.

Everyone and Everything Teaches

Ethel Mae is the sister of my friend's father. Ethel Mae was born severely mentally deficient. She cannot see, little to no hearing, does not talk, she will make moans when distressed. All she has done for over sixty years is sit in a chair and roll a ball around with her hands; that is all. She has to be completely cared for; fed, cleaned, put to bed, and put back in her chair in the morning. She can do nothing for herself but sit there and play with that ball. Most people would look at her and think, "What is the point? What good is she to society?"

She is a teacher. For those that are willing to learn she teaches patience, caring, and understanding; lessons that are very difficult to teach to others. Yes, she just sits there, but does she do nothing? No; she teaches. By being in her state she is a tool to learn compassion and caring. She has never been able to live a "normal" life or enjoy the wonders of this existence, but she has been a very good teacher to those willing to learn.

Life lessons can be found everywhere, to those that are looking, or to those willing to see them. To look at someone and think that they have nothing to teach you; nothing to offer you, is to miss a valuable opportunity. Do you think Helen Keller ever taught anyone anything? She was blind and deaf but she taught many, many things, not the least of which was the strength of the human spirit. Everyone has something to offer if others are only willing to learn.

The hardest thing to learn is how to learn.

Reese mentioned, "It is easier for me to learn from someone if I respect them."

Jos approached Reese to discuss respect. Jos felt respect was a very important feeling. He often spoke of respect and the need for it.

Respect is Earned, Not Taken

You earn respect from another human being by giving respect to them first as a human being. Most people want this to be done the other way around. Most people want other people to give them respect ... first. But in order to get respect, you must first give respect to the other person. Respect is something that is given freely, not taken.

If you look at someone with a scowl on your face and cold, defiant eyes, they are probably not responding to your skin color, sex, size, or culture. They are probably responding to the fact that you look mean and possibly dangerous. Unfortunately, in today's popular society that is the way people want to look; fearsome and dangerous. Then they get upset when someone treats them with suspicion and caution instead of respect. Do not confuse *fear with respect*.

How many times have you come in contact with some other person and they did not even acknowledge you? Did that not make you feel slighted? Then when they said something to you and you ignored them, *they* got offended and felt disrespected; that is all it takes. Something as simple as that has been known to start physical fights between two strangers.

Adam asked, "So, what about when I don't even know that I've done something like that, something wrong or disrespectful?"

First, give them respect. Second, give them the benefit of a doubt that they did not know, or were not aware of the fact that they showed disrespect first; or, you did. Give them an honest chance to show proper respect. When you first come in contact with another person, acknowledge them by looking into their eyes; then you know if they see you or not. Give them a little courtesy.

"If a man strikes your cheek, turn to him the other." Jesus said that; does that phrase mean something to you now? The more often you give someone a chance, the harder it is for them to feel disrespected and retaliate.

It took only three days for everyone to get the restaurant cleaned and decorated, updated and ready to go. Near the front door, I had a podium with a register; very fancy for this area and kind of place. Two intimate tables were at the back and the other nine tables were in the middle with decorative Japanese-like partitions around them. The walkway between everything was just wide enough to be efficient and convenient. Up at the front near my podium were three loveseats in a U shape and in the middle of them was a glass display case with pies, cupcakes, and muffins. The display case and seats were positioned in just such a way that if everyone sitting knew each other, they could talk among themselves, but if they wanted more private conversation it was easily done.

Earlier, while Natashia and Billy were making pies, cupcakes, and muffins, and Adam had his team prepping food, Reese and Rudy along with Connie and Mariam went all around the small little town announcing opening night. They handed out fliers they made off the computer and printer, using up almost all of the ink that was left. Ahmed, Curtis, Jos, and I stayed back and continued to do the little things to make everything just right.

We had decided on the first opening night to start about six o'clock and stay open until ten o'clock, just to get a feel for how all of this was going to go. I don't mind saying that I was a little apprehensive that any of this could actually work. When you listened to Jos talk about how things were going to work, he just made sense and you felt confidence, in theory, anyway. Maybe the nervousness came from thinking about how humans can react.

Everybody was back at five o'clock, and the excitement was palpable with everyone except Jos. He just walked easily around doing things like he'd been doing them all his life, with this slight knowing smile on his face. It was like he already knew exactly what was going to happen or he knew there was going to be problems and the gang would handle them just fine. The only thing I knew was that Jos was the calmest.

Just before six o'clock, Jos asked everyone if they were ready. With a mix of excitement and apprehension everyone nodded. I took my place at the podium and braced myself; I was the first one anybody would see, and I knew very well about first impressions. But just before Jos opened the door, I heard in my head Jos say what he had said before; be the first to give respect freely and people will respond to it. The door opened and I was totally amazed. There were a bunch of people standing there already waiting to come in and see the new restaurant in their neighborhood. And Jos was absolutely right; I felt at ease greeting people because I was feeling real warmth for everyone for just being there and waiting. It was like greeting friends and neighbors and wanting to introduce them to other friends and neighbors that I was genuinely very proud of. It was actually very enjoyable. I felt really good and energetic; it was almost like being a little intoxicated.

Once people came in and were seated, the gang was on their toes smiling and talking with everyone. You could tell they felt the same way I did. It all just seemed to permeate the whole place with a great atmosphere. The first thing the table captains did as they came out to greet people was to bring them fresh baked bread from Natashia, the smell of which was still thick in the air. There were so many people to start with that after everyone was seated there were still two couples left. I gave my apologies and had them sit in Connie's great idea of a waiting area and got them some bread and took a beverage order. The place was absolutely vibrating with conversations and laugher, the gang was moving like they had done this all of their lives and the smiles were endless.

Surprisingly, Ahmed and Billy had, on their own, decided to clean off tables together and even had a routine down so well they looked like a military precision group, complete with hand signals and secret salutes. They completely floored the guests, not to mention the gang, and had become the entertainment of the night; just cleaning up. It was so fascinating.

By the time ten o'clock came around, it had seemed like only an hour, but also like a dream. Jos walked over and turned the "open" sign around to "closed" and, with that knowing smile, looked over the room that was still filled with people obviously having a great time.

The first night went off without many mishaps. There were a couple of dropped glasses and a broken plate or two but for the most part, the first night of the new restaurant was far more than just successful; it was astonishing. The only real snag that happened was trying to take money; everyone wanted to pay with plastic. Luckily, a quick call to Jack found that he did have a merchant account that we were able to use.

Jack couldn't resist stopping by about eight o'clock just to see what was happening. I didn't see much of him after that, I was kept quite busy myself, but he was there for a little while then left.

Maybe he was there to make sure the little café was not burning down, or to see if it was a flop, or maybe to see if Jos really pulled off a miracle and got the place business. I don't know what he thought, but he had to be pleased. After all, this was ultimately his restaurant and any success would be of benefit to him. He must have seen that Jos, a younger man in his mid-thirties, that had talked him into letting him borrow his business must have something to teach. But Jos had told us that before. Everyone can learn; people are learning all of the time. That is the beauty of age and experience; the longer you are alive the more you learn, unless you're hiding under a rock.

Everything Affects Everything

Connie was helping clean a table with Jos and said, "That was a great opening night. Not to be pessimistic, but do you think it will continue? I mean, here, in this neighborhood. Do you think it is going to make a difference? Do you think it will have an effect?"

Oh, yes, it will definitely have an effect. It is important to understand that everything affects everything at some time. Everything in the universe started at one point and at one time. At that one point and time, everything in the universe was just one thing. As the universe expanded, everything was still just part of that one thing, it just continued to become increasingly bigger and diverse. Now it is incomprehensibly big, but it is still all just one thing. So, anything that happens, anywhere, will have an effect to everything else in it from that point on.

It is like looking at a human body. At one point in time it was microscopic in size. It was just a fertilized egg, it was just one thing. But even at that it was made up of a countless number of atoms. As time went along, it became bigger and bigger until it became the size you are now. But it is still considered just one thing. Everything that happened, as it was growing, affected everything in it in some way. Everything affects everything. The change is irreversible.

It never ceases to amaze me the arrogance of man even to be able to conceive of a philosophical question like," If a tree falls in the forest and there is no one around to hear it, does it make a sound?" Of course, it makes a sound. Do the laws of physics cease to exist without humans? Do you think the squirrel that the fallen tree almost hit wishes a human had been there so he could have heard the tree falling and run?

A tree falling on Earth, anywhere, affects the things around it; the air, the ground, other trees, everything around it. That, in turn, will affect everything coming after that in some way. It is known as the "Butterfly Effect."

Humans would not be on earth if a star about ten billion years ago did not go super nova. One thing happens and it causes another thing to happen, and then that causes something, or many other things, to happen and it just keeps going. It is never ending, that is why I say that everything affects everything, it is only a matter of time.

The trinity of time is the future, the past, and the present. That is why the present is so important; it is the fulcrum. It is the point that everything starts to affect everything else. Will this night have an effect? Yes. Will it continue? That is for time to tell.

One day, when we had some time, I found myself walking alone with Jos; a rare occasion but, as always, cherished. There was just something about this man that made you feel calm. Just walking with him in the quiet, neither of us speaking, you still just got a sense of what he was about. You noticed his breathing; occasionally he would make the very slightest of sounds, almost completely imperceptible. You could just feel his enjoyment of life, his wonderment with living, and his appreciation of the moment. Many times, he would suddenly stop, hold up a hand to get your attention, and then casually point at something of interest. It may be a small creature running across a yard or field, or it may be a vehicle making a maneuver, or a person saying something or just making a particular movement, or it may just be something as simple as a bird flying by. Everything seemed to have a meaning to him. Everything had a reason; and, like he had said, everything affects everything. Maybe he was just trying to figure out how what he was looking at was going to affect the future.

On this particular day, it was several weeks after the opening of the Burger Steak restaurant, he was in his usual mood and we were heading down the street to look at an old, large building he had seen several blocks down. It was morning, before we opened the restaurant for the day. By this time, the restaurant was doing so well the gang started opening early enough for the lunch crowd.

Without stopping this time, he raised his hand to direct my attention to two boys about to race each other on their bicycles. A great smile grew on his face. He thoroughly enjoyed watching people take pleasure in living. The two boys started at it with all they were worth; pushing their bicycles as hard as they could. Suddenly, the boy falling behind inexplicitly fell off his bicycle, landing in the grass next to the road. As Jos and I hurried over to his aid, we could hear the boy exclaiming, "You made me fall. I was just about to pull around you and you swerved and made me fall."

That was really not what I had seen; but everybody has a different point of view, I said to myself. Then I thought; Wow, Jos is really getting me to see things differently than I use to. The boy was unharmed and after a curt refusal of assistance he was on his way with the other one. Jos was laughing, not outright or aloud, but laughing all the same.

He looked at me and took this chance to tell me ...

Excuse or Reason

You can either do something using an excuse or by using a reason. The difference is an *excuse* is something people use to assign blame. A *reason* is something that people use to assign credit. Anybody can come up with either to justify their actions to others, and in their own minds.

An example would be when a child is abused in their youth. If they grow up to be abusive, then they often use the "excuse" that they were abused as a child. However, conversely, if they grow up to be very kind and would never hurt a child they often use the "reason" that they were abused as a child. See the point: it is all a point of view and the different words in language that can be used.

That is why when I say whatever influenced you in your life can either be used as an excuse or a reason.

As we walked along, Jos expanded the thought a little more.

Each and every one of us has blessings and burdens. No one person is devoid of either, it is just whether or not they wish to see it for what it is. Most blessings we have we bring upon ourselves along with most burdens. When we recognize a blessing, many religious people will refer to it as a gift from God. And they are right. Even if we bring the blessing on ourselves, it is a gift from God. As each one of us is part of God. The same is true with a burden. Most burdens are brought onto the person themselves as well. Some would say that it is God's punishment. It is your own punishment. That statement, again, is one and the same thing yet sounding so different.

He stopped suddenly and looked right at me.

Is not human language so exquisite? One word spoken, or misspoken, at any given time can change the whole meaning of the idea attempting to be conveyed. A gift from God; a gift from you; different words yet both mean the same thing. Yet others can turn it around to mean something different. Fascinating, and it is not specific to any particular language; it can be done in all languages ... manipulation. Fascinating! Communication is so tricky and treacherous. Do you not think? That is why it is said; the pen is mightier than the sword. It is just words.

But back to what I was saying. The only difference is: do you wish to see the blessing or the burden, and where do you perceive it coming from. That is your choice and your responsibility.

Because of the yin and yang of life, to every burden there is a blessing; and vice versa. It is up to you to perceive anything the way you want to.

He looked at me and winked. We walked a short distance in silence.

"Sometimes I wonder," I said in reflection. "What the purpose and meaning of life really is."

Without even an apparent thought, Jos replied ...

The Purpose of Life Versus the Meaning of Life

What is the purpose of life? That is simple; the purpose of life is to survive, period.

What is the meaning of life? That is one of those most asked, seemingly unanswerable questions philosophers have been struggling with since humans were able to ask it. But the *meaning* of life is quite simple too. It is to learn and experience as much as possible *and* to pass along as much of that knowledge and experience as possible to others, to further the species in a positive direction.

The reason for "living things" is it is the only way that *living* can be experienced. You must have an instrument that is made up of matter to manipulate the world of matter. That is the meaning and reasoning for life, to be able to experience and to learn as much as possible about all aspects of living, in all the different ways that can be done, from all the different points of view.

Life is Precious

Everyone thinks that life is precious. If human life was precious, it would be indestructible. God does not see life as precious; *humans* do. God knows that life only has a finite period to survive anyhow. What God sees as precious is energy; what we commonly refer to as the soul or spirit. The energy that makes us who we are as individuals. And that energy, or soul, cannot be taken or destroyed by anybody or anything; not even by ourselves. That is the piece of "God" that existed before the human body did, and the piece that will exist after. That is what is put here to learn and experience. *That is what is precious to God. That is God.*

The human body is nothing more than a mass of atoms assembled together to make a living human body. That mass of atoms is constantly being recycled into other things on earth throughout time. The atoms that make up your body were acquired from your food. Just prior to you eating it, those atoms made up other plants and animals.

Life is precious; I am not disputing that. It is a gift that has to be nurtured and taken care of. Life, of every kind, is magical and mystical and full of wonder. Life should be cherished by anything intelligent enough to know how special it is; all life. *All lives matter.* Life is precious, but it is not the most precious thing around. The most precious thing is knowledge and life experience. Life comes and goes but knowledge is forever.

At the end of several blocks, and just as we turned the corner, I saw the old, really large building. It was not far back from the road. You could tell the building was very old from the style and the brickwork that made up the walls. You could tell it had been painted several times and even at some point had some sort of picture painted on the side. But now, what paint survived was just in patches with curled edges. Most of the few windows it had were still intact, surprisingly. I would guess that its original purpose was some kind of factory; of what and for what was anyone's guess. Just how many different times in its history had that purpose changed was again, anyone's guess. The fact that it was not in use at present was quite obvious.

The biggest guess for me right now was its interest to Jos. What was he thinking? As he was staring up at the huge, ominous building, a phrase blurted out just under his breath, like voices had been going around in his head and one just suddenly broke free. I heard Jos utter
...

The Church of Understanding

Now he was talking more to himself than to me; almost in a whisper.

We should call it the Church of Understanding. The Church of Understanding is not just a teaching church but a place to understand others. It is where people will learn ... everything. That is how you praise God; that is how you really worship God. It is to learn. It is to praise and worship other living things.

Now he turned to me. He had a blaze of excitement in his eyes.

Here is what I see as a good thing to do on a Sunday morning. You go to a big building with a bunch of other people, people from your community, all different kinds and ages of people, and instead of sitting around listening to some person's interpretation of a book, whichever book of any religion, you sit around talking to the other people about all kinds of things there in that great big room. People, all different kinds and ages of people, have a whole lot of knowledge about all kinds of things. Knowledge that would be of benefit to others, a lot more benefit than some interpretation of a book.

Yes, a building where people can go to learn from others. People in their community; and get to know people in their own community. The community you live in is far more important than any fantasy community on television. The people that live close around you are far more important, and interesting, than those that live in communities far away, with their own gangs, interests, and problems.

All you have to do is afford the people of the area a place to gather and get to know one another. Once they do that, then it is just a small step to get them to start teaching each other things they know. Mostly just simple things like hobbies. But some people, especially the young, can make hobbies into careers. And it really does not matter what you learn, everything you learn can be beneficial at some time.

Here are a few things Muhammad said:

"To spend more time in learning is better than spending more time praying."

"It is better to teach knowledge one hour in the night than to pray all night."

"Whoever seeketh knowledge and findeth it will get two rewards; one of them the reward for desiring it and the other for attaining it; therefore, even if he does not attain it, for him is one reward."

"One learned man is harder on the devil than a thousand ignorant worshippers."

"He who knoweth his own self knoweth God."

He who knoweth his own self knoweth God. That is more correct than most people know.

A good and true Church of Understanding would be built with tables and basic tools so that others could show and teach beneficial things like wood working, machining, computers, sewing, design, house maintenance, and the list could go on and on. Different kinds of artwork, musical instruments, basic photography, the arts, the sciences, philosophies; anything and everything that people can think of. It is the very *meaning of life*. In the process of learning and sharing knowledge of different things people learn and share knowledge about themselves and their cultures and backgrounds. People learn firsthand about other people. Your knowledge and understanding of the things that interest you as well as other people would grow exponentially fast and would probably be a lot of fun in the process.

Life experience is knowledge; knowledge of the most valuable kind. Life experience is knowledge that cannot be bought or paid for; it is acquired through time.

Knowledge Is Compassion and Power

The more you know about people, the more compassion you have for other people. If you know nothing about another person, why would you even care what they think, or what they are going through, or what they have done, or what they know? There are so many people on this planet how can you possibly care for all of them like you know them?

Knowledge is a precious thing. Compassion is priceless.

You tend to care more for the people close to you; in fact, it is generally proportionate; the closer someone is to you the more you care about them. This is a point when and where the "gang theory" comes into play. The smaller and tighter the gang, the closer the group gets to one another, and the tighter the bond becomes.

The Passion

So many people fixate on the "Passion of the Christ" and its importance, but fail to focus on the true importance of Jesus which was the "*Compassion* of Jesus." Whether or not Jesus was, or is, divine is not important. What is important is his message and what he was trying to teach.

Everyone has become so determined to prove his divinity that they completely lose sight of what he was teaching and the reason, in his own words, for why he was here to start with. "To love one another as I have loved you," and "to testify to the truth." Jesus said he was here to pass along the good word: that God is love, and that God was within you and all about you. Jesus preached tolerance and compassion for all, at all times. In every action and every word and every implication that he gave was to promote tolerance and compassion and respect, not to prove his divinity. Look at the way he was with the tax collector and with the Romans and with the Sanhedrin, even at the time they were brutalizing him. Even the most poignant example when he forgave the Roman soldier for crucifying him. "Father, forgive them, for they know not what they do."

He was not judgmental; he did not care how someone else lived their life as long as they did not harm another in any way. In fact, about the only time you read about Jesus getting mad is when some living thing was being harmed "in the name of God."

Once a person can develop a sense of compassion for all other people regardless of the circumstances, then that person will gain immeasurable power. Look into your heart, you know this to be true.

The only reason the "Passion of the Christ" was important was simply to make Jesus stay in the minds of men. In a time when many miracle workers and prophets were around, rivals of Jesus, like Mithras, Simon Magus, Apollonius of Tyana, Simon Bar Kochba, and Isis, even John the Baptist, just to name a few. The "Passion" is what makes people remember Jesus over them.

The next time you want a serial killer to be put to death, think about the compassion of Jesus. What does it say about you if you want to kill, even a killer? That is just vengeful. If you cannot give compassion, give them nothing. Understand that they will feel what they did when they become their victim for eternity.

"Understand that they will feel what they did when they become their victim for eternity." That line stuck in my head. What an odd thing to say.

We were walking around this massive structure, viewing it from all sides. Jos would walk up to the building as close as he could then look back. He appeared to be getting different perspectives of the building and its surroundings. My mind started drifting over the things he had just said. Then I kind of just blurted out, "Isn't that what religions are about? What is divine and what is not? What is the right thing to do and what is not?"

He gazed at me for a second. The question jarred him from his thoughts. Then he remarked out succinctly ...

Most people think so but, really, not so much.

The Main Reason Humans Have Religion

The main reason humans have ever had religion is one primary purpose: to answer the question "What happens after I die?" From even before recorded history, there is evidence that humans have entertained this question in earnest. Of all the other reasons people have developed different religions the number one main purpose is to either answer the question. "What happens after I die?" or "Is there an afterlife?" The only reason they really even consider God is because they think that God determines their afterlife. Even religions that do not really even have a designated god consider the afterlife.

One of the hardest things that humans have to deal with is their own mortality. They know, without a doubt, that one day they are going to die. Probably the most frightening thing for most is to think that this is the end of everything, the finale, and nothingness for evermore. Or for some, the frightening part is not necessarily that they will never again exist, but that a loved one will never again exist. For some people, religion is only meant to be a comfort when someone they love, very dearly, dies, especially if it is early or abruptly. It is hard for them to except the end as finality.

Jos had picked up a rock and was tossing it back and forth in his hands as he talked. Now he cast the rock aside and said ...

Well, that is about all I needed to see here for now. Let us get back to the restaurant for service.

As we headed back down toward the Burger Steak Jos continued to tell me things. I felt quite privileged to hear this information as none of the others were with us. I listened intently.

Here is where another unique trait of human beings is seen; the trait to take advantage of that little idiosyncrasy of the human psyche. That innate desire to believe and trust in anything or anybody that can offer hope of an afterlife. So many people in the past have used that glimmer of hope to persuade other people into doing their will or following their laws. Whole countries and governments have been set up with this ruse in place. "If you listen to me and follow what I say, without question mind you, I can promise you eternal life." Or, "If you follow my instructions, no matter how bad life in the here and now is, you will be rewarded with endless wishes for eternity." Or, even the best one, "Do what I say and you will go to Heaven, if you do not you will go to Hell." Now they throw in, not only is there an afterlife but if you follow them it will be good, and if you do not follow them it will be bad ... forever. That is classic human manipulation.

By this time, we had gotten close to the restaurant and two of the gang had come out to meet us. As they came close, they got in on the last part of the conversation. Curtis, a dark-skinned man, closer in age to Adam, meekly said, "Is there a hereafter?"
Jos looked Curtis straight into the eye and with full conviction said
...

Let me just succinctly say, here and now, that there is an afterlife. It is probably not what you have been led to believe it is, though.

First, let everyone please understand that the afterlife will consist of energy, or the spirit if you prefer to call it that; not a physical body. The physical body you have on Earth will return to where it came from; Earth. The human body is not a "person"; it is a machine, a chalice if you will, that contains the spirit, or if you prefer "the Holy Spirit," or energy, of a person.

Bodies can be damaged, broken, and burned all without harming the spirit. Once the vessel that contains the spirit is gone, it disintegrates back into its chemical components sooner or later.

For right now, just for the sake of argument, let us just say that there is an afterlife. If there is, what would it really be like? Again, let me say, that Heaven, Jannah, Olam Haba, Shamayim, Valhalla, whichever word in whichever religion you want to use, is not a place; it is a time. You will not go to that place; you are already there. When Jesus was asked, "Where is Heaven?" He replied, according to St. Thomas, "The kingdom of Heaven is within you and all about you." That pretty much describes "everyplace." The "Land beyond" or the place where you will spend the afterlife is all around you; it is this universe.

You are creating the afterlife right now with what you do and how you treat others. The afterlife is where time exists all at once. All things are known in the hereafter.

Curtis and Reese joined me and Jos walking back to the restaurant. Jos seemed preoccupied, you could tell that he was still thinking about the old, large building even as he talked about other things. It was as if he was so knowledgeable about what he was talking about he could just explain things as if he had firsthand experience of it and it was second nature to talk about it. It was like he could be in two completely different places and function with complete concentration in both.

Time and Matter and Energy

Time, matter, and energy are what make up the known universe.

The science of these things has taken the lifetimes of some of the smartest people that have ever lived to understand. It is far too much to describe in detail now, but there is one thing that is very important to know; that is time.

Matter is made up of an unimaginable amount of infinitesimally small things. Even smaller than atoms. Everything combined together make up everything you see.

Time, on the other hand, is something altogether different. The "time" that I am talking about is merely a point of reference. As anything else in the universe time has a yin and yang to it; the future and the past. Time into the future moves in a linear progression. The possibilities of what can happen to any type of matter in the future is vast. Now, once it is in the past whatever is going to happen to that material has happened and cannot be changed. Anything in the past can be referenced at any time. In other words, you can remember or think about anything that happened in the past at any given moment. So, essentially, the past exists all at the same time; it is all encompassing.

Here is the point I am trying to make regarding time and matter: matter exists in a perpetual state of possibilities until a particular, instantaneous point in time; then, at that moment, it is confirmed and defined and never to be changed. Time, on the other hand, is in a constant state of linear progression until that particular, instantaneous moment of the "present"; then it is no longer linear but all-encompassing at once as a memory or "history" and, again, cannot be changed, only reflected on. In conclusion: the only thing that changes *matter* is *time*, and the only thing that changes *time* is the "present"; a very specific instantaneous point.

Now Jos stopped, smiled, and held up his hands. He looked at us to see our response to what he thought was a valuable secret.

The Most Important Thing In the Universe Is the Present.

The reason this is important to understand is that to truly understand life and to truly appreciate living is to understand that the *present* is the determining factor to everything. I have said before, often, that everything changes everything and the only thing that changes everything from possibilities to factual history is the very instant of the present. All things begin and all things end. The only question is where anything is at in its particular timeline.

I like to say, "We are living in the past of the future. We are living in the future of the past. We only live in the present."

I hope that you can now grasp this so very important point about the universe and everything in it. If you do not understand anything else that I tell you, please understand this. The most important thing in the universe is the present.

I remember this so clearly because it seemed so important to Jos. It was still somewhat vague to me however. "The most important thing in the universe is the present." It was a sentence that really did not have the impact it should have had on me at the time. I would come to learn its true importance as my time with Jos went along.

As we came back up to the restaurant we could see what looked like an older, disheveled man with a scraggily beard standing at the side of the building. Jos was saying something about how the old place could use a facelift or at least a little tender loving care.

"Some new paint would be nice," I heard someone say. I am not sure who said it, though, because at the time I was preoccupied by this rather lost looking man on the side of the building.

Like I said before, this was a part of the town that had already seen its better days. This was not where you were going to find the rich and famous passing through. This man was obviously neither rich nor famous. In fact, he was a little unnerving. I was not sure what to make of him just by looking at him, but he did make me feel somewhat uneasy. He was unkempt with a tattered old jacket and looked as if sleeping in a bed was not his normal practice. As we came up to where he was, he just stood there frozen, staring like a deer in headlights. It was obvious that Reese had noticed him, too, but I was not sure that Curtis or Jos had, as they were consumed in conversation.

Just as we were parallel with the man, Jos stopped talking to Curtis and addressed the man standing there as if he had been with us the whole time. Walking up to him, Jos said ...

I have an idea that I want you to think about. If you were to do me this favor, I would be honored to give you a fine meal.

The man looked startled for a moment, wondering who this was just walking up to him without any regard; in fact, like he had known him personally. The man had a bewildered look on his face. It would have made me slow down with cautiousness. However, Jos was not fazed, he walked right up to him. Jos talked to him for a second, looking straight into his face. The man was looking back with a mixture of confusion and defensiveness. Without wavering, Jos continued to talk; at one time, he kind of leaned back to look behind the length of the restaurant, then right back at the man. Before long the man's expression softened and he shrugged. Jos put his hand on the man's shoulder and walked out to the sidewalk with him. The man was not completely steady with walking and was a bit slow in step. With his free hand Jos waved the direction he wanted the man to go, toward the front door.

Jos asked Reese if he would obtain enough money from the restaurant's maintenance funds to purchase the needed paint and supplies to paint the outside of the restaurant. Then he asked Curtis to find Connie and use her talent for design and go get the right color of paint.

With the move to open for lunch the menu selections had grown. The lunch crowd was brisk and to capacity because of our successful nighttime operation. The reputation was out that the Burger Steak was the place to eat in this area. We had been quite busy and really surprised with the immediate and overwhelming success of the business. Nice atmosphere, great food for the right price, and a friendly staff all working together. As Jos would say, "How could it go wrong?"

We walked into the front of the restaurant and found Mariam. She had been working with Rudy and Billy to get the tables ready to open. Adam and his team were in the kitchen, judging by the savory aroma emitting from there. With the man still in tow, Jos walked up to Mariam and spoke to her. Mariam had her usual sweet smile on her face, looking kind and gentle, but her brief gaze to the man was quite obviously cautious. After a moment, Mariam reached up and replaced Jos' hand with her own on the man's shoulder. The two of them walked into the back of the restaurant toward the dishwashing station.

Not Everyone Has Read the Same Book

Watching Mariam walking to the back with the man in tow, I remembered something she had said once. I don't know why that suddenly came to mind. Mariam was a very kind person and you could see her genuine concern for this stranger. I think that's what brought this to mind and what Jos had to say about it.

Mariam said, "When I was a nurse working the ICU, one night a man came in complaining about discomfort in his left foot. He was sweaty and a little short of breath, but his main complaint was his left foot ached. Now, he didn't have any chest pain. No indication of a heart attack at all. But because of his age it was routine to run an EKG. So, *they did one in the Emergency Room when he came in and found that he was having a heart attack. It seemed funny that he really didn't have any of the usual symptoms of a cardiac event, but there you go. He was having a heart attack and the symptom for him was pain in the left foot. Funny."*

"Guess he didn't read the book on the symptoms he was supposed to have, huh?" Connie commented.

Mariam agreed. "Yeah, that's what we said."

When they spoke about that, Jos said ...

That is a great point. Everyone has not read the same book. This you see all the time; a very common problem when you have many viewpoints.

All people have different interests, different curiosities, and different points of view. This is why you have so many different points of view with humans. But, that is the point; to have many different points of view. However, those different points of view sometimes clash with other points of view and there you will find conflicts. This happens with beliefs, cultures, and customs. They even have different medical symptoms for the same problems. This can create confusion.

It is hard to find a similarity with other people when you have nothing in common that you can identify with. Although, if people did stop long enough to investigate, or at least tolerate a little curiosity about others, people would find that even being quite different they really do have a lot in common. Most people want to live a good life; they want to enjoy laughter, have good friends, make a living, look at pretty things, eat good food, have children and raise them well. Most people desire the same things regardless of the culture, language, location, and beliefs.

When trying to relate or communicate with someone else, you have to be able to find some common ground in which to get started. You both need to have "read the same book" or something is going to get missed. Humans around the world have many, many things in common; most people are *"on the same page,"* they just do not know it because they have not read the same book the other did.

They all want the same things in life, they just have been taught a different way to go about it. That creates a conflict when trying to agree on just about anything.

Muhammad said it pretty well: "No man is a true believer unless he *desires for his brother* that which he *desires for himself.*"

While most people are on the "same page," they are just reading from "different books."

"So, are we just going to feed this guy?" Reese asked nonchalantly. "I mean, I don't care. The guy could definitely use a good meal, but we really can't just do that to everyone that comes by."

You could tell that Reese was feeling a little uneasy bringing this up, so he kept it as matter-of-fact as he could. "I mean, this is a business."

Jos understood completely what Reese was saying and knew that some of the others were feeling the same way. Even though Jos was looking at Reese he was talking to everyone to see if he could get them in the same book ...

The Food Gift for Work

A lot of times many people are struggling just to eat. Many people, for whatever reason, just need a meal; whether they are homeless and "down on their luck" or they use what money they can get to feed a drug addiction or some other circumstance. Some places there just is not an opportunity to acquire food. Almost every person that sees this wants to help. Nobody wants to see another person starve regardless of their situation or reason.

Many good charitable organizations assist with this endeavor. But they can only operate with charitable donations and generally do not ask anything from the recipients at all for the service. There is a yin and yang to that. It is good to give food away without question, and it is also bad to do that. It is like putting food outside your house for a friendly raccoon; it has its pros and cons. It is generous and kind to feed the raccoon, and it may be fun to watch the little critter come up and eat, but you are inviting the animal close to your house and you do not know what it will do at any particular time. Plus, what will this animal do if it gets use to having this charity and then it suddenly stops? Charity, for all of its good, costs somebody something.

There are many missed opportunities, even today, for those that want to help. Where they could set up opportunities for people to earn their way. Because in many countries you have certain laws that mandate that if someone works, they have to be paid, in currency, a certain amount at least. That keeps many opportunities from materializing because of legal requirements and ramifications.

You have got to understand that there are those people out there that cannot hold down a job for various reasons. Either they choose not to, or they just cannot seem to be able to work what would be required of them for a regular job. However, they can wash dishes or clean a kitchen for a meal. They can clean a yard for a meal. They can do some simple chore that does not take long or is too involved, like fixing a fence, for some kind of gratuity and stay perfectly legal because it is not an actual job with legal employment requirements. It is just humans helping each other.

Be forewarned, however, unfortunately in this time, people have to be very careful about how they go about assisting others with opportunities. So many well-meaning people have been harmed and killed for allowing complete strangers to work close to them and for them.

If you can provide *safe*, *responsible*, and *monitored* opportunities to those in need, then many people could obtain what they need without loss of dignity and self-respect, on their own terms. That would be a balance that would lean heavily to the good for both.

When Mariam and the older man came back into the restaurant from the back, it was shortly before opening for the day. The man looked totally different. He was cleaned up; his beard was shaved and mustache trimmed. He had on a clean shirt and pants. He actually looked younger. Mariam escorted him over to one of the two place tables and had him sit down. He sat there staring out into the dining area with a rather blank gaze and a lost facial expression. He looked like he did not know what to do, where to look, or what to think. Rudy and Billy had finished what they were doing. Billy went back into the kitchen and Rudy was sitting up in the waiting area casually wiping down the display case. His back was to the dining area. Jos and I were standing at the entrance podium just about to open for business.

I mentioned that the man had returned and was sitting at the back table, just in passing. Jos had talked to this man while he was in the back. He informed me that the man's name was Jordan and confirmed that he was a "street person." He relayed what little he could find out in a short amount of time in talking with him. He had been living on the street for a few years now and his drug of choice was alcohol. He pretty much just begged for money for any drink he could get. Otherwise what he could find on the streets to recycle he cashed in, and anything he could "find" he would pawn to get some money for food and the rest went on drink. Jos found that he was willing to put in a little work for a decent meal and maybe an extra sandwich or two to go. After a short talk with the man, Jos felt comfortable enough, especially with Billy and the other guys around, to bring the man in, let him get cleaned up, have his clothes cleaned, and feed him. In return, he asked the man to scrape down the outside of the restaurant and paint it. He made a deal with Jordan to give him a full meal and some spending money for each side of the building he painted.

By this time, Curtis and Connie were back with the painting supplies. After telling Jos where they put the supplies, they went on about their own ways. Everyone kept busy doing what needed to be done to run the restaurant. No one needed to be told anything, and other than polite chatter, the only thing you would hear was someone asking for some assistance and an immediate obliging response. I had noticed over the last several weeks that we acted somehow different than normal employees of a business. For the simple fact that everyone received pay according to their percentage in the business. Everyone acted more like respectful partners than co-workers. They were always trying to come up with a better idea or way of doing things and constantly discussing it among themselves. Everyone seemed secure in their position and content in doing it.

I saw Jos walk over to Jordan, who was just starting to eat the plate of food Mariam had brought him. Jordan continued to eat as Jos spoke. He would glace at Jos occasionally and nod. You could tell that however he looked when we first saw him was slowly fading away. He was more alert and responsive. After a few more minutes of talking and some animated hand gestures in the air, Jos put his hand on Jordan's shoulder and stood up. Jos started to head back toward me at the front.

A few of the guys got with Jos and straight out asked him how much he trusted Jordan; one, to do a decent job on the restaurant, and two, how safe he was to have around? They were concerned mainly for the patrons of the restaurant, for the restaurant itself, but also for each other's safety. It was a valid concern and Jos acknowledged that. He also commended them for promptly coming up to him to voice their concerns and question his judgment. He expressed appreciation for their honesty and his delight that they felt comfortable enough to confront him immediately about it. He then called everyone to him. He apologized for making a "business" decision without consulting everyone first. This was a combined effort, he told everyone, and he had just made a unilateral decision and for that he apologized. He then asked how everyone felt about having Jordan trade some work for food and a little cash. Of course, everyone was on board with helping anyone but still had reasonable concerns. After giving them some assurance he and I walked over to the door. He indicated that it was time to open the door and I noticed that there were already people ready to come in.

Amusingly, I mentioned to Jos that there were quite a few people ready to eat. He nodded, commenting that this is the way of things. "All machines must have fuel," he would always say. When Jos talked about humans, he always seemed to differentiate them into two parts. It would depend on whether he was talking about how they thought or what they did. When he talked about what people did, he would talk *about them as being like, as he put it, a chemical processing plant or like their bodies were just machines. When he would talk about how they thought, or what made them who they were as individuals, he would talk about them totally differently.*

The Human Machine

What most people do not really understand is that the human body is just a machine like any other machine and "our spirit," energy, gets to inhabit it for a period of time. Then the machine, like everything else on Earth, is reclaimed back by the planet. The human body is a functioning, living organism, but it really is no different than a car or any other complex, multifaceted functioning mechanism. The only difference from a car is that the body is made up of living tissue; biological tissue.

The chemicals, or food, that go into your body, make other chemical compounds inside your body by its own machinery. Chemicals go in, get processed and used, and come out. Your body reverts back to what it has been conditioned to do or expect. That is why if you eat a good diet for just a short period of time, like a day or even a week, you do not generally see any changes; you have to be on a diet for a while for your body to process the changes. You cannot just exercise once in a while and expect that your body will maintain any particular shape. Your body is *always* in a constant state of change and will always, and only, reflect what is demanded of it for any period of time.

Once your body is conceived, I mean the moment two cells come together to start the process of conception, it is on a journey to death. Your body is on a constant timeline to the end. You can speed it up and you can slow it down, but you cannot stop it and you cannot reverse it. All your body is going to do is constantly change to maintain the vessel that is demanded of it to house and supply the brain with what it needs at any given time.

There are three parts to any human being: the physical body, which is the living tissue that is the machine; the physical brain, which is the nervous operating system of the body, the computer; and the living spirit, which is the consciousness or the energy, the thoughts and feelings and memories, that inhabits the physical form during its time on Earth, and *influences* the physical brain. That is the trinity of the human being.

Another part of the "trinity" of the human being is time-based. The beginning, the end, and the time in the middle; the time in the middle has a fulcrum. I had a friend whose father was a soldier in

World War Two. I asked his father once how he managed to survive the war being shot at in battle and all. He told me, only half-jokingly, "When I was young, I was not very smart but I could run really fast; when I got older I was not very fast but I was a lot smarter."

In a natural lifetime, as the body decreases, the intelligence increases; the body is not at the best at birth and the mind is not the best at death. There is a point where every human that lives a natural lifetime crosses the center of the fulcrum and that is their peak; of body and mind. Before the fulcrum, the body is in better shape; after the fulcrum, the mind is better. That is just one of the things that make living things, "living things."

Adam had come out from the kitchen earlier and was listening to the conversation; or I should say he was listening to what Jos had to say. Because he had come in a little late he had a question. "Let me ask this," he said. "What makes a living thing? When you talk about memories and machines and that kind of thing, what makes us different? Let me put it this way, what makes 'living things' different from, say, artificial intelligence machines? From what I understand, which may not be much, but some quantum based computers are many times faster than current computers and can hold vastly more information. In the future, what is going to make them any different than living organisms?"

Without missing a beat Jos explained ...

What Makes a Living Thing a Living Thing?

Living things are living things because they have an internal energy that controls processes. They are not built, they build themselves. An example would be: If you put down all the parts needed to build a car on the floor and left the room and given enough time you could walk back into that room and the car would be sitting there, self-made. In real living things, you do not even put down all the parts needed, you just put down one nut and one bolt, one reproduction cell with another reproduction cell, and leave the room for enough time and not only does it self-construct it develops and manufactures all the parts needed. Now, granted, it does have to have a source of materials to draw from, namely nutrients, but it assembles itself.

Because they are able to develop their own needed parts, they are also able to mutate, modify, and change as needed. I mean that things change for a purpose or for a desire. The mutation is generally of benefit to the organism. Non-living things just cannot do that.

Living things grow on their own, like the universe. Non-living things have to be put together.

"So, what you're saying is that the human body is a biological machine," Adam went on, *"a gift from God."* He gleefully smiled at Jos.

Jos smiled right back. Jos nodded, big nods, like you would see from a horse.

The Human Body Is a Chemical Plant

People have looked at the human body as a miracle; one miraculous living thing that is singular onto itself. That the human body is separate from all other things and what belongs to that individual body belongs to that individual body and nothing else.

The truth of the matter is that the human body is nothing more than a chemical processing plant. Nothing in the human body is unique or exclusive to that body.

Nutrients obtained from foods are essential to life and are foremost in rule number one, survival, and have therefore been well programmed into the brain to discern exactly how to acquire them. Whether you grow it, kill it, or steal it, the body will do what it has to do to obtain it. If you do not obtain nutrients you will die. This is one of "God's laws" and is therefore non-negotiable. This is where humans can, and do, exploit other humans.

I had been so busy bringing people in for lunch that I had not even noticed that Jordan had gotten up and left. It was not until I needed the table he had been sitting at that I realized that he had gone and the table was already cleaned. Without too much thought on the matter, I just used his table to seat another guest. It was about two hours later that I saw him come back in and ask if he could get a drink of water. I had him sit in the little U-shaped waiting area with dried paint flakes in his hair and all over his face. His hands were absolutely covered in teal-colored dust, the color the restaurant had been on the outside. Jordan had the look of someone that had been working harder than he had in a long time, but instead of looking beaten he looked surprisingly invigorated. He had a glow about him that was quiet and brighter.

I asked him if he wanted to go wash off a little. It was with a kind of pride about him he absently got up and mumbled, "Yeah, I probably should, huh?" Off he went toward the back of the restaurant with Mariam and Connie swinging around him with full plates to deliver. The girls didn't even react to him except to dodge him like a pillar or a table, like he had been there all the time. When Billy came through the kitchen door, he paused just for a moment with his foot holding it open for Jordan to go in. Then Jordan disappeared into the back.

A few minutes later I noticed Jordan sitting patiently in the waiting area not bothering a soul. I asked him if he would rather have a soda. He shook his head and said, "Just water would be great. Thanks." After a glass of water and a few more moments, I came back to my station to see an empty waiting area and an empty glass. All I could do was smile. "How simple was that?"

Then I remembered something that Jos had said before when we were just starting this adventure. He had been referring to new beginnings when he talked about ...

Hope

Hope is probably the most powerful, least understood emotion of humankind. Hope can be extremely powerful; when you have it and when you lose it. Hope will give you the desire to proceed; a reason to get out of bed in the morning, the inner excitement and giddiness that make you dream a dream and continue to make that dream come true. Hope will give you the strength to fight. Hope gives some people a reason to go on. Hope will make you do things that you would not normally do, or go places you would not normally go. Hope is a driving force. Hope is what gives light to the darkness. As long as there is hope, there is a glimmer of a chance and that can be a very powerful force indeed.

Losing hope can be just as powerful. Hopelessness is an emotion that puts some people into such a depression that they can lose rule number one, the drive to survive. Hope builds one up and gives you strength and determinations, whereas hopelessness can tear you down and make you go weak and defeated. When a person feels hopelessness and allows it to overcome them, you will see people shrink down, whither, withdrawal, and fade. Hopelessness can also clandestinely make you easier to anger. Hopelessness often leads to an addiction of various kinds; most frequently drugs because of the immediate numbing of the emotion. Sadly, drug addiction leads to more hopelessness, which begins a vicious cycle.

The worst part about hope is that it is generally not recognized. People have hope for or about something and are not even aware of it sometimes, which also goes with hopelessness; some people will have a sense of hopelessness and not be aware of it. Hope is quiet and generally kept deep down in a person's subconscious.

Humans must have hope, however, to continue. Set goals, dreams, aspirations, and then stay on track with hope of succeeding in those endeavors. Hope keeps people alive and living. Hopelessness can be very destructive, but, again, it is how it is acted on. Hopelessness can also be a powerful motivator but it is very difficult to bounce back from hopelessness; and sometimes it is very difficult to recognize it.

Hope is what creates miracles. *A hope that comes to fruition is often considered a miracle.*

If it is a realistic hope then now is the time to stop and plan, set goals, and get a direction to make the hope come true. Remember, the most important thing is the present.

It was getting close to dark when Jordan came back into the restaurant. His hair was again disheveled, only this time from hours of sweat and not days of being unwashed. His head was sprinkled with rusty orange-colored speckles and his hands and arms were smeared with the same color. I guessed the new color of the restaurant was going to be a rustic, dark orange color. He came up and looked at me, stating he was done with the back of the building. I looked at him without really knowing what to say. Dinner service was just now really starting to kick in with people coming in and already waiting. About the time I was going to suggest getting cleaned up again, Mariam walked up and told Jordan that his clothes were clean and in the back. She guided him once again toward the cleaning area. He was in the back of the restaurant for quite a while.

Later he came out from the back, cleaned up and in his original clothes, now cleaned. He had an uncharacteristic spring in his step as he popped through the dining room. By my podium, he gave me a "Thanks" with a thumb up as he passed. "See you tomorrow," was the last thing I heard him say on the way out. In just a few hours I had seen a disheveled, dirty, downtrodden man transform into a vibrant, energetic, happy guy that I would have never recognized as the same person.

Jos later informed me that while in the back, Adam and the crew had fed Jordan again and gave him a stuffed baguette to take with him. Jos also gave him a little cash with a promise of more when he came back to do more. As Jos explained to most of us, he did not really want to give Jordan a large amount of cash right now. Not because he was trying to cheat him out of a fair day's pay or even to tempt him to come back. Sometimes, Jos explained, if you give an addict a windfall of cash you could be the means of their demise. In other words, they may get and take too much at one time. It may not be as dangerous with alcohol as with something like heroin but still. Also, he really wanted Jordan to come back so Jos could have a little more time with him. Nobody really had the chance to find out where Jordan was going to go for the night. At that time, I did not know if Jos had been able to find out. I later found out he knew.

The next day came and went without any sign of Jordan. The following day Jordan was still a no show. The restaurant had an old, worn and chipped teal front and sides, but had a beautiful rustic, dark orange back to it. Jordan had really done a good job on the part that he had worked on, but now it looked like it would have to be finished by someone else.

The third day when the gang came up to the restaurant in the morning, there was Jordan. Standing at the front door looking very much the same as when I first saw him. I remember thinking: How could he get that dirty and disheveled in such a short time? Without skipping a beat or any hesitation in his voice, Jos asked him if he was ready to do a side or two today. Sheepishly, with his head down, Jordan nodded. I think he was a little surprised at Jos' reaction of no reaction, and I think that made him feel a little ashamed, even though Jos had done absolutely nothing to cause that emotion. Either it was no surprise to Jos, like he had expected it, or it was of no matter to him. Jos just went on like business as usual. He had Jordan do essentially the same thing as before; come in, get cleaned up, get some food in him, then off to work.

A few of the gang lightly questioned Jos about his judgment of Jordan. They thought Jos might be a little naïve about Jordan's true state of being. Maybe Jos was just being a little too kind, to the point of being taken advantage of. As one of them harshly put it, "He is an alcoholic. He will never be dependable." "He will never have any drive to change. Especially if we keep feeding him," another said.

Jos put his head down and reluctantly nodded. Then he looked up and spoke ...

Drugs Take, Not Give

Sadly, one of the major problems in today's society, if not the number one major problem, is drug addiction. It is prevalent in every country, every region, every culture, and every social-economic group around the world. There is nothing and no one immune to it and there is no immunity for it. It can attack anyone, any sex, any race, any sexual orientation, any religion, any cultural background, any age, whether you are considered attractive or not, whether you are considered fortunate or not, whether you are considered smart or stupid, or even if you are disciplined. Drug addiction is truly one of the only things on Earth that is completely unbiased to any human. And at the beginning it is extremely subtle.

Drug addictions are so much more prevalent today than in centuries past that it was rarely addressed in religious texts. If Jesus were here today, one of the more miraculous notations written of him would be the "curing of the addict."

Drugs are artificial ways of stimulating the pleasure centers of the brain immediately; sex is another way of stimulating the pleasure centers immediately. This is the reason that both of these things are so easily, and so commonly, addicted to and abused.

The worst thing drugs do to you is hamper your free will. Drugs interfere with your ability to exercise free will. The longer you are free from drugs the more "free will" you can exercise.

This is where humans have to govern themselves using self-control. This is where it is probably the hardest. But nothing else can do it. Others can help, others can assist, and it behooves everyone to try to help those in need; and these are the neediest of all. However, only the individual can control the addiction; no one else can.

With Jordan, we have a lot of people around; all he has to do is scrape down the old paint and put on the new paint. It is relatively hard to mess that up, and there is really nothing to harm or steal. To me it is worth a chance. I would like to know more about him, and the only way I can do that is if he is here. He may be wanting to change, but he has to be ready.

This is why I would like to see Jordan here working. Maybe with him around people, like you that truly enjoy life and all it has to offer, he will notice and desire that instead. Many people do not truly understand the affect they have on other people. I would like to give Jordan a chance, and besides, the old building does need a facelift.

"Wouldn't it be great if we could get Jordan to stop drinking?" Mariam said. "He would be so much happier. You see how happy he is when he's working and socializing with the rest of us. I think he could really be happy and have a good life if he could stay out of the bottle. I think we could help him." She looked at Jos. "Isn't it our obligation to help him get and stay sober? Isn't that what you say?"

Want To and Ready To

It is our obligation to *help* him. But that means to assist him when he is ready and not to hinder him when he is trying to make it himself. Too many people think that their "obligation" is to try to get him to quit; *make* him get sober and stay that way. Again, that is trying to force their sense of right and wrong, their way of thinking, onto him. It is not going to work. You have seen what happens when you try to force someone to do something. It only serves to push them farther away. Like teaching and learning; you can assist, you can influence, but only the individual learns what they want to learn.

Here is the thing about any addiction: you cannot "*want to*" quit and succeed, you have to be "*ready to.*" The more other people push for someone to stop an addiction, the more reason you give the addict to continue; it is an evil twist.

Even if the person wants to quit, that is not enough for them to do it. They will always find an excuse to slip back into it and then they get the feeling of, "Well, what is the point? I failed." That is just another excuse to fall back into the addiction; a sense of failure, then leading to hopelessness.

The difference between *wanting to* and *ready to* is: when you "want to" you choose a point, or time, to initiate it, like, "I will quit smoking after this pack." In contrast, when you are "ready to" quit, you just stop. At that very instant that you are ready, there may or may not even be a conscious effort.

The only thing you can do as a friend is be realistic when looking at someone. Be aware and cautious at all times. No matter how much you like someone or how much you "want" them to change and hope they do, and no matter how much you "think" someone is really ready and is changing, never drop your guard of self-preservation. Be aware that drink and drugs makes people do unpredictable things that are completely out of character, even for them. So, be kind, be tolerant, be helpful and assist when and where you can, but also be extremely careful.

A physician once told me: "Sadly, there are two rules to life. Rule number one: people die. Rule number two: you cannot change rule number one." You have to accept that there are things that you, yourself, cannot change. That can be frustrating.

Maybe with Jordan we can have an effect.

THE BAKERY

The first part of the day Adam and his crew would use part of the kitchen to prepare food. Natashia and Billy would beat them to the restaurant and already be preparing and baking for the day. They would have breads and muffins and donuts made for the morning. By the time Adam arrived, they would be making dessert items. Everybody worked very well together, but Natashia and Billy seemed to get along particularly well. Whatever was their secret, they put out a lot of pastries and baked goods.

Jos had talked to all of us and asked about expanding. He thought Natashia and Billy were productive enough to create a separate business. Jos indicated that if we all put in an investment we should be able to rent and fix up that empty shop down the street and make a bakery. It can continue to supply the restaurant and, with their production rate, could make enough to stand alone. They could even start selling pastries before the restaurant opened for lunch. Natashia gave Billy a glance of excitement and trepidation. Billy just looked excited.

Billy suggested that if they were going to do that it would be helpful to have just a few more hands kneading dough. Jos assured him that anywhere you go, if you are willing to take a chance and give a break, helping hands are abundant. He just wanted them to remember to bring people in that needed the help and were willing to be part of the business. That is a risk for many people that need to be able to count on a paycheck. Just think of the right thing to do. You have something very valuable to offer, so does a potential business partner. If you do not lose sight of both of those facts, then you will make the right decision. Be smart, give yourself options, look at all the options; that was the advice Jos was giving both of them.

Jos talked about options in such a way that it meant more than just looking for a new business partner. It pertained to much more; and what he had to say could be used in all aspects of life for anybody.

Options

I have talked before about options. There are generally many more options than most people think about in almost any situation.

That is the reason so many professionals that have to act quickly, like emergency medical personnel, firefighting personnel, policing personnel, military personnel, commercial pilots, and many others, practice many different scenarios and practice them often. The reason is that it gives them many different options and makes it almost automatic to choose one quickly.

The best way to get options is to get as much information as possible. Knowledge is the key here. The more information you have on any subject leads to the most options available. Everything that needs a decision has a time limit on it. But do not let that time limit push you into making a bad decision. Find out your time limit and use that time to obtain as much information, accurate information as you can. Completely exhaust all the time you have before picking an option. Then you will make the best decision possible.

People with many options are calmer. Calm people are happier and more satisfied and make better decisions.

What Do You Cost?

"We want someone who is going to work with us," Billy told Natashia. "I don't want someone to just stand here and not jump in and help. You know what I mean? I want someone that is not only going to work but also pitch in ideas and be creative."

"Of course. What you say I understand. Until you give a chance, how you can know what someone will do?" Natashia said in her Slavic accent. She looked up into Billy's face. "We could give people a chance, a few, see which is best one. Like you say; if they do nothing it costs us nothing."

"Well, not until we hire them." Billy gazed up in a thoughtful look. "We won't know until we give them a chance. Let's give them a tryout period first. Like, just one day and see what they do. Like a test."

Jos was listening to the two of them more or less thinking out loud to each other. He seemed fascinated by the process by which they were working things out. He was interested in their train of thought and how it was progressing. You could also sort of see a glint in his eye at the way the two of them looked at each other. Jos always seemed to find some inner pleasure watching other people with each other. Maybe that is why he had such insight into people or why what people did, good or bad, never seemed to surprise him. He was a people watcher. More than that, he was a people "understander." But Jos had to speak up and tell them something they were losing sight of. Again, what he was talking about could pertain to much more than this particular incident; it affected all aspects of life and living.

If humans are alive, they are costing something. People think if they do not do anything, they do not cost anything. For every minute you are breathing, you cost something. The human body is continuously processing chemicals. Just the process of breathing uses oxygen and glucose, or sugar. There is oxygen in the air, thank goodness you are not charged for that directly. But sugar, on the other hand, costs something to obtain and to consume. That is the cost of being alive at the very basic level. The truth of the matter is that you cost a lot more in a normal day to day living. Somebody has to pay for it; if you are not, then someone else is. The only way to not have any cost associated with you is to not exist.

What Is Free?

Oh, and by the way, *free* is a word that gets used, abused, and thrown around by many people wrongly. It gets thrown around, especially by businesses and marketing ploys. You see everywhere people are offering "free" stuff.

"Free" means you walk into someplace, get something, and walk back out; no questions asked and no money exchanged and no law broken and no person harmed. Everything else claimed as "free" is a ploy to give up something. Buy one, get one free; no, really it is just get two at half price. If you have to pay something, anything, even information, then it is not free. Just keep that in mind. Think about it; if businesses gave away things for free, I mean really free, they would not be a business at all. They would be a charity. But even charity is not free. Somebody had to pay something, they had to make donations.

When you say that you can have someone come in and essentially demonstrate their skills, aptitude, and desire for the job at no cost to you, you could be right. But it will cost someone something. If you do not pay them, or compensate them in some way, then they are paying the cost. Their time costs. It costs somebody, something.

If you want to do that, however, which is not really a bad idea, you have to let them know what you are doing and offer some kind of compensation. Tell them if they work and show you what they are about for one or two hours you will let them take home what they make. That will give them the incentive to do well for the job and have at least something good to take home. Does that make sense?

Natashia and Billy had big smiles on their faces as they were nodding. Obviously, they saw the point and thought it was a brilliant idea. They shared a smiling glance at each other in confirmation.

Jos also told them that they should consider bringing whoever they get to help them with the business into the business as partners; not as employees. He wanted them to do just like he had done with the restaurant. He explained that it really was a harder way to start a business, but it was always a better way to run a business.

Share the Wealth

Be as fair with everyone as you would want them to be with you. I wish I could say give equally but people are just not equal.

The only thing that everyone gets equally in life is: one life. You get one life; each and every person. Now on this, I did not say fair; I said equal to everyone. That one life is not necessarily "fair" to each person. Some people get a healthy body and some do not, some get a pretty body and some do not, some get a trouble-free life and some do not. I did not say that everyone got a fair life; I said everyone got *one* life equally. Every individual person, even in conjoined twins, gets one singular life experience that is their own.

You cannot give equally, but you can give fairly.

All I am asking of you is the same thing that I did with the restaurant; share the wealth. I made a deal with Jack to share the profits or the debt after two weeks, whichever, if he would give us a chance to run the business without him. At first, I asked him to take a two-week vacation and I put up my bus as collateral in case it turned out to be a debit at the end of two weeks. I knew it would not be a debit because I knew what kind of crew I had. But I was willing to sacrifice my bus.

The reason I *knew* that it would not end up a debit is because I was going to share everything with everybody. I was going to share the ideas, the responsibilities, the pride, and the success and profits. That gave everyone a vested interest to work together to make the business a success. You have seen what humans can do when they put aside their differences and come together for one purpose. So, I knew that the restaurant would be a great success; and it is. Now, because everyone involved with the restaurant is investing, and therefore trusting, in you two, I only ask that you do the same thing.

Anyone you accept in here to help you, give them a fair valued share of the business. You will have to determine their share because their share will be different than yours and the others; especially at the beginning. You two and the others are putting in an investment that you have already obtained. Anyone new will be coming in at ground zero; that is to say, with no initial investment, but that can be obtained in tandem as they continue employment.

Now, if they know that their pay will be directly reflected in the health of the business, then they will be very interested to make sure the business is healthy. The healthier the business, the healthier their paycheck and there is no limit to that.

Billy and Natashia looked at each other and nodded. I noted a slight upturn in the mouth of Jos as he noted the slight glint in each of their eyes as they looked at each other.

A few days had gone by with the restaurant running smoothly, Billy and Natashia cleaning up the new bakery and making it their own, and Jordan coming in, most of the time, to finish the makeover.

Jos had found out who was in possession of the old factory he had looked at. He found out what they had wanted for rent. After a little negotiation, he was able to get them to give him the keys almost rent-free. He explained: what with the state of disrepair, the almost poverty-stricken neighborhood, and the lack of any other options, other than just sitting on the property. Jos had made a deal to renew the place and have it used as beneficial to the community, as opposed to just being target practice for the neighborhood window bullies.

The building was an old, World War Two-era red brick two-story structure. The first floor was almost entirely open the more-than-an-acre size of the building except for several load-bearing brick pillars. The second floor was sectioned off into more than twenty large open rooms, like massive sewing rooms or rooms for assembling many pieces into large parts. There was a huge lavatory on either end of the structure, both top and bottom floors, apparently added on after the original building was constructed. The building had dirt and debris strewn around both floors and it had an old musty "not been used in sometime" smell to it, like moist brick, but it didn't seem moldy or structurally unsound. The window openings had been boarded up long ago even with that however some of the windows had been broken. Looking around the place Rudy had commented that just fixing the windows was going to be somewhat expensive. Rudy was good about keeping a running total of any type of costs in his head and it generally slipped out his mouth unconsciously. The bottom floor had normal doors on two sides on one end and two incredibly large drive through doors on the other end; all were wooden in nature. There were three staircases; one on both ends and a central staircase. Jos was obviously excited and his voice echoed throughout the bottom floor as he spoke in a slightly louder, exuberant tone; or maybe that was just the acoustics of the room. On the second floor, he would point out things that needed attention and his ideas as he kicked through the debris.

His suggestion for the second floor was to make some of the rooms into nice comfortable ward like sleeping areas with cots that could be used by the homeless and destitute at night to get out of the weather. However, he warned that we would need to come up with some nightlong active human security to keep everyone safe and the whole building peaceful.

Jos was well aware of human nature and what was possible when you get more than a few people in one place, especially those that had little to nothing to lose. However, during the day, the rooms could be used for individual instruction areas for musical instruments and the like. So, sound proofing would have to be done but that would be a benefit also for "sleeping rooms." Some of the rooms could be used by us for information storage and office like work. Most of the rooms were big enough to partition them into sections and make some of them permanent quarters for some certain people in exchange for services; like nighttime guard duty and building maintenance and general assistance when needed. We would have to build in some fixed securing lockers or closets into the rooms so these people could feel safe leaving their stuff there, he suggested.

His suggestion for the first floor was exactly what he had described earlier about the Church of Understanding. It would be a large, open room that could be used for gatherings, teaching, building, constructing, creating, and just general networking with others. In different areas, you would have wood working equipment; in another part, you would have metal working equipment. In another area, you would have large tables of different sizes and many different chairs to carry out all kinds of different functions from fabric work to large design drawings to leatherwork to different kinds of artwork, all the way up to different electronic projects and the like. The first floor was large enough to build a full size 747 aircraft with all the parts; it was big enough to accommodate many different hands on skilled projects at one time. That was the point, he kept pointing out, was to have many different people teaching many different things to many other different people where all could witness the others.

First things first, he explained. The whole building was going to need to be cleaned and what few repairs that needed to be done get accomplished; like on windows and door frames and such. Then what partitioning we needed to do and securing structures that needed to be installed needed to be done. Then we would have to start acquiring some equipment and start making furniture. Jos mentioned that we already had Jordan and his "most-of-the-time" willing, helping hands; maybe he had other people he knew and would recommend that could use a meal or two for some simple labor.

As far as getting the message out for needed equipment and the whole purpose and idea of the Church of Understanding, Jos thought about the restaurant. A very large portion of the working class of the surrounding area came in for lunch at some point during the week. At night, the restaurant had been rather successful attracting the more affluent in the area for dinner because of the phenomenally good food and service along with the quiet, friendly, romantic, and charming atmosphere.

Jos and the gang had made quite a few good contacts that now considered them friends. No one in the group had any reluctance talking and asking for help for what Jos considered a very worthwhile cause. Jos also wanted everyone to let everyone else know that Saturdays were going to be the day of general gathering and wanted them to let people know the purpose and proposal for the place. Anybody that didn't mind sharing some knowledge and anybody wanting to learn anything should come by.

Jos said that we could all guarantee a good time and that he would make sure that none of us would be disappointed. Up until now Jos had always been good to his word, so no one in the gang had any doubt about what he was saying. In fact, everyone in the gang had acquired the same enthusiasm about the project as Jos had. We all wanted to see what was going to happen and how it was going to turn out. He had talked about the idea several times before, now we were going to put it into practice. Jos was one of the best in making people see a vision, believe in the vision, and then making the vision a reality.

When everything was over, people would look back with incredible pride and marvel at how really easy the endeavor was to pull off and why it hadn't been done before. I had seen that in just my relatively short time with him. Things that some people thought could not be done, or were not practical, Jos showed them that not only was it possible, but with the undaunted help of others it was actually rather easy to accomplish. That was just another unique and genuine quality of this man.

Now that the restaurant had been up and running for quite a few months, everyone stopped to think about what they had made in such a short time; they were amazed. Even the owner who was only taking a share had over doubled his income. The business was healthy and solvent with actually a little extra income to make necessary improvements. Each of the gang had realized that they had made far more than they would have if they had just been employees of the business making the average pay for their job title. But even more than that they had made a fantastic business from a failing one and *had real fun in the accomplishment. They worked as a team and it showed.*

"*It just amazes me to think where we started,*" Reese said. "*I can't believe this little restaurant business caught on so fast and did so well.*"

Never underestimate what humans can do when they set their mind on something and work together. Each of you had a vested interest to work together. You overcame your differences for the sake of the whole because helping each other only helped yourselves. It is not amazing to me that humans can be so productive when they work together. It amazes me that humans do not recognize how that would work with everything everywhere every day.

When humans come together and work for the good of a project with a singular goal in mind they can have amazing success. People have an incredible ability to problem solve when they work in unison.

World peace is obtainable, despite what most people think. But it can only be obtained when every single person works for that goal, and puts aside prejudices and preconceived notions.

Open Mind

One of the most important things to remember with learning is to keep an open mind, otherwise you cannot learn anything. Because what can a man learn when he already knows everything. You must keep an open mind.

An Islamic extremist group known as the Boko Haram, translated means: "Teaching Western Education Forbidden." It is so adamant about prohibiting outside influences that they actually kill other humans. This is an extremist group that is so closed minded that they do not even want anyone else to have an open mind and to think for themselves. What do they think the others are going to learn? Anyone in the right, and doing the right thing, wants everyone to learn as much as possible because that will only bring to light the righteousness of their cause. Anyone who tries to sustain another from learning is trying to hide something and/or knows the wrongfulness of their cause. This is not only what I say, this is what Muhammad taught vehemently.

The only way ... *the only way* ... to understand and comprehend the real God is to have an open mind. The real God is so complex and profound that it is completely impossible to comprehend, understand and appreciate the concept and truth of God without an open mind.

Jos had made arrangements to rent the storefront for the bakery in his usual manner, although no one really knew what that was. Whatever it was, it made the rent quite affordable. When everyone was asked about using restaurant funds for a fair percentage of the company, everyone agreed. Working between times they were at the restaurant Billy and Natashia, along with the occasional help of the others in their spare time, had the bakery ready to start operating within a single week. Everyone at the restaurant had become so efficient at doing their jobs and assisting the others that covering for Natashia and Billy was accomplished relatively easily.

They decided to call the place Hot Buns Bakery, after an off-sided, and completely unintentional, remark Billy had made to Natashia one day while cleaning the ovens. It had just been one of those comments made when the different meanings of the language used could be interpreted in different ways. After the comment was made, a slight pause ensued while both contemplated the different meanings applicable followed by continuous laughter and snickering snorts.

Billy and Natashia, after a couple of days of looking at a few different people, had decided on two people. One of them was a single mother of three children in her early twenties living within walking distance of the shop. Her name was Syria, and she could start right away. The other was an older lady from around the corner named Saliha. Billy and Natashia really didn't need two, but Saliha was older, wanted to help out, could use a little extra money and probably brought untold riches in old school knowledge that they just could not pass up. And she did not want to start until later, which worked out perfectly for Billy and Natashia.

Syria had been living on public support and had been desperately trying to find a job that she could do within her restrictions. The inevitable result of her past decisions had resulted in her living in an apartment that she could barely afford in a neighborhood that offered few employment opportunities. She had no form of transportation other than public, and because of where she lived made even that difficult. Two of her children were school-aged and the youngest was eligible for part-time nursery care. All of which restricted the time she could devote to employment, especially the time of day. She had a sister that lived reasonably close that could watch the kids before school and then take the youngest to the nursery before leaving for her job but after that the kids were on their own. Syria had to be off and available for her children by three in the afternoon. Syria had no baking experience, but her enthusiasm and energy had impressed Billy and Natashia and her willingness to learn was easily apparent.

Fortunately, because of the nature of the bakery business most of the work was done in the very wee hours of the morning, before most people even got up. For that reason, and because of the arrangement with her sister, the hours worked out well for Syria as long as she could train her body to get up at about two in the morning. Also, her walking distance from the shop was ideal for her. Billy and Natashia were quite pleased to find her enthusiasm and eagerness resulted in her becoming a quick study. Not only had she learned very fast, she quickly excelled in creating new and very delicious baked concoctions, all on her own.

Syria had been somewhat dubious about the pay arrangement when Natashia explained it to her; that she would be making a percentage of the business instead of a fixed hourly pay. Her biggest concern came when Natashia informed her that the business had to make money before Syria would be paid. That sounded totally unacceptable to Syria because she had to be able to depend on a steady paycheck. And she would need to start being paid within the normal two weeks so she could start to get caught up on her debts. When Natashia explained that it should not be a problem for her to get her first paycheck within two weeks that relieved some of her anxiety. Also, when Natashia explained the potential of the amount of pay in this manner Syria was willing to take the risk. Natashia did not fabricate anything to entice Syria; she told her very realistic probabilities based on just the past performances of the baking endeavor by Billy and herself.

Within a month Hot Buns Bakery had exceeded even the most optimistic expectations of success. They were all in the building working by three in the morning and were open for business each day by five. By that time, they had almost all of the baked goods for the restaurant done, especially the coveted breads and rolls. The only thing left to do for the restaurant was the popular and daily special desserts, which they completed in the afternoon. By the time they opened the doors, donuts and other assortments of breakfast goods had been prepared and people were already waiting to come in.

At first, construction and factory workers that frequented the restaurant at lunchtime were their stable customers, having heard about the forthcoming opening of the bakery. Not to mention that both Natashia and Billy had developed an admiring following from the restaurant, customers that were eager to see them succeed. Soon word of mouth and the quality of the goods brought people from far and wide to make frequent and routine pickups.

Originally, Billy had been a little apprehensive about opening a store in this type of neighborhood and especially at this time of the morning when no other business was open. He had felt a little secluded and isolated, making him feel a little vulnerable and unconsciously responsible for the safety of the girls. But it wasn't long before he realized that you always ran that risk almost anywhere, that this time of the morning was not really a common time for the unsavory of the neighborhood to be up and moving, and from the moment the door opened the little store was almost never without customers.

Billy had been concerned enough to mention safety to Jos, who talked to him for a while and put him at ease. Looking at it as Jos had put it: life is a series of taking chances. If you use common sense and due precautions, generally you will be safe in any situation, but you always are taking a risk, especially if you are doing something worthwhile and righteous. Billy was bringing a business to an area that desperately needed a positive presence and he was making an opportunity for at least one person to work. It may only be one person and in the big scheme of things it was not that much but to that one person it meant everything in the world. So, Jos challenged Billy: was it worth the risk? Without hesitation Billy bowed his head and with a proud smile nodded.

Natashia was talking about Syria working out well. She started to fit right in and took off. "She very motivated, yes," Natashia said. Her accent was delightful. "She makes really good pastries, by the way. And, she makes ideas how to improve storefront." Billy seemed excited too.

Natashia added, "I guess she just meant to be here." Looking right at Jos, "Like you say, get all information you can then make decision and take chance." She grinned and gave a perky, little shrug. Billy concurred and reiterated that it was meant to be.

Jos was genuinely happy for them both. They really were excited and happy. Not only had that helped out their little business but now if the bakery did really well it will help out the others at the restaurant. Like Jos had said so many times, one thing affecting another thing. Jos went on to say ...

The "It Was Meant to Be" Theory

Was it really meant to be? I hear so many people say that. "It was meant to be." Like it was preordained or predestined to happen. I hear the religious say, "It is God's will." I am not sure people really understand the true concept of time and possibilities. How can someone talk one moment about "free will" and endless possibilities and then the next moment talk about destiny or something being "planned" or "designed"? It is either one or the other; it cannot be both.

Was it meant to be? Yes. Why? Because it happened. That does not mean that it was predestined. If you think it was, then you should not get upset with what happens, because it was already going to happen anyway. Right?

Now, from here on into the future there are a multitude of possibilities, but once something occurs then it was meant to be. Syria could be the key to your wildest dreams, she could be the force that takes this business so much further than either of you could ever imagine. She could also be the thorn that brings everything down, the biggest mistake you have ever made. She could be here until the business ends decades in the future or she could have a mishap in her life and be gone tomorrow. I do not want to sound gloomy or negative. Quite the contrary, I am just pointing out that anything is possible. I encourage you to see the blessing now and enjoy it to the fullest. This is the present, and the future is full of promise, regardless of what happens. It only depends on you for how you will look at it and how you will respond to it while you are alive. Enjoy what is most important: the present.

Later, back at the restaurant during the evening dinner service, Jos had noticed that Reese was a little on edge. For some reason, he just didn't seem to have the same intensity that he normally had. It made Jos wonder why. After dinner service, and after Reese had finished helping Ahmed and Billy clean up, Jos went outside with Reese and had a talk.

Reese had been doing more of Billy's job at the restaurant as hygiene officer in concert with Ahmed. Billy was getting overwhelmed with the duties at the bakery and long hours and finishing his days with his routine with Ahmed at the restaurant. The routine they had for clearing tables was still a hit with the guests even after this much time doing it. It was almost like a trademark of the restaurant. Now Reese was taking over the position, especially as he had perfected his bookkeeping and ordering duties so well that they really did not take that much time anymore. By this time everyone really had their duties and responsibilities in hand.

Reese confided in Jos that he was just a little depressed because so many things were changing. Jos had often commented that humans are generally reluctant to change. Everything, as Jos so often explained, had its own timing.

Timing

Timing is very important. Like a living thing, if a business remains stagnant for a very long time, it will die. A business must constantly be fed and it has to grow and evolve or it will age and eventually die, like all living things.

Timing is extremely important to everything tied to it. You have heard all of the different expressions that bring this point home: "He was before his time" or "That guy lives in the past" or "Strike when the iron is hot." Timing is extremely important.

Adolf Hitler is a good example of how time affects outcome. If Hitler would have died, for whatever reason in early 1935, he would have been regarded in history as a great man who brought a country out of ruins and made it productive and prosperous. During the 1936 Olympics, the *New York Times* wrote that "Germany was a nation happy and prosperous beyond belief and Hitler is one of the greatest, if not the greatest, political leaders in the world today."

Instead of dying and becoming known as a great man, he continued on until he destroyed the country and many human lives; an estimated forty to fifty million dead in the European theater during World War Two. Most of which were civilians. So now he is looked at as the epitome of evil. Just one more example of the affect that timing has on all things. Because of her suicide, Marilyn Monroe will forever be considered a beautiful woman. No person will ever think of her as an aged woman.

Time changes everything and everything changes in time. The events that take place at any particular point in time will forever determine the rest of events in the future from that moment. That instantaneous point of time considered "the present" is unimaginably and unspeakably important for every future event coming after it. You will see.

It was a Sunday morning and most of the gang was still in the old factory building cleaning up but were slowly starting to slip away to get the restaurant started for the day. Earlier in the morning Billy had come by with quite a few delicious "mistakes" that had been produced that morning in the bakery. It was becoming a routine that the baked breakfast goods that were deemed a flop, and Natashia would not sell, came here instead of being thrown out. A couple of the gang thought they were as good as the approved pastries; who cares if they were a little misshapen, they were still very tasty. And with the early morning abundance of sweet pastries came many of the neighborhood children. For a little assistance in carrying trash and sweeping, they could have all they wanted. Before long, even this old building was gleaming. Within a month of free coffee, sodas, and the available pastries, there were more than just the neighborhood children; some mothers started coming along with some of the older, retired neighborhood residents. To be truthful, I didn't know that many people lived that close in the area. There were enough hands to accomplish amazing amounts of work in a miniscule amount of time. One day the old building was a wreak, a worthless cause, and it seemed like just the next day it was a brand new, recently-built commercial building.

Jordan had made an appearance along with three of his "friends." The same courtesies were given to them that were given to Jordan. In exchange for painting, and now some window and frame fixing, they received clean clothes, a chance to clean up, and food throughout the day. Again, like the bakery, it was food that Adam didn't want to sell for whatever reason but it was still very tasty and good. It wasn't just food for Jordan and his friends, it was food for all of us. Jordan and his friends became more dependable on a daily basis and they started to build the security closets and tables and chairs. I have to admit, they did a really good job.

By now, the knowledge and the purpose of the Church of Understanding was becoming well known within and outside the community. Donations of all kinds started to come in; spare and outdated equipment like power tools, hand tools, two sewing machines, leather and woodworking tools, and machining equipment. Even a couple of stove and oven combinations. It was a virtual cornucopia of hardware showing up along with literally tons of supplies of all kinds: wood, cloth, metal scraps, and even some leather scraps from a shop about a mile away. At one point, I didn't know if people were really helping out or they were just using the old place as a new dumping ground; someplace to get rid of all their unwanted scraps. Whatever the case, Jos was visually ecstatic. He kept commenting that this is what people were really about, given the chance; helping one another any way they can. And he kept adding and pointing out that this is what he was talking about when people work together and put away their differences. What should have taken a professional crew six months to accomplish was completed in less than a month and a half. Essentially, everyone felt as if they were paid for their services as well. Everybody got something out of the deal; and what most felt they received is a productive day in the company of good people. They shared laughs and grunts and hopes and exhaustion; but most of all they shared sharing.

That was the purpose of the Church of Understanding: to bring people together to help one another, to learn from one another, and to share with one another. As Jos would put it, that should be the purpose of any church, regardless of the specific religion that it represents. When you come together to do good things for many people, that is when you do many good things for God. If every person is a small part of God, then the more people helped the more of God is happy. For the Church of Understanding to already be this far ahead of making people happy and helping people out even before it opened was a very good start. I could start to understand why Jos had such intense passion to see this come about. It was the personification of what he had been teaching.

That afternoon there were about fourteen other people along with a few of the gang when everyone took a minute for a break to have a drink. Everybody was talking amongst each other with occasional glances toward Jos. People had come to be interested, like the rest of us, in what he had to say. And, like I said before, Jos was one of those kinds of people that had good chemistry with virtually everyone he met. Jos had this calm, knowing smile on his face and really moved down his own path but always bringing some kind of assistance for another with him. It seemed like whatever Jos was doing at any given time, it was a process of helping someone out. It was just that when Jos was thinking about something, it was about someone else and what they needed.

One of the mothers had made a comment about the old building and how it had evolved. She stated that she had been living in the area for many years now and how the neighborhood had seemed so stagnant. She also mentioned how this old building was such a dark and gloomy presence in the middle of the block. Almost like an old, haunted relic of some dark and ominous past. She for one was glad that someone finally made the place turn around into something more inviting.

With a shine in his eyes, Jos sat there listening to the woman. Many times, he had spoken of the difference between evolving and revolving; this seemed like a good time to tell her. As he started to speak to her, everyone else slowly finished their conversations and attended to his ...

Evolve Versus Revolve Theory

There is a difference between evolving and revolving. All things are always in a constant state of change, sometimes moving constantly forward and sometimes moving forward and back again. But things are always changing, even if it is just aging.

Humans are not an intelligent species because they have a big brain and can work out solutions to problems and questions. Humans are an intelligent species and have advanced to their state of knowledge because they can, and do, pass along information, experiences, and knowledge from results they have discovered. Their intelligence, not just their bodies, has evolved. This is what is needed from us and what is asked of us; to learn, and just as importantly, to share and pass on this knowledge.

Here we have not only shared an experience of transforming a building we have been sharing a piece of each of us with others. You have learned something about everyone here, and everyone here as learned something about you. If nothing else, that gives a better understanding of you to everyone here. It is far better to interact with other living people than it is to sit in front of a TV watching only what you want to see. That is just revolving. When you get out with different people and share an experience together that is when you are truly evolving. Evolution, even as frightening as it is, is good because evolution is tantamount to improvement.

One of the older women in the group said something jokingly to Jos about how he was an evolutionist and then started laughing. Jos quickly understood the play on words, or the play on meanings, I should say, and started chuckling himself. Then, Jos jokingly commented that he was actually both; an evolutionist and a revolutionist. He was playing with the meanings of words also. Which made the older woman keep laughing. For her age, she was very quick witted and easily entertained.

Those comments, however, had somehow sparked a deep-seated chord in Rudy in some bizarre way. Even though Jos had not been talking about evolution in the context of evolutionism that was what was going around in Rudy's head through the night. He kept thinking about what Jos was saying about the creation of humankind. It had him conflicted between what Jos was saying and his religious teachings and long-standing beliefs on the subject. Rudy was not of the character that took easily to change. He, of course, had heard of the theory of evolution but was not completely sold on the whole idea that life happened by chance and then evolved.

Creationism Versus Evolutionism

The next day, Rudy sat down next to Jos. "I can sort of understand what you're trying to say about God and the beginning of man," he said. "But I still believe in creationism. I am a creationist, I guess. I tend to believe that God is an intelligent entity and that He designed all living things. We didn't just evolve from some kind of soup by chance. I've just never believed that."

Jos, taken a little off-guard, listening intently, understood the conflict. With that he said ...

Many people feel that life is far too complex to have come about without some intelligent entity engineering it. Nothing in the universe started out complex, however. Everything started simply and continued to evolve to more and more complex states. Evolution is the very definition of creation. Everything has to start somewhere, simply, then build on the success and eliminate the failures to become viable.

It has been taught for thousands of years that God made man and put him on Earth. Just because something has been taught for thousands of years does not make it factual.

It was understood over a long period of time that everything revolved around the Earth; that Earth was the center of the universe. That was even easy to see and understand; just look up at the stars and Sun moving around this planet, it had to be the center. Then to be told that it was not the center, that the Earth was just a very small piece and one of many revolving around the sun was heretical. In fact, it was so offensive that it had one of the greatest scientists in history locked up and almost executed, Galileo Galilei. People refused to believe something so horrendous and completely wrong. Now, of course, it is understood to be correct. But in the course of history, when something is being taught to be correct, regardless of the emerging facts, it is difficult to abandon the lessons of the past.

If a person remains close-minded to basic evidence, then they will never grow and understand the truth.

Simply put: thinking is better than believing.

The simple fact is that all life creation is a process of evolution. I am not just talking about the life on Earth but all things in the universe. Every star, every planet, every moon, every solar system, every galaxy, even the universe itself started at some point and was very simple and continued to evolve into something more and more complex.

The human species is constantly in the process of evolving. It is the process of evolution that has been going on since the creation of the universe to now and is continuing on into the future. Only two thousand years ago, life expectancy was half what it has evolved to today. Why is it so hard to understand evolution? What is the reluctance to realize the true nature of the human species?

Does it make more sense that a master designer masterminded the universe and all the processes that are contained within, or, that the universe is itself a living entity that is growing and evolving? Look at the science that has been acquired over eons of time, consuming the lives of countless intelligent humans and put it all together.

God is not the creator; God is the creation. Just as you are not your creator; you are a creation. Your mother and father created you. What came together to create God is unknowable, but the God humans know is the creation; not the creator. Therefore, I believe evolutionism is creationism.

Then Rudy said, "What about those that say they have never seen any real proof of evolution. I have to agree that I understand what science says about things changing slowly into other things. But I have to agree with these other people. I have never seen real proof of evolution in our time. You would think that you would see some proof. How can you prove evolution?"

Jos looked at Rudy, closed his eyes tightly for a moment, then opened them again looking at Rudy. In an almost exacerbated, breathy voice, he said ...

What do you mean that you have never seen evolution in your time? If that is so, it is only because you have not looked, or you refuse to see. There are many that believe what you just said. They are so intent on convincing people of a "creationist" God that they never observe the obvious.

Have you never seen a human grow from a baby to an adult? Have you never observed the evolution of the very bone structure of a human being in one single lifetime? How can you say that you have never seen any proof of evolution? You see it on a daily basis, every day, throughout your life. Have you not seen and even felt your own body evolve in your short time already?

If you want to stay fixed on an idea and not look at the obvious truth, then there is nothing anyone can do to change your mind.

Rudy, I can feel you agonizing over this. That is only because it is hard to hold up a falling archaic wall. Just allow the truth to wash over you and you will understand without the agony.

One day just before the Church of Understanding was opened, one of the community's business owners came up to Jos and asked him about his success. He praised Jos on the success of the restaurant and wanted to know how he did it. He had a couple of cleaning businesses, some were doing well and some were not. He wanted to know if Jos had some strategy or some formula that made businesses successful.

Jos let him know about letting everyone be part of the business. That was the first rule and most important principle to him. Everyone gets a percentage of the business; no one is paid by the boss. But if you are talking about how to manage a business when the structure is already set up as most businesses are then Jos had some advice. As Jos told him, there is a simple rule: do what is right; it will always pay off in the long run. It may not be quick and it may not be hugely profitable especially in the short term, but it always works if the intentions are true.

A Great Manager

The measure of any great manager is how they treat those they have some control over. Treat others like they are you. You must care for the business, but care for your employees as you would care for yourself.

The man's face was blank for only a moment. Then it lit up like a candle. You could see in the business owner's face that he knew what Jos was talking about and he was already making certain decisions about his own businesses. His head had this slight, continuous knowing nod.

THE OPENING

The time came for the gang to open the Church of Understanding. It was a marvelous day and remarkable in the number of people that attended to witness the official opening. The late morning was one of the busiest times for both the bakery and the restaurant. By this time, Saliha had joined the bakery crew, as the business had bloomed so fast they needed the extra help. Just like Syria, she had come in enthusiastic and immediately beneficial.

Everyone from the bakery with some of their finest confections, had made it to the opening. Along with everyone from the restaurant, except for Adam and Sochin, who stayed back to finish some last-minute preparations for the lunch rush. Jordan and his three friends were there, along with about four other "associates" that came with them. Amazingly, a very large portion of the community and beyond showed up. I saw mostly people that had been involved with either the restoration of the building or the donation of equipment and supplies. I also saw many of the influential people that had contributed to the cause. And I also saw many people that I had never seen before. Of these people, some were other residents of the area and most of them were teenagers. Some looked curious, some looked bored with nothing else to do and looking for something to keep them entertained. Some looked a little foreboding like they were not sure who these new people to the neighborhood were, how they got here, what they wanted and/or what to do about it. It was almost like we were invading their "turf," and they did not like it.

Jos talked about this often ...

Neighborhood Control

The main reasons for war, historically, are religious convictions, freedom from persecutions of different types, and probably one of the most common is land and property control. The belief that "this area is mine and you cannot have it or even walk on it unless I say so" is a leading cause of many wars. It does not matter whether the land actually does belong to an individual or group or not. There are always those that want control of it. You see it on small scale within neighborhoods. You see it on a grand scale like countries or regions. You see it all over the world, where residential neighborhoods are "controlled" by an individual's group as to who and what comes into the area, for what purpose, and who or what leaves the area.

These are not elected people or even people the residents of the area want. These are just groups that have "taken over" an area for their purposes. Only because they can inflict unrighteous horror on innocent people can they take control of what is not theirs. The non-violent people of the area suffer at the hands of these selfish few. They are terrorized and harmed at the mercy of the greedy. And until they can be caught and contained or eliminated, their persecution of the innocent will continue, sometimes for centuries.

Just think of how many neighborhoods, areas, countries, and regions have produced refugees because people rather leave their homes and possessions for the safety of a foreign area? An act that can be avoided if every refugee were to ban together and refuse those that would terrorize them to accomplish their goals. But that can be more than difficult; in most instances, it is impossible without advanced weaponry.

Unfortunately, it does not take many to come into a neighborhood and terrorize the residents to obtain control. Those that are willing to harm others without reason or restraint terrorize and obtain control quickly. Until a sound, non-corrupt, well-equipped policing or military force can come in and restore and enforce justice and peace for all of the citizens of an area they either have to live under the cloud or move away like a refugee.

This all just shows that to some human beings the *land* is far and away much more valuable than human life.

Land and Humans

There is probably no better example than Jerusalem. How many countless lives have been slaughtered over that reasonably small piece of land? By everyone's accounts in the Abrahamic religions, it is the Holy Land and nobody owns it but God, yet everybody fights for control of it. It is not about Yahweh, God, or Allah. It is only about control. Just humans wanting to control other humans.

Can there ever be any real justice to that blood-soaked sand? Can it ever be truly controlled by only one people without any future conflicts? Will it ever truly be the Holy Land or will it forever be the killing field of the religious? I personally, humbly beg this now, *May Jerusalem someday find lasting peace.*

Jerusalem can find peace; it is obtainable. When everyone puts away religious beliefs and just lives with the others, regardless of their religion, or if they even have one, then that city, too, can find peace. Only then will it truly be the city of God.

Jos was quiet for a moment, bowing his head in respect for the countless millions that found their demise in that city.

The Fear of the Church of Understanding

Jos was perfectly aware of the area we were in. He knew that it had a substantial "street gang" population and influence. Up until now, they had not bothered any of our gang or the restaurant or bakery. But the obvious few that were here at the opening did draw his attention. He did not voice any concern nor did he in any way show any concern in his manner or actions. In fact, if anything, he almost looked keen on meeting them and learning about them. I do not know if it was his nature, his experience, his knowledge, or just his ignorance that always made him appear fearless in the face of any danger; however, I really never considered it to be the latter.

Jos made a little "thank-you" speech for everyone coming and everyone helping out in the restoration and creation of the new place. He explained the purpose of the Church of Understanding. It was a place for people of all kinds, ages, experiences, social-economic levels, religions, and sexes, whatever, to come together and learn from one another. There was enough equipment here to learn all kinds of skills and trades and enough room for people to get together and share knowledge and experiences of all kinds.

Looking specifically at the younger people without being too obvious, he stated that this was the place to take full advantage of the opportunity to learn and advance into a safe and honest future. He encouraged anyone with a generous nature to come by and afford whoever was there with any and all of their knowledge. Then he let everyone dive into the delicious treats that Natashia, Billy, Syria, and Saliha had brought.

Jos clandestinely made his way, without being obvious, to the young men by the back door that looked a little menacing. He remained quiet and uninvolved with all the spontaneous conversations. Before long one of the older guys in the targeted crowd spoke to Jos, asking him what he thought he was doing and what he thought he was going to accomplish with this place. In a completely disarming manner, Jos respectfully addressed the man. He explained that this was one place, even better than a church, which could help the people of the neighborhood with something better than money or food or handouts or consolations, it could help them with knowledge, self-respect, and self-appreciation. This was the one place that would give them real-world skills and experience that they would have to pay for anywhere else. Here it was offered free. Here, all they had to do was come with an interest and curiosity.

Then he explained that if he could make people know that this was the one safe place in the neighborhood that people could come without any regard to any association and try to better their lives, it would be greatly appreciated. Like any church, a sanctuary to all that would be respected by honor. It was almost a plea that was not lost on the young man. Surreptitiously watching this, it fascinated me that Jos was so deft at making himself understood and obtaining the cooperation of even the most unlikely of allies. The young man nodded in an obvious pact and what Jos had asked was understood and granted by the man that could grant such a request. Jos reiterated so that it was clear that anyone, regardless of any association, was safe inside this sanctuary. The young man stared at him with dark, fiery eyes in an almost challenge that Jos obviously met satisfactorily when he gave him another confirming nod of agreement. I noted just the slightest imperceptible smile on the young man's face that indicated a real respect for Jos and his character. Then he crammed one of Natashia's delicious cherry tarts in his mouth.

Jos respectfully introduced himself and the young man reciprocated. He let Jos know his name was Toro, and that was what he expected to be called. Toro was not tall but he had enormous bulk. He stood and walked with an air of superiority. He introduced a couple of the other gang members; making it quite obvious that he was the top man of this area. All of the other people there also made it obvious that Toro was one to be cautious of. Jos did not show concern of the type most people thought he should. His concern was different, and it was apparent that Jos had the assistance of Toro in mind.

Jos explained later to our gang and to the many of those that stayed around after the ceremonies ...

One of the frightening aspects of the Church of Understanding is the bonding and close proximity of other classes, or gangs, in one place. If you mix the desperate and needy with the affluent and wealthy, you are opening a proverbial can of worms and opening the door for some not so healthy acquaintances. If the Church is successful, you are going to have well-meaning knowledgeable, kind, and generous, affluent people coming here to help those that are less fortunate and realistically desperate. That is the purpose and whole idea of the new church. That could obviously put them in peril if not closely monitored. Harm could come to them, even from people that really appreciate what they are doing and genuinely love who they are. Just because they are that desperate and can see no other option, or the temptation is just too overwhelming.

Desperate people will do unthinkable things even to their own loved ones and family. Especially drug addicted individuals. The psychology of drug altered individuals is wholly different than their normal psychology when clear of intoxicants. The worst thing I can think of is to bring good, kind people together with those that need their assistance and end up getting one of them harmed in the process. And I know that this is a very real possibility. But the benefit, the great benefit to all of humankind, really does outweigh the risks. There is nothing that can be nobler than to share the wealth of knowledge with those that so desperately need it. Just as Jesus said, "Give a person a fish and you feed him for a day, but teach him how to fish and you feed him for life." We just have to make very sure that we protect the teachers at all cost.

That is what Jos said to us. That was the hope and concern of Jos with the Church of Understanding. I, for one, was willing to do anything and everything to assist him in realizing his hopes and suppressing his concerns. But, more importantly, there was another one that seemed far more suited for the job.

Lorne was huge. Lorne was about six feet four inches tall and weighed about two hundred and sixty pounds of rigid muscle and had rough facial features that would stop a lion in its tracks. His voice was softly spoken at the pitch of a big diesel engine accelerating. He came up to Jos and thanked him for his vision of the church and asked if he could help. Jos conversed with him for a while and learned that the two of them had mutual desires and that Lorne was a welcomed, needed, and a perfect addition to the church. Lorne needed a cheap place to stay and study and Jos needed someone that no one would argue with.

Lorne lived a couple of blocks over with his large family in a small apartment. He lived with his single mother and brothers and sisters of different ages and temperaments. One thing he really liked to do was read and because of the size of the apartment having quiet time was virtually unheard of. He was intrigued by the offer of his own living area and readily agreed to the terms Jos asked for. Jos was delighted, for now he had at least one person to provide safety without great expense. Lorne went off to claim his room and make it his own. He would be moving in that night. Even though Lorne was a big, quiet, and reserved young man, it was still easy to see his enthusiasm at the prospect of having his own space.

Jos knew that the simple generosity that was going to be offered here at the church was going to lead to some difficult times. It was inevitable because humans are human after all. All he could do was incorporate everyone involved into feeling like they had a personal investment to make this adventure work; just like any business. People must govern themselves because they cannot be governed by anything else if they do not want to be. That also meant that people would have to be "encouraged" to clean up after themselves and help keep the place clean voluntarily.

Not so surprisingly, within a couple of hours there were already instructions going on. There was an older man over by an old, rusty donated lathe machine showing a couple of teenagers, how to turn a block of wood and make a table leg. In another section of the room were a few women almost competing to make pillow like cushions from the scraps lying around; there were even two boys standing quietly watching them. People were naturally curious and genuinely interested. It would be interesting to see how this all worked out over time.

Later that day, actually in the evening, Jordan asked Jos if it would be alright if he and a couple of his associates spent the night in the sleep rooms. Jos explained that they did not have enough cots for everyone, but that was of no matter to them. They were used to sleeping on the ground, and they were grateful that this ground was inside and close to a real bathroom. Of course, Jos welcomed them in and he asked that in return they clean up after. They understood.

The Church of Understanding notwithstanding, there were still other businesses that had to be supported and kept addressed. So, the restaurant crew went back to the restaurant, the bakery gang went back to the bakery, and Jos stayed back to talk to the new people he did not know.

Jos started talking to one of the ladies who was using the sewing machine. She was a middle-aged woman wearing a hijab, named Desha, that was obviously quite adept at sewing and designing. She addressed Jos very formally and reservedly. She asked many of the same questions that many others asked and then added, "How long before you think someone will allow themselves to do something wrong in here?"

It all depends on what value people put on themselves.

The woman looked at him mystified. What a strange response, she was obviously thinking, and Jos could see that. So, he explained ...

Self-Value

How much are you individually worth to yourself? This has to do with putting a value on integrity, honor, and reputable activities. To put this in a different way, all our actions have a price. We decide what that price is. It is we who decide at what point we agree to be bought.

There is a long-told story. One of the many versions of the story is of a conversation between a very sophisticated gentleman and a very respectable lady at a party. They are talking about prostitution. "Well," says the gentleman, "just for the sake of our argument, suppose I offered you $100,000—would you spend the night with me?" The lady, smiling flirtatiously, answers: "Why yes—I might very well!" The gentleman then asks: "Now, suppose I offer you $10 for the night?" The lady, indignant, replies, "Of course not, what do you think I am?" The gentleman remarks, "We've already established what you are. Now we are just haggling over the price."

The actual question arises frequently; at what point are you willing to sell your values? It is a valid question and one that should be often asked of an individual's self. At what point are you willing to sell your integrity, your honor, your self-respect?

I will tell you this; when an addiction, any addiction, is involved, your self-value drops significantly. To most people, the answer to the question is very much dependent on need. If you are cold, starving for food, or scared, the price to get you to abandon your principles and self-respect may be very low. Some people are in such need for basic survival necessities that they have succumb to indignities that they would never have imagined.

To answer your question; at what point in here will someone finally be so tempted that they succumb to temptation and do something that they will regret? Time can only be the judge of that. I will try to raise the bar of temptation for every person that comes in here. Just think if everybody just tried, anyway they could, to raise everyone else's level of self-respect everyplace would be safer and everyone would be happier. And then, of course, think of the cost of not trying at all.

The woman just shook her head, saying that Jos was an incurable optimist. But she liked that, she said, smiling and she vowed to do whatever she could to help. She also knew that if she could help improve the area, it would benefit her as well. On leaving for the day, she made a comment to Jos to the effect of, "May Allah be with you," on her way out. Jos smiled, knowing that Allah was with everyone all the time.

Much later on that day, at the restaurant, almost closing time, Rohm finished with his sous chef duties in the back and came out front just to help the others get caught up, then stopped at Jos. Rohm was born in India to well-to-do parents and was still young when he set out to see the world, even though it was against their advice. Having a Hindu background, he was very respectful of the elderly but he had a question he said that had been going through his head. He was wondering if the young people around here, specifically for what Jos had wanted, would be inclined to listen to the older people. Like he told Jos, respect for the elderly in his country was much more common than other places in the world. In the Far East, like China and Japan and some other places, the older people were really valued. But in many parts of the world they were not so regarded. Most of the time, he saw older people just pushed aside like they had outlived their usefulness. Jos knew sorrowfully that Rohm was right and that was really a great unrecognized tragedy. With few people left in the restaurant and most of the gang patiently waiting for those few to finish, most of them gathered around to hear what Jos had to say. As Jos began to talk I noticed that most of the patrons that were left actually stopped to eavesdrop clandestinely in the conversation as well. Jos noticed this and spoke in a tone that was easily heard ...

The Young and the Old

When people look at an older person, most see an old person. Rarely does anyone look at an older person and see the young child that was there. The elderly *rarely* sees themselves as old, except when they start to hurt or start to slow down unwillingly because of aging. They can clearly remember their hopes and dreams of younger years. They still have the desire to be young and act young and think young. Only the aging process shocks them into reality.

When you see an older person, you must realize that at some time they were a baby, completely helpless and dependent on others for survival. As you look at an older person, you must realize that at some time they were young and "stupid" with hormones that had them doing all sorts of things they thought were fun at the time. It is hard to look at one's own parents and think of them giddy with dreams and desires and infatuations. It is hard to look at a crouched over, frail old man using a walker as someone that was once formidable and strong, able to wage a strong fight in a battle. It is hard to look at someone in their eighties and nineties as someone that was sexually attractive and active at one time. But, at some time in the past, every "old" person was young and experiencing many of the same things the young are experiencing today for the first time.

The only thing that separates the young of today with the old of today is time. Many of the same things plagued each generation: wars, famine, poverty, strong governmental rules, the upper class versus the lower class. It is the same story of "same page," just "different book."

Unless you really sit and think about it, it is hard to imagine that many of the same things that concern you now were also the same concerns of generations past. Many people think that the times have completely changed and things are completely different today than yesterday. They are not. Young men still get erections and young women still giggle about it.

Life is a constant progression. Life is a constant state of evolution. You start off young and you grow old, if you are lucky and live long enough. This is another one of the real "God's laws," so it is non-negotiable.

If I can get the young in our midst to understand anything it would be the treasure they have at the Church of Understanding. They would stop idolizing the "celebrities" they see on TV and start exploiting the wealth available at their very finger tips. The elderly people around here are a treasure that is eager to give them knowledge that is far more valuable than money.

Wisdom

Wisdom only comes with time. Wisdom is a matter of having the intelligence and using it wisely. Wisdom can be considered a state of being. If you allow the aggravation of age and the intolerance of the young to slip into your thoughts, you lose wisdom.

The reason you generally only see wisdom in the more mature individuals is because it takes knowledge and the control that comes with time to apply the intelligence that is true wisdom. It is very hard, even for the very learned, to control emotions to the extent needed for wisdom to emerge. And it is very hard for others to take the time to listen and learn from the very wise.

Wise people will not try to push their knowledge onto others. Wisdom is like a rough diamond laying in the middle of a field of quartz rocks, it is very rare, very precious, easily overlooked, and once found has to be handled very carefully to bring out its pure worth and beauty. Wisdom has to be coaxed from another with patience.

Wisdom is not something that you go and get; it is something that comes to you in time if you have the willingness to accept it once it is available.

That, to me, is far more valuable for the young to listen to than some religious teacher of any kind telling them what their prophet had to say and what they meant by it. The old and wise of today have much more to give than the prophets of antiquity. Forget the teachings of centuries past and listen to the elderly of today, they are familiar with the contemporary world. They were the ones who created it. That is what I want from the Church of Understanding. That is what I want for the young around here. That is the meaning of life; to share knowledge and experience. That is wealth.

Jos stopped talking and looked at Rohm. A second later, spontaneous clapping started in the middle of the restaurant from one of the patrons listening in. We all looked over to see tears in the eyes of an elderly man sitting there with his wife.

The gang quietly got up and went on about their duties. Jos gave a slight nod of recognition to the older gentleman there and went on about his work. I just stood there at my station, quiet.

Later on, after all the customers had left and the gang was about to go to their respective residences, we all sat down to unwind. All of us sat drinking a beverage and talking about the events of the day. The new project of Jos was a central topic for most conversations. Some talked seriously about the expectations and others joked about what could happen.

Connie had brought almost everyone's conversation to a focal point when she asked Jos if he thought that there could ever be a utopian society. She wondered if there could ever be a society that lived in perfect harmony. The question did not even give Jos pause to contemplate.

Utopian Society

Yes, and no. It depends on your definition of utopia. If you are talking about a place like most people think of as heaven, where everything is good, there is no want, all there is around you is love? Then the answer is: no. As long as human beings are mortal and biological, chemical processing plants, then you are always going to have those that need more than others and for that simple reason alone there can be no utopia on Earth.

In order to have a perfectly utopian society, every person in it has to be the same as everyone else. They have to be the same in every detail as well. Not only do they have to have the exact physical attributes, but they also have to have the same desires, same experiences, and same outlook on the myriad of different philosophies.

Fairness and Equality

As far as fairness and equality goes, that is another matter. You may not be able to develop a completely utopian society but you can certainly obtain a society much closer in fairness and equality.

The simple fact is that humans are born unequal to each other. Then, of course, you have to take into account the circumstances that people are born into. Specifically, the parents the child is born to and the environment the child is born within. Obviously, there is no equality and certainly no fairness to a child born into royalty as opposed to a child born unwanted into poverty. The child has no control of these factors and, conversely, these factors may not determine the child's eventual outcome.

Treating someone "equally" does not take into account their human differences. If I was concerned about a patron in the women's toilet, would you want me to treat Mariam and Adam equally in asking them to check on that patron? When I am making a determination as to who to ask for assistance with an unruly patron, should I consider Natashia, who is petite, or Reese, who is a two-meter tank? People say they want to be treated equally, yes, but more than that, they want to be treated fairly.

If I am a woman and I do exactly the same work as a man, then I want equal pay; that is fair. However, if I am a woman and my work is considerably superior to the man's work, I do not want equal pay; I want to be paid fairly, I want to be paid more than the man.

Think about this. You have a person from your country's military that, while doing their duty, they had their legs damaged and ultimately removed. They currently live in reasonably adequate housing with a reasonable food and amenities allotment and even have enough to watch a sports game occasionally. The person playing this game makes more money in one year than the wounded military person will have the rest of their life. So, when it comes down to talking about equality and fairness, where do you go for your standards?

What I think most people would like to see is fair and equal *respect* shown to everyone. *That is obtainable.* The inequality and unfairness that is facing the world of today needs to be addressed by those that can address it, or the problems that it creates will continue to worsen. Like the unequal compensation for work in some countries, like Mexico, by other countries, like the United States.

A simple question that every person should ask is not, "What can I get away with paying someone because they are poor and needy?" The simple question that every moral person should ask is, "If I was doing that job, what would I think is fair and equitable?"

The first step in an improved world for every person is fair and equal *respect* for each individual as an individual. Next would be the fair and equal, and more importantly, appropriate compensation for work performed or services rendered.

That is the moral I have always tried to live, and that is the direction I have tried to show to others with everything I do.

A few weeks had gone by and the Church of Understanding was really starting to catch on within the neighborhood. Many more people than I thought were coming over throughout the week to learn different things. I could not believe how many women, not girls, women in their late twenties and early to mid-thirties, were coming over on a daily basis to practice things like metal work, welding, and woodworking. I would have thought jewelry making or sewing, but no, hardcore stuff. In fact, it also surprised me the few men that were learning sewing and jewelry making. At first, I thought it is not what I would expect, but then, when you think about it for a minute, it did start to make sense; this is not how most people are directed in school. When given the freedom, and released of the stigmas, why would a man not want to learn how to make jewelry and sew to attract and impress a woman? And, why would a woman not want to learn how to make things to be more self-sufficient, or be able to bond with a favorite man?

Saturday was really the day that everyone came over from even outside the community. Saturday was "Church" day. The diversity of the people coming took my breath away. That was the day that most people could get off and come over either to teach or to learn.

Many people were just like me when it came to Jos. We did not know what it was about this man that drew us to him, but he was a kind and generous teacher of many things, mostly life in general. It was also more than a little amazing to me how many manual skills Jos had. He was quite adept at many different tools and techniques for many different disciplines. His ability to teach and his own eagerness to learn were infectious.

The one day that the building was light on people was Sunday, because many that came were religious and went to their own church, or synagogue, or mosque, or temple that day. But, as the weeks went on, I started seeing more of them coming in on Sunday also. Jos had always said that people really do like to teach but not when they are forced to and not when they think they are just wasting their time. Also, people really love to learn things that they really want to learn, but again, not when they are forced to.

The Church of Understanding wasn't just a place to come and teach and learn but also a great place to socialize. Without any person planning or even suggesting it, people started bringing in stuff to eat, and before you knew it, Saturdays turned out to be a big pot-luck-type-lunch day. I think that some of the people there were almost in an unspoken competition trying to out-do some of the others in who could bring in the best item. It was a great and friendly competition that benefitted everyone who came, so everyone encouraged it.

As time went on, from time to time you would hear some people talking about different religions and what they believed. This was really kept to a minimum from the people there just out of respect for each other. There were quite a few different opinions on many different topics of discussion. Again, however, people didn't elaborate much because they were keeping a very decent and relaxed atmosphere. But the people there knew that many of the others were of many different faiths; there were Muslims, several different sects of Christians, some Jews, a few Hindus and Buddhists would also come by, along with a significant agonistic or atheistic few.

When it came to religion, the people that came in were a vastly mixed group. Which, in and of itself, fascinated me. But, like I said, the diversity of all different kinds of people astonished me all coming to this one little place on Saturday to share interests. It was not only fascinating; it was humbling as well.

The Confusion of God's Plan

So many people in the world today believe that if you do not follow the teachings of the old prophets, you are somehow a non-believer. If you choose to see the world for what it is, then you are a heretic. People believe, if you do not believe in what some human wrote thousands of years ago, even before the Dark Ages, then you are not religious. Many people of religion think that if you do not believe in an "intelligent designer," then you are an atheist and do not believe in God.

Some people are so resigned to their own belief that even in the light of new truth they refuse to even concede logical evidence. That is exactly what was happening in thirty-three CE, when Jesus went to the Pharisees. They absolutely knew without a shadow of a doubt that they were right and that Jesus was preaching nonsense and was a heretic. They believed it so vehemently that they orchestrated his demise. They were unwilling to bend in their beliefs as well.

A rather large man who was standing asked Jos if he thought there really was a God or not. Jos answered succinctly, yes.

Almost in unison two women from either side of the room along with a man to the side but closer asked essentially the same question; a question that Jos had been asked often. Which religion do you think is the right one?

What is the general theme of all religions? One, that there is a God of some kind; two, there is an afterlife of some kind; and three, to be kind, humane, and tolerant of your fellow human beings.

The *difference* with all religions is what that God is, what the afterlife is, and *how* to go about living respectfully of others and nature. Same page; different book.

That is why when I hear someone say, "You just have to have faith. You just have to believe what I am saying is true and believe in me." If you do not believe what they are saying, you are either considered Godless or an infidel, or they just walk away from you considering you to be tainted or corrupt. My problem with that is the phrase, "You just have to have faith. You just have to believe what I am saying is true." That is exactly the line a con man uses to get something from someone surreptitiously. When someone cannot prove what they are talking about or cannot, at least, give something in evidence that makes sense, they always fall back to the line "You just have to believe me, you have to have *faith*."

Think for yourself. No person is helpless to acquire new knowledge unless they are restricted by another. That should be the struggle of every human being all over the planet; the struggle to let every human being, regardless of who they are, learn everything they can without harming others.

That is the very central idea of this Church of Understanding. It is not to teach a belief. It is to teach anything and everything that can help everyone understand better the world humans live in and the people in it that we live with. It is for exactly what the name says: understanding.

Once you understand, then you do not have to believe; you will know.

With that Jos explained he had to go to the bakery. He paused for a minute for any questions anyone might pose, and left. Everyone around just sort of slightly nodded their heads and went back to what they were doing. To me it seemed like they went back to what they were doing with a little more intensity, vigor and purpose.

The bakery was an absolute madhouse during the daytime immediately after opening in the morning. It was beautifully controlled chaos that was surprisingly and deftly handled by Natashia and Billy with the help of Syria and Saliha. With all the different and delectable pastry offerings that they had accumulated, their business was utterly skyrocketing. The business had blossomed into quite a successful adventure for Natashia and Billy. It had not only become wildly profitable for the two of them but for Syria and Saliha also. Of course, the rest of the gang at the restaurant were benefiting as well, because all of them shared a percentage of the profits due to all of them investing in the startup of the business.

The only thing that was blossoming more than Billy and Natashia's little adventure into baking was their affection for one another. Over the last few months, it had become more and more apparent to the rest of the gang that Natashia and Billy had an attraction for each other. Needless to say, Jos had realized this far earlier; he just did not want to have any influence on it one way or the other. Love, Jos said once when we were all standing around, is a very strange and powerful emotion. When Jos said that Billy barked out a chuckle, completely uncontrolled and unexpected. Natashia, with her head turned, glanced at him and as clandestinely as she could, she gave him a slight knowing smirk.

Jos would say there is no explaining it; why one person is attracted to another person and not some other. Far too often it seemed to be a complete mystery to him. Not love in general but romantic, physical attraction that other people had. I do not know if Jos had ever been in love, that kind of love, nor did he ever talk about it if he had. He talked of love many times; all the different kinds and forms of love.

Love

The word love can be used in relation to a friend, a distant or a close family member, or a person of idolization, a romantic interest, or a sexual interest. The word love can also be used to describe strong feelings for many things other than people as well. The word love, just in the context with other human beings, can encompass a vast amount of different degrees and contexts. Now you see why I think the word love can be extremely confusing.

Affectionate love is such a powerful emotion. It is the romantic love that two people have for each other; when they just want to be close to the other person, they cannot stop thinking about the other person, and they want to see that other person happy all the time. And, there is no greater yin and yang in the universe than this particular kind of love. It can be the greatest thing to ever happen to a person; it can also be the greatest disaster to ever happen to a person. In a very literal sense it can be the cause of the creation of another human being, and it can be the cause of the demise of another human being.

Romance at the Start

Romance is strong; strong enough to change religion and politics. It has been one of the few things that can, and has, actually changed the course of history. Just one example: King Henry VIII wanted a divorce from Catherine of Aragon so badly, because he was in love with Anne Boleyn, and the Catholic Church would not allow him to divorce. It caused him to separate from the church and make his own church. This caused such a rift in the politics of the land that it is still felt to this day. You continue to see conflict between the Catholics and the Protestants. That is just one example of what romance can do. The list is endless: Helen of Troy, the face that launched a thousand ships, and Cleopatra; it just keeps going.

Romance is the spice of life. Romance is an enzyme; it makes things happen that would not normally happen. People say that romance is like a drug, but they are wrong; it is not *like* a drug, it *is* a drug. Romance is a chemical release of neurotransmitters in the brain. It is indeed, by any definition of the word, a drug. It enhances some senses and it mutes others.

That is the rather humorous yin and yang to that. The act of sex, especially the most passionate, appears as a very brutal act between two people; including the sounds of slaps and moans; the spanking and pinching, the fingernails and bites. Even the face of someone having an orgasm is almost indistinguishable from the face of sheer agony. The after effects are even such that it appears as if one has just been through a lifesaving defensive action with panting and sweating and muscle shakes.

Romantic love, however, is a treasure and should never be wasted for any reason.

Sex is, without a doubt, one of the strongest desires of the human species and of all other species as well. It is the very essence of the purpose of life. The only drive that surpasses it is survival.

You might be able to say that sex was the original obsession. It is known as the oldest profession, and it has also been referred to as the original sin. Any way you look at it, sex has been around since the first human being; of course, because what came first the chicken or the egg?

By the way, the answer to that question is the egg. I know that the response to that is: then where did the egg come from? Who knows; maybe from a dinosaur and it developed into a chicken. The simple truth is the reason the egg is the answer is basic biology and mathematics. An egg is the first step in any advance species. It is only one cell that continues to divide into a complex organism; it is one thing that becomes a million things. You have to start simple and then advance to complex.

Many times, when Jos was talking about love, he would also talk about "the closet." That special place in an individual's mind where thoughts and feelings were very private to the individual.

The Closet

Everybody has a closet. The closet is a secret place in a person's mind that no one else on earth knows about or is allowed to enter. In the closet are kept the secrets that an individual person has about themselves that are not even shared with their closest confidant or spouse. No other person on earth knows what is in another person's closet. It is a secret place.

People keep things in their closet that they find embarrassing, or it may be something that they do not want other people to know because it would hurt their feelings, or it may be something that they think other people would find silly, or it may be something that they feel would let other people know just too much about them. It is their special closet that makes them unique and individual from everyone else ... and *every person has one.*

Forms of Control

Jos noted that sexual desires and fantasies were probably the most common item kept in the closet. One time, I heard Adam comment, "Sex is one of the ways some people control other people." He looked to Jos for confirmation of that statement.

Jos responded with a nod.

That is correct. There are five ways to control people and populations: through governments, the laws of man; through commerce, the laws of money; through religion, the laws of God; one of the most powerful forms of control is the human sex drive, the laws of desire; and a very effective way to exert control is through mass media, the laws of public opinion. Not only is mass media a form of control it is generally the major assistant to all other forms of control.

Throughout history, you can see where, in different areas, the predominate control means would change from time to time. Jerusalem is a great example of this concept. At first it was dominated by religion, then the Romans came in and controlled it with government, then commerce had a stronger hold on the local inhabitants, then religion came back into the picture. Today the area is just a mess with so many things trying to exert control by religion or government or commerce or mass media. It is, as you would expect, a perpetual "war zone" within and between many different control methods.

Those that always suffer the most are the majority who are not in control; the ordinary people that live there and actually make everyday life possible. They do not want to control anything but their own lives. They just want to live, work, have a family, enjoy the pleasure of life itself, and not harm or intrude on anyone else until they expire from this life-form.

"That is kind of normal, though, isn't it?" Adam said. "People trying to control others. I don't know why when I think about it. But that is sort of the way of things. People are always trying to control other people"

Jos agreed. He would refer to what he called the third rule: the drive for control. Almost everyone had some form of it. Either the drive to control others or the drive not to be controlled themselves by anyone. It was for these reasons that people made laws. It was also for these reasons that some normally law-abiding people would break laws.

When we would talk about laws and rules, or long held customs, Jos would always say things like ...

How Do I Affect You?

How is what I eat going to affect your life? How is who I want to sleep with going to affect your life? How is who or what I pray to going to affect your life? Unless, of course, who or what I pray to is instructing me to harm you. How is the lack of personal protection while I am driving, walking, swimming, or anything else going to affect you? Why should anything I do that affects only my life and does not affect your life give you any right to comment, or interfere with my decisions? Who gave you the insight to know what is best for me? Who gave you the right to determine what is best for my life? If we are all children of Allah, then Allah can instruct any of us the same as any other.

People will use whatever influence they can to obtain that control; whether it is terror, commerce, politics, laws, religion, mocked kindness, or deception, or sex. Whatever it takes for them to obtain and maintain control, people will use it. Religion has been the number one means of exerting control over others throughout recorded history. Jesus never advocated control over anything but one's own self. It was those that came after him, using his name, that set up controls.

Forms of Control: Are They Needed?

Humans think that these controls are necessary in order to have an operational civilization. Other species show that without these controls a society can coexist and be extremely productive and prosperous. Termites, ants, and bees are highly organized societies that have no religious, governmental or commercial restrictions and produce phenomenal works of construction and productive interaction. Other species recognize the value of the others and respect them for their value to the whole.

People always marvel at the splendor of the pyramids without giving any thought to the towering mounds of the termites that far surpass any human endeavor in comparative size relationship.

Other species have shown that, if all know their respective place in society and are working for the betterment of the entire group and not for themselves, then they all share in a bountiful reward. Only individual desires cause people to manipulate others instead of working within a society. Then some control becomes necessary. But then control very quickly gets abused. Control should only be used to keep people from harming others.

Freedom

The idea of having complete control over one's own life and future is the yearning of every human being. The freedom to carry out one's own choice is every person's desire.

However, with great freedom comes great responsibility. If the freedom is going to be individual, then the responsibility is also individual; which means that if an individual wants a great amount of freedom to do or say what they want, then it is also up to them not to abuse that freedom and to exert individual control and restraint.

Sadly, most individuals have proven that they must have laws, rules, customs, however you want to define it, in order to cohabitate with other people without invading on their freedoms. In this situation, it is usually the largest group of people that come to some general consensus that dominates the area.

This is why you see in every generation throughout history some rebellion by the youth of the time to long standing rules or customs or opinions. The younger generation is always the driving force for change, which is just another way of saying evolution. This is why the human species has evolved from caves to earthen enclosures to rock buildings to wooden structures all the way up to marble palaces and steel towers. This is why humans have evolved from thinking thunder was Thor's hammer, an eclipse was the hand of God, and the Sun orbited the Earth to what we now know.

One day when Jos was talking about freedom, he said this ...

Like It or Not, Majority Rules

It does not matter the right or wrong of it; when most people agree on something, then it is right and the few that disagree are wrong. That is the way it has been throughout history. People in the past have always had to conform to what the majority advocates whether they liked it or not. It is still that way today. Not everyone agrees with everything.

There is power in numbers. You have heard that many times. It does not just apply to physical space it also applies to knowledge and beliefs.

Looking back on history, it is easy to see just how many customs, beliefs, and rituals have changed throughout time, and all of them fueled by the collective majority.

Reese spoke up. "But that is the way that it has always been. It is probably never going to change."

Now I hear you say, "But that is the way it has always been." Throughout history of the human species, it has always been the haves and the have-nots, the givers and the takers, the fortunate and the unfortunate. It is not going to change; not now, not ever. You are absolutely correct; if there were not two sides, two opposing forces, then nothing would move; there would be no motion. If everyone were to remain happy with the status quo then people would still be living in caves sitting around a fire telling stories for entertainment.

When humans stop getting angry at other people's religion, culture, race, politics, looks, clothing, sexual orientation, food choice, lifestyle choice, when humans allow others to have their freedoms and stop abusing their own freedoms that allow prejudices onto others, that is when you will start to see some really quick and wonderful progressions. That is when life will start to be more equal and fair for everyone.

Alcohol Versus Marijuana

I remember one time when Jos was demonstrating how the opinions of the majority can dictate certain laws that affect everyone. Even when those opinions were really not completely correct. It was just the desires that drove the majority and hence the results. Jos explained it like this ...

There are a lot of similarities that go along with the arguments that can be made about two different but similar things. I will take for instance the arguments about alcohol and marijuana. Two substances that are mind-altering and used, primarily, regardless of what people say, for recreational purposes. In short, people use the substances to feel good. One substance is generally legal virtually everywhere and the other is generally illegal virtually everywhere.

Let us look at how marijuana and alcohol compare to each other. Both are psychologically addicting, but *only* alcohol is strongly physically addicting. That is why when a sufficient quantity is consumed it produces a "hangover"; marijuana does not produce a hangover. Those that use alcohol in a sufficient amount for a sufficient amount of time will incur physical withdraw symptoms when they stop drinking; *they can even die*. Those that use marijuana in a sufficient amount for a sufficient amount of time will *not* incur physical withdraw symptoms when they stop. Also, you can drink enough alcohol to overdose and die; you *cannot* smoke enough marijuana to overdose and die.

When alcohol is used, the more you drink, the more intoxicated you become, until you become comatose and even die. However, when marijuana is smoked, you will reach a peak and that is it, regardless of how much you smoke you will only become intoxicated to a certain level and that is it; no more.

Ask any emergency medical provider or emergency room physician and they will tell you that they would much rather deal with someone that is "stoned" than someone that is "drunk." A person high on marijuana is generally docile and calm, whereas a person who is drunk is generally obnoxious and belligerent and can become violent quickly.

With those criteria, I would classify alcohol as a hard drug and marijuana as a soft drug.

It is just interesting to me that not only is alcohol legal in most places, it is also socially accepted and even encouraged, especially through the media with advertisements and visions of how much fun people are having with it. On the other hand, what a stigma that marijuana has; it is generally illegal in most places, and it is not socially accepted. In fact, it is discouraged and vilified in the media. It is almost like locking up a thief and inviting a murderer to a party.

It is just another good example of the "right and wrong" of society that is dictated by the desires of the majority without looking at all the information available; or using confirmation bias to prove their point as to what is good and what is bad for others in society. If alcohol is legal then marijuana should be legal; if marijuana is illegal then alcohol should be illegal, that would only be the fair thing to do.

Jos stopped suddenly. He raised his hand up shaking it.

This is not my bid to make marijuana legal or to promote its use in any way. Nor is this my way of showing objection to the use of alcohol. Rather it is just my way of showing how many things are not fairly considered because of the power and control of the "majority" of a group, or region, or society. How many times in history has the human race seen something become popular only to later be vilified, and then later, sometimes, to become popular again?

This is just a way for me to show you how people change, the constant state of evolution in human development that is occurring at all times even within your own lifetime. What is in "fashion" or even the "accepted normalcy" of any group, or region, or society, or culture is generally dictated by the majority of that group, regardless of the facts one way or another. It also shows how quickly people can either become intolerant of other's choices or tolerant of them.

"Then how are we to make laws?" Connie asked. "What would be the right way to impart certain controls? You cannot just let everyone

make up their own rules within a society. That would be complete chaos; even dangerous. What rules should be imposed for the safety of everyone?"

The Law

What people want and what people need are laws that "protect me from other people, and protect other people from me." People do not want or need laws that "protect me from myself." The motorcycle helmet law is a good example of the point here.

If I choose to not wear a helmet, it is not going to affect anyone but me. If I get into an accident without a helmet, I am the only one that will be injured. I am not going to injure any other person in that accident if I am not wearing a helmet. So, to make a law that says when I am of the age of consent that I have to wear a helmet is "protecting me from myself," *it is someone else pushing their ideas on me.*

I want to be free to make decisions about my own life without other people meddling in my life if it, in no way, affects them. I do not care if other people think that I am taking unnecessary chances. This is my life, not theirs. It is my individual choice, not theirs. Those are two very individual opinions. No person appreciates another person's opinion about how they choose to live their life. You would not want it done to you, so, you should *never* do it to someone else.

If you feel the need, then offer me any information that you think I do not know to make a more informed decision. Give me the knowledge to make an informed and responsible decision. However, just telling me that I am "stupid" is not giving me sufficient information.

Was it not Jesus who said, "Why do you complain about the splinter in your neighbor's eye and take no heed to the plank in your own eye?"

Do not make laws to protect me from me. Make laws that protect me from others, and protect others from me. Only!

Even Jesus taught, incessantly and continuously, about tolerance, understanding and the right of every individual to make their own decisions about their lives, loves, beliefs and convictions. There were two places in the Bible where Jesus chastised someone; one was in the temple with the money changers; the *"moneygrubbers."* The other place Jesus chastised someone is when they criticized others for what they did or who they were. "Judge not lest ye be judged." If it does not affect your life or livelihood than allow other people to live their lives as they see fit within their beliefs and convictions and choices. If they make a bad decision that is only going to affect them then they have to live with it; others do not. "You who is without sin, cast the first stone."

No matter, how the *"majority"* feels individuals have the *God-given right* to be individual as long as they do not harm any others in the process. Yes, that is right, I said "God-given right." That is the reason and purpose we have individual bodies. Without that individual freedom for the spirit in every one of us God does not learn new and different things.

You should have respect and tolerance for other people's choices. You do not have to like them or agree with them for yourself, but you should have respect for their life choices and decisions. If their decisions do not harm you. I do not mean "offend" you. I mean physically, psychologically or financially harm you or your loved ones, then you should at least tolerate them.

When you listened to Jos speak about that topic, you could tell he was very vehement about the subject. It did not take a person very long to understand that Jos felt very strongly about each and every individual. It was almost like he was living their life with them and knew just how they felt at any given time. His power of empathy was stronger than any other person that I have ever encountered. It was like he never even had to hear what a person said about something as long as he was in proximity to them. You could see him feel the pain, anger, joy, apprehension, pleasure, or any other emotion that they were feeling in his body language. It was almost unnervingly uncanny.

He was stern about every person was an individual and every person had the right to be individual and he wanted every person to practice that individuality. Non-harmful and unobtrusive individuality was, to Jos, a miracle in itself and a wonder to witness. He said that often.

The wonder of life is individuality.

THE FABRIC STORE

Jos had talked to Desha at the opening of the Church of Understanding. She said, "How long before you think someone will do something wrong here?" Jos had explained to her about self-value and the levels of temptation. Since that time, though, Jos had seen Desha here almost every day. She was using the sewing machine and most of the time teaching others sewing and different sewing techniques. Desha was always covered in traditional Muslim attire but her designs, however, were very modern and flamboyant in fashion. She had a way about her that other people responded to very positively. The creations she made together with others were very popular, and they sold them easily to buy more supplies of materials and fabrics.

After a few long talks with Desha, Jos had convinced her that she could use her talents and time to advance her eager "students," give them a chance to enjoy and understand the fruits of their labor, and create a legacy of benefit to the community. He suggested that, along with the restaurant gang and the bakery gang, they invest in a private shop to provide clothing and other garments. The restaurant crew had been begging for tablecloths and napkins. The bakery had been asking for special hot pad holders. And everyone had been talking about uniforms and just the need for some new clothes. As Jos told Desha, "You already have a clientele and a demand for your services. Before long, and with a deserving gang to back you up, you could have a great influence on this community."

Desha thought about it for days. She had reservations and discussed them with Jos. Whatever they were, he was able to quell her reluctance. Desha was older. I was never really sure what her age was, but I guessed between mid to late fifties maybe even early sixties, it was very hard to tell with the covering that she always wore and maintained. Her speech was quiet and reserved, she never raised her voice. She was one of those that did not need to; her silence was louder than a yell.

Soon, however, Jos brought the whole restaurant and bakery gangs together to propose the investment into a design and clothing store. Without any hesitation, everyone was onboard and willing to offer any additional assistance as necessary. The gang I came here with was very diverse. Over time I got to know their stories and reasons for being here. Some had left their old lives behind, some were like me, just now leaving their old life. Everyone still kept in contact with their families and friends but now we all had a new family and new life. Every day was a new adventure for all of us. Every day we met new friends.

Everyone that I knew had met Desha, and they all loved her and her design aesthetics. Desha wanted to call the place "Cover Your Heart Designs." For some reason, that brought a smile to Desha's face every time she said it.

Jos told us about the desire to help Desha build a business. It was not for the financial possibilities but because she was one of those people who needed that kind of outlet. She had something inside of her that was special, and she had found the way to make it accessible to other people. When that very unique part of someone was realized Jos liked to encourage it and share it with others, every way possible. He said, "That is the blessing we give to God: it is the sharing of our unique creative self with others."

Art and Artistry

This is the beauty of humans: the ability to create art and perfect artistry. This is what makes humans that much more interesting. It is one thing that makes us different from other animals. Humans commonly make works that can be looked at for many years and be appreciated.

Desha has a definite artistic way with fashion design. She also has a very artistic way with teaching the craft to others. That is why I want to see her have her own shop. She can do a lot of amazing things; not only making fine garments but passing on that enthusiasm and creativity to a new and younger population. She knows things you cannot learn from books, and knowledge is precious.

Shortly after starting to put together the clothing store for Desha, the gang sat down for a break. Jordan and his two friends were coming in from painting outside. They went over to the sink to clean up a bit. Reese, Jos and I came over to a table in the middle of the room to sit with our drinks.

Desha and Adam had been involved in a conversation between them *for some time; just talking back and forth in common conversation. They were religious and had been in a discussion regarding religion. Both had spent enough time with Jos to be tolerant of other views to the extreme. But both were also very committed to their beliefs. At one point Adam was able to catch the attention of Jos.*

"We were always taught about the Holy Trinity: The Father, Son, and Holy Ghost." He looked at Jos. "We were taught that the Holy Trinity was one and the same thing, yet all three things were different and separate. How can the three be separate and different, and at the same time be one in the same thing?"

Nodding, Jos looked at Adam and, cocking his head, continued nodding. It was an expression of "Very good question."

The Holy Trinity

There are many "trinities" in the universe that are one and the same thing in essence yet are made up of three different things. You have heard me speak often that there are two sides to every story and the truth lies somewhere in the middle. That is a trinity; this side, that side, and the truth. This is a trinity, the left, the right, and the middle; the three different parts of something that cannot exist without each other together. The birth, the death, and the lifetime of something, anything; all things have a beginning and an end and some timeline between the two. That again is a trinity; three things that are separate but make up a whole.

Many times, you hear God the Father, Jesus the Son, and the Holy Spirit used almost interchangeably. There is really no difference between them.

He leaned over toward Adam like he was about to tell him a great secret and almost whispered ...

That is because there is not a difference between them. They are one in the same thing; it is all the same thing. The difference is not in the three parts, the difference is how humans look at the three parts and separate them. Humans have made the difference.

This is really going to get the Christian in you steaming: Jesus was a human being. He was not a lion, or a whale, or a great ape, or some other species. He was a human. His body was a human chemical processing plant like every other human body.

There are many things that people just do not talk about; especially devout Christians. Jesus was human. He had a heart that pumped human blood. He had a liver that helped digest food. He had kidneys that made urine. He ate food that included animal meat. And by the way, he drank alcohol; not because he liked to drink an intoxicant but because in his time it was the safest fluid to drink. Water was often contaminated but wine was fermented and safe. He ingested nutrients; he had to just like all other humans. He processed them into necessary body parts and body functions, produced waste products and defecated just like every other human before his time and since.

When you look at a human being, you can only see a very small part of them. Just what is on the outside. Most of the human body's mass is inside and cannot be seen. But that is just the material part of a human being. The biggest part of any human being is the energy that is their thoughts and feelings, emotions and memories.

When you look at the universe, you only see about four percent, which is light matter. Eighteen percent is dark matter. And the largest part of the universe is dark energy; about seventy-eight percent.

Both of these things are composed of three different things that are, in essence, all the same thing. There are many "trinities" within the universe; of which the universe itself is only one.

When you are talking about a human being, a person, you are talking about all the things put together that make up a person: your essence. It is not only one thing. There are far too many things that make up a human being for any one of them to be considered that one individual. Even your thoughts are just a part of you, your feelings, controlled and uncontrolled, are part of you, your kidneys are part of you, your heart is part of you, your past and memories are part of you. Everything that has ever affected you and everything that has ever influenced you is also part of you. When you are talking about a person, a human being, you are talking about many, many things all put together much like the Holy Trinity. All parts being completely different yet everything is the same thing.

Adam looked at Jos with silent understanding. Jos looked at him with a big smile. Slowly a smile grew on Adam's face. "That was pretty deep for a simple question at break time."

Jos kept smiling and shrugged. He got up and put his hand on Adam's shoulder and said, "You do not ask simple questions."

Natashia and Billy came over with some snacks and to see how things were going. They seemed to go everywhere together these days. Billy commented on how the place was coming along while Natashia was talking to Desha. Break time was taking a little longer this time probably because of the unexpected treats.

When Natashia came over to the group that was sitting there next to Billy, she looked up at him. Her eyes had an unspoken question in them that only Billy knew. Billy directed his attention to Jos that was just walking over to a window.

"Jos," Billy said, "I was wondering. Well, really, Natashia and I were wondering. You had said earlier that you really wanted Desha to begin this business. It was like the same way you, kind of, encouraged Natashia and me to start the bakery. You seem to want these things to get started, but it doesn't really seem like it is because you want to see the business get started. It seems like you just want to see us get started. The question is, why? What is your motive? What's going on?"

Jos was standing there with the bright light from the window blazing behind him. It put a glow around him. His face was almost completely obscured by the overwhelming light behind him, putting his face in a deep shadow. You really couldn't see his eyes, all you could hear was his voice saying ...

Influences

All that human beings can do in their own lifetime is *influence* the future. That is what life is all about: influences. In the vastness of time, there is the past, the present, and the future. One cannot change the past; it is but a memory. One cannot change the future once they die. All anyone can do, and all everyone does do, is influence the future while they are alive. The very moment of the present that they are living.

People often talk about the *reason* they did something, or the *excuse* why they did something. Nothing and nobody makes another person do something. Things and *other people* can have a profound *influence* as to why someone makes a particular decision to pick a certain option. But it is just an influence.

While human beings are in a physical, material form, they can initiate actions. They can manipulate other physical, material forms; whether it is by actual physical manipulation, touching it, or by words. What is sometimes lost on people is that everything they do or say will have some reaction.

The reason that I wanted you and Natashia and Desha to start the business is because of the influences you have, and will have, on the future of everything around you.

Everything Just Influences Other Things

"So, let me get this straight," Billy questioned with a bewildered face. *"You wanted us to start these businesses to influence others? That puts an unusual responsibility on us, doesn't it?"*

Influences do not control anything they only encourage a response. Many people run around saying that *this* made them do something or *that* made them say something. In truth, "this" or "that" only provided an influence, it did not really make anything happen. It was only how the individual chose to react and respond to the influence that created their response.

Everything that happens creates an influence for something else to happen. That particular influence can create different responses at different times and on different things, which, in turn, creates other influences. This continues to perpetuate on down the line into the future.

This influence is what gives everything multiple possibilities until the moment of the present arrives. Then, an action is taken, one of the multiple possibilities that could happen does happen. The influence did not make anything happen. Once the result is done, it cannot be changed; it only influences other actions and so on.

Responsibility

Every decision to act a person makes is based on experiences in their lives. But every decision to act a person makes is their *responsibility*, completely and totally.

A couple of people in the group started to say something. "Well, uh," was about as far as they got before Jos waved a hand in the air to stop them.

I know. I know. Listen, so there is no one going to push the hypothetical boundaries with the "Well, what about this," question. Let me say this. You know what I am trying to say. When something bad happens to us, or we do something bad, do not just point a finger and pronounce fault without looking at what *your* responsibility is in the situation.

You know what I am saying. If a man molests or rapes a woman, he cannot avoid responsibility because of drugs or pornography or an unfair childhood. It is his fault and responsibility for acting on his impulses. However, if a woman goes to a bar and has a couple of drinks and walks out of the bar and gets molested or raped, it is not her responsibility for enticing the rapist or "for being there in the first place."

Too many people are quick to blame something else for their actions. And too many people justify other people's actions on other things. "Well, he is this way because he was abused as a child." No, he is not this way because of his childhood. He is this way because that is the way he *chooses* to be. I hear many people blame bad actions on the media, pornography, alcohol and drugs, poverty, race, and racial issues, even video games and movies and music. None of these things make anybody do anything. They may influence many people. I will give you that. But none of these things make anybody do anything; what they do is their decision. They are responsible for their decisions; more than that, they are responsible for their actions. You are not responsible for their actions because of your influences.

This is the major reason that I wanted to see the whole gang start a business, like the restaurant. This is the reason I wanted to see Billy and Natashia start the bakery, and this is the reason I wanted Desha to have this clothing and fabric store. All of you are excellent examples. When people see excellent examples of anything, they become influenced. Look at how Syria and Saliha have blossomed and grown because of the influences of you and Natashia. Look at the influences they are now giving and passing along.

Positivity is as contagious as negativity. I just think that all of you would be good examples and your influences would be well received. People must take responsibility for their own actions and not blame an influence for the action they took. I have seen many times all of you take full responsibility for your own actions. You are good examples.

"Well," Billy said, "Natashia and I were just trying to be nice. Like you said, 'Do nice, do not do not-nice.' We are just trying to be good."

I could see that statement click a switch on in the mind of Jos. He closed his eyes and nodded while he brought up his hand and slowly pointed the whole hand at Billy. With a sigh, Jos spoke ...

One of the major problems of the world today is that just being nice all the time is very, very hard. It is becoming increasingly harder to be nice to every person in today's society. It seems like the more people get packed into a smaller area, the closer people have to live with many others, the more they keep to themselves. It is very hard to be respectful, tolerant, and just plain nice to people today because of the way they act. But that is the very reason why it is so important to continue to try and why it is so important to succeed in being respectful, tolerant, and nice to everyone you have contact with. It is very difficult but it is very necessary at the same time for all humans; because even just one act will radiate to all others. It is hard but necessary and that is the yin and yang of that.

Jos stopped, and just stood there in the twilight between sunlight and shadow as he continued ...

Good and Evil

Good and bad is alive, but never more strong and evident than in the more intelligent of species. It is said that nature is neither kind nor cruel; it is merely indifferent. But you start to see a difference between mere indifference, and actual cruelty and kindness become more evident the higher the intelligence of the species.

Plants show no affinity to either good or evil, neither do bacteria, algae, jellyfish, alligators, or even sharks; all of them are more primitive and of lesser "intelligence" and are merely indifferent to what they are doing. But start to look at dolphins and primates and other more intelligent species and you start to see either a little more cruelty and/or kindness in their character. When it comes to humans, theoretically the most intelligent of all species on this planet, and you see a very clear and defined difference of cruelty and kindness attributed to character.

Here, I have spoken before about killing. The Ten Commandments state that one shall not kill ... anything. However, I submit in order to preserve life, one may be forced to kill. In order to protect yourself or another person from harm caused by another, if there is no other way to prevent it, one may be forced to kill. That is not to say that one can go looking for that opportunity. Only if one is faced with it and cannot prevent it in any other way. *A human should never take any pleasure in the act of killing another living thing.*

Killing for entertainment, for punishment, for revenge, out of rage or for any other reason other than protection and survival is wrong and an obscenity. Everyone knows the truth of what I say; it really does not need to be explained except for those wanting to find a loophole that they can exploit to their advantage.

Good and bad thoughts go through almost every person. The only question is how are they going to act on those thoughts, those influences. It is not your thoughts but your actions and words that create influences on other people. People must try to do good actions;

regardless how hard it may be with their thoughts. Even as difficult as other people may tend to make it.

Jos was quiet now and strolling toward us.
Desha asked Jos, "Why did you choose me?"
Well out of the blinding back light now, Jos walked closer to Desha.

I have been watching you. You are one of those very rare people that reach across all human lines and find the very best in others. Then you bring that close to you and together you work to make great works of art. You have that natural tendency to combine with others to bring out the true creative essence of humans.

Pentatonix

I have to tell you something. I had the good fortune to watch a singing group while I was in North Europe; they called themselves the Pentatonix. They were an a cappella group consisting of five young people. The fascinating thing to me was that they were a mix of many different "types," you could say that they all belonged to different individual gangs; different sexes, different races, different sexual orientations, and different cultures. But all that did not matter because when they worked together, their five voices blended together to make one sound and it was absolutely angelic. Completely without any instruments, with just their voices, they sounded like a complete ensemble of finely-tuned instruments. That is because they were. They were the instruments of the living voice; the voice of God.

God has a voice. God has action. You see this example every day when you understand that the essence of God is every living thing together. It is amazing what people can do when they work together. You see it every day in Formula One racing, cruise ships, the Pyramids, space programs, and many science endeavors. All examples of what can be done when many very different people from all walks of life, all different cultures, religions, backgrounds, points of views, all come together to work together. It is an example of many parts making one body with one purpose and goal.

God Recognizes No Color

When speaking of gangs and gang affiliations, the fastest groupings will be associated with how a person looks. Obviously, unless you are a blind person, the first thing that you have to start making associations with is visual. That starts before anything else because that is a long-distance sense. Of the visual sense, some of the first things noted are sex, skin color, height, weight, age, and attractiveness. These are all very important glues for people to assess a threat; friend or foe. That is nature.

This was especially important in early development because you want to recognize a threat from a distance. One of the most obvious traits is skin color, because it generally denotes same or different culture origin. Now, whether a particular skin color will be regarded as friend or foe is completely a learned response. You are not born with that information; you learn it through experience and teachings. This is where prejudice rears its ugly head. What were you taught and what were your actual experiences? But, that is not exclusive to skin color; it also pertains to sex, height, weight, age, and attractiveness.

In order to experience all life, you must have a vast range and the most diverse differences between all people for different experiences. To be non-racial is not to be color blind but, quite the contrary, to be perfectly aware of all the different skin colors and to recognize that skin color is only skin deep. The wisdom of Dr. Martin Luther King Jr., who said, "I have four daughters, I hope one day they will not be judged for the color of their skin, but by the content of their character."

Let me go one step further than Dr. King: Judge me not by the color of my skin, or my height, or my sex, or my weight, or my religion, or my sexual orientation, or my family heritage but by the content of my individual character. When we start looking at individual people and not at their group characteristics then we will stop hurting innocent, peaceful, kind, and tolerant individuals. That is when we will have true justice.

Now Jos walked over to the table and sat down in the middle of us. He leaned back in the chair with his arm across the back of another empty chair. He was gazing across the room at nothing in particular.

A Bad Person is a Bad Person Regardless of Associations

A good person is a good person no matter who they are otherwise. The whole essence of what I am trying to say is simple: regardless of any particular gang association you are affiliated with, if you are a good person then you are a good person, individually. If you have kindness, respect, and tolerance for other people regardless of their associations, then you are a good person. If you try to assist other people in need in a responsible manner, then you are a good person.

However, conversely, regardless of any association you are affiliated with, if you are a bad person then you are a bad person. If you are not kind, give no respect, and/or have no tolerance for other people regardless, or because of, their associations then you are a bad person. If you refuse to assist a person in need, in any manner, then you are a bad person. If you knowingly harm another, then you are a bad person.

I do not care what religion you are or if you even are religious. I do not care what your social or economic status is. I do not care what your sex or your sexual orientation is. I do not care what your culture is or your race is or your traditions are. I do not care about any of your associations, or gangs, that you belong to. You are your individual character. I say this: If you look at another person and judge them for any other reason but for their sole individual character, then you are unjust and wrong. You are prejudging.

A few weeks had passed and Desha's little Cover Your Heart Designs store was open for business and was already over its head in requests. She had gotten two other ladies and two young girls and two young boys to come in and help her on a "when they can" schedule. To avoid hourly wages and how awkward and time consuming that can be, especially with their schedules, she had followed the advice of Jos as far as compensation in this circumstance.

She decided to pay a percentage of the sale price of the garment or piece sold. The way Jos had explained it: an appropriate percentage to the one who made it, an appropriate percentage to the shop and equipment for the space and tools to make it, an appropriate percentage for the material used to make it, and an appropriate percentage to the one in charge of selling it and accounting for all the other aspects of making it. That way, the garment itself supplies the appropriate amount to everything having to do with its creation and sale. No one can take advantage of another in the line.

It also allowed for some individual creativity. Once the requests were filled, then everyone was allowed to create their own clothing and have a venue to sell it. It gave an incentive for everyone to work well and fast; it also gave them someone to look to for advice and instruction. Desha was the perfect influence for an aspiring individual interested in the textile industry.

Then one day, while Jos and I were at the Church of Understanding watching some amazing woodwork being made, Desha came in. She was concerned with one of the girls that came to work with her named Lajita. She started out very promising, but now seemed to have lost interest and was not doing as well as she could. She was promising with so much potential Desha didn't want to lose the young girl because of some unknown reason that she didn't know about. She knew that Lajita wasn't doing drugs, and Desha had talked to her about other troubles that might be in her life, but there were really no notable things that would cause the change. Desha was hoping that Jos could help. Jos thought about it for a moment. He confirmed that Lajita was the girl he was thinking about because he had met her before, here, in the Church before the clothing shop opened. Desha confirmed she was who he was thinking about and he agreed that she was very gifted.

Self-Standard

Lajita sounds like someone who puts very high standards on themselves. That is not a bad thing, but it can be disappointing sometimes and at times destructive. When they feel like they cannot meet their own standards, then they just give up. That is the worst thing anyone can do.

Every great person on Earth present and past has had their own trials, tribulations, and doubts to contend with. It just was a matter of time, and in most cases the guidance and/or influence of another to help them get to where they were going. *Most important of all is that the person must not give up on themselves.* They must continue the struggle and they must fight to obtain the good that they want.

All you can do is encourage, support, and provide a trusting influence with complete tolerance to their vision. *Do not tell them* that you believe in them, for that will only give them something to disappoint, which they do not need. *Show* them that you believe in them, for that is what is missing in them.

Keep working with her, I plead with you, for if she does turn to the dark side, the path is much easier and much harder to recover from. She has the talent; she just has to find that talent, in herself, which is just the first step. If she takes the next step, developing the skill, which is much longer, she will have a bejeweled future.

Desha thanked Jos for his insight and promised that she would do what she could and she would keep him informed. He thanked her for that.

She said, "I will pray for the girl. That will help." With that Jos smiled. Desha looked at him. "You do not believe in prayer?" she queried.

Where we were standing, in the middle of his Church of Understanding, the question seemed almost obscene. With the smile still on his face, Jos looked down. It brought many strange looks to his direction. It seemed like an odd reaction to a simple, straightforward question.

"Do you laugh at me because I believe in prayer?" Desha asked. With that Jos instantly stopped smiling, assuring her that was not the case by any means. When he looked to tell Desha, he suddenly saw all the faces that had stopped what they were doing and were now staring at him. So, Jos spoke up ...

I would never laugh at anyone in prayer or wanting to pray for someone. And if I in anyway made you think that, I ask to be excused. I understand the meaning and purpose of prayer. Anybody wanting to pray for another is only wishing them the very best. I would not take that lightly. Anyone wanting to pray for someone only wants to do whatever they can to help. That is the epitome of kind and caring. But you asked me, so let me tell you what I know about praying.

Hold on to your chair, because I am about to say something that is going to have you flying up in protest. Ready, here it goes; *what is the point?*

With that, it seemed like every jaw in the house just dropped. Everybody looked stunned.

If you truly feel something in your heart, then there is no need to say it, except to show other people. All of the parts and pieces that compose the entity that is God already knows what is in your heart and how you really feel. Live it, do not say it.

Prayers, Praying, and How God Works

Sochin, one of Adam's sous chefs that rarely got a chance to get out was standing there, he started questioning Jos about the workings of God. Even though he rarely spoke about it, Sochin was religious. He never defined which religion, he would just say things like, "I pray to God," "May God bless you," and "You can trust in God." And he would say them with conviction.

Sochin said, "I have prayed to God and have had those prayers answered." Staring at Jos he said, "The way you describe God you can't ask him for anything. To pray is useless."

Praying is not useless. Again, I tell you, God *does* exist.

The only way that God intervenes with humans is through the mind of humans. This is what is so hard for people to understand about God. The conscious energy of God is made up of all the conscious energy in the universe, including yours. So, that part of your conscious energy that thinks and reasons and imagines is the conscious energy of God.

Sochin rolled his eyes. "You see? You sound like you are talking in circles. You sound like a politician. I just want to know one thing. Does praying do any good or not?"

Yes. Have you ever noticed that when you talk to yourself you are able to work things out a little better? You can say you figured out on your own, or you can say that you talked to God; either way you are correct.

When you have a complex question and you try to work it out for yourself, it can be hard. If you take the problem to a few other people, the problem is generally much easier and quicker to solve. Some people do not think that is the work of God, but it is. The more minds you put together the more parts of God you put together.

I am not saying do not pray, because it does do something very important; it makes you feel as if you have done everything that you could possibly do to help. And, sometimes, in that prayer you now hear the request out loud and anything else that can possibly be done you now become aware of. Sometimes, *that* is when the answer comes to you. "Oh, God answered my prayer." To pray is good because then you actually face the real question of what you want. That is the first step.

If you want God to help you with yourself, like with a problem you have or something you want to change about yourself, then prayer can be very helpful. Each time you pray, you reinforce the recognition of the problem. Like I have said before, we do not live life day to day but moment to moment. Each time you pray, you reinforce the goal and allow the moment to assist in obtaining that goal.

Here is an example: if someone wants to quit smoking and they pray for help, the first thing they have done is stated the problem and recognized a goal they wish to obtain. Then, as they are trying to quit, they will have "powerful urges" to backslide and smoke. Each time they pray, they reconfirm their desire to obtain the goal and it gives them a moment for the urge to pass. It reinforces their drive to succeed. The more they pray, the more powerful and in control they become because they continually reinforce their desire. This works the same way with every other thing a person wants for themselves. Now, did God really help them? Yes. Because they are God and they were, in essence, asking themselves for help on a moment to moment basis, and it worked. Again, this is not to say that God does not exist; it is to confirm the true nature of God. God does exist in you!

It comes down to the question: what do you think is really going to happen when you pray? Do you think some magic is going to happen or a miracle? Do you really think there is an entity that is going to change the course of events just on your request? To understand the true nature of God is to understand prayer. You have heard the phrase, "God helps them who help themselves." To understand that you are part of God, is to truly understand the power of prayer and how to use it.

Desha was quite obviously offended by what Jos had to say. She said, "I do not only pray for help, and I do not only pray for good things. I pray mostly to show my devotion to Allah. Allah be praised. That is why I pray."

I do not wish to offend you. Allah must be praised. I agree to that. But Allah knows what is in your heart. Muhammad would agree to that. Muhammad stated that. Allah knows what is in your heart. Do you agree with that?

What good does it do for people to stand and praise Allah, as if Allah does not know what is in their heart? I say to you now, if you want to praise Allah do not waste time saying it; do it. Every time you help another human being you praise Allah. Every time you learn something new you praise Allah. Every time you praise another living thing you praise Allah.

I would never say not to pray to Allah for Lajita. I say help Lajita, and by helping her, you praise Allah much better than praying. I do not understand why people cannot see the connection. Actions are much more powerful form of praise than words. Allah needs people to act to help other people. That is how Allah answers prayers.

You wish to praise Allah? Assist all other people to make a better life for them and their families. How much more praise do you think Allah wants? Look into your heart; what do you feel?

The only ones that see devotion and praise to Allah when you are praying are those people that are there to see you pray. Only other people need to see you pray to believe your devotion, because they can only see your body. Allah does not need to see you pray, Allah sees your heart.

Desha stood there looking at Jos. You could see in her eyes the understanding coming over her, but you could also see the turmoil that she was going through. She had a lifetime of teachings and beliefs that were now being modified, and she clearly didn't know what to think about it. Desha was very devout and circumstances in her past had guided her feelings. She heard the kindness in the voice of Jos. She knew the wisdom of Jos. Yet, all of this seemed somehow contradictory to what she knew and confusing because she didn't know why it felt that way.

Desha at one moment looked as if she wanted to slap Jos and walk away, and at the same moment she looked as if she wanted to hug him. Her face then suddenly seemed to just go blank. This was something she was going to have to think about in order to understand how she really felt about it. She gave Jos a cursory nod and turned to leave.

Jos' head tilted to a side as he watched her walk away. He knew that he had given her a lot to think about, and you could tell he felt her anguish. As he continued to watch her, I looked around the room. All of the activity that had been going on before this discussion had come to a stop. Jos just kept his eyes on Desha.

As Desha disappeared out of the door, Jos brought his attention back into the room. He now noticed the multitude of silent stares. In an instant, he realized that Desha was not the only one caught in a quandary. Praying was something that humans had been doing since before recorded history. In fact, for all anyone knew some of the cave drawings found from thousands of years before recorded history may have been ways of appeasing the Gods. It is certain that praying has been going on since before anything was ever recorded. Now, suddenly, here comes a man to question the validity and value of prayer in the traditional sense. Was he insane or just mentally inept? People here, and everyone that had heard Jos, happen to think that he was somewhat gifted with an unknown wisdom.

He peered around at all those in the room. He then walked over to a high stool and sat down with everyone watching his every step.

With that, Jos stopped. He looked around at the division in the room. All the sudden uncertain questions clashing with the stern certainty of belief. He just instinctively knew that this was a time for rest. He bade everyone to take some time for self-reflection. Encouraged them to go back to teaching and learning what they were doing. This was a time for understanding. He strongly suggested contemplation before reaction.

I had heard Jos speak often of well-meaning people, even well-educated people, just naturally having a closed mind because of years, even a lifetime, of training and rigorous compliance. I have heard him say often ...

120

Open the Possibilities

The one thing that is very common with humans is that they come to a point when they learn some basic beliefs and they stop. They no longer continue to investigate other possibilities. They tend to learn these beliefs very early in life, when they are still very young children. Some will continue to look at other possibilities further in life. But, generally, by the time of late adolescence or early adulthood, most people have a belief and stop looking at other possibilities.

It is always best to continue learning, continue investigating and always with an open mind; and then just using some pretty common sense when coming to a conclusion. You *cannot* learn if you already *know.*

I thought about that and what he had said before. He was just trying to get people to open their minds and allow new possibilities. I liked that a lot. Because it has been shown all through history that one person thinks about something, then another person hears about it with an open mind and they think about it some more, then years down the line someone proves the thoughts through experimentation and that is how things are learned. That is how the human species evolves and advances. I liked that a lot.

When everyone was back to doing what they were doing, I saw Toro, the leader of the local street gang that Jos talked to before, walk into the building with four of his associates, shall we say, and cruise straight up to Jos. He gave Jos some greeting signs with a nod or two and then low under his breath he started talking to Jos. Toro was talking while mostly looking at the ground with an occasional glance up into the face of Jos. Jos, on the other hand, was steady looking at Toro as he spoke. After a long converse Toro looked right at Jos. Almost immediately Jos vigorously shook his head no. Then he started conferring back with Toro. You could see all of the guys that had walked in with Toro tense up and get into a battle stance like a cobra puffing out its head. Toro made his eyes look as mean and evil as he could. Which I have to admit was pretty effective. All of this was obviously to intimidate Jos into compliance. I had been with Jos quite a few months now and, to be honest, I didn't think this tactic was going to work on him. Jos just didn't seem to be intimidated. In a soft, imperceptible tone, Jos just talked to Toro.

For some reason, I just happened to glance around the room and noticed a few of the others on the floor were clandestinely watching the exchange. While I was turning around, I caught the glimmer of Lorne standing at the top of the stairs. Now, if you want to talk about something that looked intimidating, he was it. I don't think he was even trying to do that. He was actually unnoticeable because he was so big, he looked like part of the building itself.

I don't think that Toro or any of his crew noticed any of the others, especially not Lorne. They were too concentrated on Jos. But as they conversed I could see all of their expressions changing from intimidation to more pleading. First, they were going to force a result and now, they were just wanting the result. Jos had a way of saying no. I do not know what was said or what was being discussed, but I do know that if it was a request for help, in any way, Jos would be quick to accommodate; unless, of course, that request was going to result in some kind of harm. I had a sneaking suspicion that was just what was going on.

Shortly, Toro threw up his arms and hands in an expression of defeat. I heard him say, "Think about it. You could make some easy money." He turned with his arms still up, dropped them then walked out. The rest of his crew turned and followed him with a certain rhythm to their steps indicating they were tough and not to be messed with. They were just about to the door when Jos yelled after them to hold up. He walked over to Toro, said a few things, then they broke up with Toro going about his way.

When I inquired about the exchange, just in passing a little later on, Jos tried to explain that Toro seemed to have a business proposition for him. He looked at me using a line from a movie, "An offer I could not refuse." With a smile but not looking at me he continued, "I refused." Then he moved away, on about his business. I wasn't so sure that this would be the end of it. Toro didn't seem like the type to just let things go.

This was not the first time Jos had to deal with the unsavory type of society. There are people of all kinds in this world and I do mean every kind you can imagine and some you cannot. Like Jos had said, there are always two sides and something in the middle. When it comes to crime and criminals, the two sides can be very extreme and most crimes were in the middle, crimes of opportunity. This is where you get people taking advantage of a situation, or people that are in a situation. For some people, the opportunity is accidental and just too tempting, and for others they tend to create the opportunity. I think Toro was more like the latter. Jos seemed to know how to reach people and understood opportunistic crime. He had told me once …

Crime

Many examples exist of good people presented with an opportunity that they "just could not pass up." After World War Two, many good people stole property that was available because no one could or would stop them. During a riot when stores are broken into by opportunistic criminals and left open without anyone watching many "good" people will break down and just "take a little," knowing they will not be caught. And I am not talking about just "minor" crimes like property theft where "no one was really hurt." Even though whoever owned the store did get hurt. I am talking about serious crimes.

After World War Two, millions, and I am not exaggerating, millions, some estimates are about four million German women were raped by the Russian army. Many of the men were exacting revenge against the Germans for what was done during the war, many were encouraged to rape for that very reason, others did it because they could, knowing that they would never have to answer for it. I can understand the desire for revenge. I do not agree with it but I can understand it. But raping the women?

The wrongdoing that I am trying to emphasize here is when ordinarily "good" people are presented with an opportunity that they feel they just cannot pass up. It takes humans with an unusually strong moral character to resist the temptation presented to them, even for the most minor of situations.

The point is you know what is right and what is wrong. Regardless of the potential circumstances, whether or not you can or will be caught, you know what is right and what is wrong. In some cases, the only benefit to doing the right thing is the satisfaction you get for your own conscience. And all that depends on your own character and your own conscience. I am here to tell you that whenever someone does something wrong, there is always at least one person that is aware of it.

Reese was there and now looking down at his hands. "I know what you are saying. And I know what you are saying is true." He looked up at Jos. "But with some crimes what if the person really needs it? I mean, what if the person is poor and hungry?"

Jos nodded, knowing what Reese was talking about.

You know the truth; within you, you know the truth.

When talking about crimes, it is easy to get caught up in legalities and severities. People like to argue that some things are not really illegal; the things they are talking about may be *morally* wrong, but they are not illegal. There are many things that are morally wrong, and anyone would recognize it, but they are not specifically illegal in certain countries so people do it.

All wrongs are wrongs for the very reason that they do harm to someone else. It may not be immediate, it may not be severe, and it may not ever actually be seen, but wrongs do harm to someone else that is why they are wrongs.

In most cases, if it is harmful physically, psychologically, or financially to another, it is a wrong. If you were to consider it to be a wrong done to you, then it is a wrong to do to another.

Now, as far as Toro goes, he was just looking for opportunities. He sees great opportunity here as a result of many people coming and going. But then any businessman would see the same thing. Anytime you have many people coming to one place it is tempting to take advantage of the situation.

Toro also considers this area his "turf" or his area to control. We came to an understanding that I think is agreeable to both of us. All "gangs" need to do business with other "gangs." No entity lives completely in a vacuum. Everything will need something else's assistance at some time. It is a very good practice not to burn bridges, especially if you have not even crossed the particular bridge. I merely expressed that we had not really even done any business together and that we should both want to stay on good terms with each other.

Billy looked at Jos skeptically. "Are we going to do business with him at some point?" Jos replied succinctly with a no. After a pause, however, he did add that you just never know what the future holds, so, all doors are open. With that, Jos gave Billy a reassuring wink.

In the time that I was with Jos, he had much to say about rules and laws, crime and punishment. He often talked about how much of the old religious scriptures had to do with rules and laws and what was considered a crime and what punishment should be employed for specific infractions.

As he would say: the basic rules and laws of a society, namely not to harm others, is still very current.

That was the major point that Jos was trying to make. As humans have evolved, so have the rules and justifiably so. In days of long ago, when the whole society was just a single tribe and someone committed a grievous act, there were no prisons to punish them. Punishments were dictated, generally, by the chieftain of the tribe, and it was left up to them to be just and prudent and effective. As society evolved and advanced, many new conditions arose to be considered. When tribes grew into villages then into societies and cities and more and more humans lived in closer and closer proximity, other rules and laws had to be established. Now, in today's society, with even a much greater involvement with other societies that are not even in close proximity to the other, new rules and laws need to be established even further.

These are some of the things he would talk about over the time I knew him.

God's Laws

The real "laws" of God are written in the genetic coding of living things, in physics and in the natural world. These are God's true laws. God's laws are non-negotiable; period. Those laws cannot be negotiated, cannot be manipulated, cannot be modified, and are unbreakable.

The laws of "God," *written* by man, *can be* negotiated and manipulated and modified to fit the lives of men. Those laws can be broken. Like: thou shalt not kill.

The laws of man should be modified with time, however. It is the natural progression and evolution of civility and society. Slavery should not be allowed by any society in modern times. Human trafficking should be an atrocity anywhere in the world today. Stoning to death an adulterer is beyond modern civil conduct in any society. Dismemberment of any person for criminal punishment is archaic and is an abomination to any entity considered to be a "merciful God."

You should not murder. You should not commit adultery. You should not steal. You should not covet anything that is your neighbor's. You should not lie.

These are basic laws that protect people from other people; they really do not need to be spelled out, because every person recognizes the obviousness of these laws and why. It is a testament to what humans will try to get away with on other humans. No person wants any of these laws perpetrated against them so why they have to be told not to perpetrate them against other people is fascinating to me.

Trust

Sometimes people will just take a little from someone; not much, just a little. It really does not harm the other person. What it does harm is the other person's "trust" in other people. That is what is happening today.

They violate trust. No amount of trust is trivial. Everyone will suffer for the deception. That is the reason that in the world of today when an automobile of a person breaks down on the side of the road, no one will stop to help. It is because of the severe lack of trust of other people. When they do stop the person that needs help becomes suspicious and is "on guard." Violation of trust is the most grievous of wrongs.

Jos looked directly at me remembering the first time he saw me. I was on the side of the road and when they pulled over to help, he was right, my apprehension increased.

It may just be a small sum but trust has no price tag, and its value is immeasurable. Once trust is violated that damage can never be undone. One of the problems with governments today is that people have lost trust in them. So, even when the government is trying to do something good and protect the people, like give vaccinations, they are not trusted and people refuse to be vaccinated. Thus, putting more people at risk.

The one principle that Jos kept instilling on us was every living experience is valuable to God. If an individual jeopardizes another, that individual needs to be stopped and contained or encapsulated. To kill, or even to want to kill for punishment, is the same as the killer.

The best punishment for killing of another person is complete isolation from society so that the disease is removed from any possibility of ever offending again. The perpetrator of murder should remain enclosed in a cell for the remainder of their human existence. No communication with any other person, except legal or medical. Why not? The victim can no longer communicate with anyone they love.

God can still obtain the living experience of the perpetrator, but without risk to others.

These are the things that Jos tried to get across to us about rules, laws, crimes, and punishments. These are just some of the things that he would talk about. As he said many times, these subjects are very vast and wide ranging. They come in such varying degrees and extremes that it is really impossible to create realistic and just laws for every person. Just like a utopian society, in order for every law and punishment to be right for every person then every person would have to be very closely the same in every way.

Each individual body is a world onto itself; allow that world to follow its own path. If one is going to collide with you, which is easier? Making the other move away or merely stepping out of the way yourself?

Over the course of time, Jos kept promoting a common theme to people and their actions. With many other ways of saying it, one time

I remember him specifically saying ...

Once an action is taken, it becomes part of the past and the past cannot be changed. That is a law of God and is therefore non-negotiable.

The past cannot be changed. Looking back, not only can the past not be changed it is also incredibly brief. It just occurred to me how fast time was moving. It doesn't seem that long since I left my friends and family to venture out. I kept in touch often with phone calls but my life was here now.

One evening over a year after the gang had taken over the restaurant, Jack offered a deal to Jos. He was the last customer of the evening. He had really planned it that way so he could talk to Jos after closing. We found out later it was an offer to buy out Jack and take complete ownership of the restaurant.

The thing that Jack had to say to Jos and the gang was that he had been watching us for a long time now very closely and with great interest. Watching, as he put it, from the outside. He noticed that even though Jos was not the designated head of operation, inside the restaurant he easily appreciated his influence on everyone. He knew that Adam had been given directional leadership of the business. He also knew that Curtis and Reese had really been given the duties of bookkeeper, in charge of daily financial, supply requisition, expense tracking, and legal and safety concerns. That Curtis and Reese had been working in tandem to keep all the little loose ends tied. He had seen Jos step farther and farther back into the dark wings and let the gang take full, harmonious control of the whole operation without him. It was a thing of beauty, he clearly acknowledged. But he was curious as to why Jos had done it that way. At the initial conversation with Jos, Jack was under the impression that Jos was going to be the head person. But right from the very beginning, Jos turned control of the restaurant over to the gang. Now, Jack was not upset with that decision, especially with the eventual outcome. He was just curious as to why Jos did not insist, because it was his idea in the first place, that he have more control of its direction; at least at the start. Jos explained that he was just planting a seed. All his job was to ever be was just to plant a seed and let it grow. Jos asked ...

Have you ever heard the story of the mustard seed that Jesus spoke of? Well, anyway, that is all I was doing was planting, a little mustard seed and wanted to see if it was going to grow. When I look at something, I try to look at as many different things as I can so I can make the best choices and the best decision. I do not just look at what I want to see; I look at everything. There is always a good side and a bad side to everything. The best is a balance somewhere in the middle. I look very openly and honestly at many sides. I hope for the best and prepare for the worse.

Over the next two weeks, Jos had much to say about the way humans work, how humans will progress, and how the gang would have to proceed with obtaining and maintaining the restaurant. For some reason, to him, it all seemed to merge into a common subject but to everyone else it seemed to be disjointed with completely different meanings. But, as Jos would remind us over and over, everything affects everything. In some mostly unseen and convoluted way, everything is connected.

First, he went on to talk about memories and their importance to the human experience and how it would affect any afterlife there may be. The significance at the time was sort of lost on me, but later it made sense with future discussions. In fact, it was necessary to have heard the dialogue in order to systematically associate and put things together. I remember thinking at one time that it was no wonder why most people did not think of the things Jos did naturally; because their mind would be forever running in all kinds of different directions at once. For Jos, that seemed to just be the ordinary way of his thought process where, conversely, with other people it would have been the very definition of insanity.

On the subject of memory, though, I remember him talking to Sochin and commenting on something Sochin had talked to him about earlier ...

Memory

The difference between awareness and consciousness is memory. Awareness is the ability to perceive the environment around you and react to it; as with a plant. Consciousness is awareness and memory of that awareness for some period of time and to be able to use that memory in an ever-expanding knowledge base.

Now, some people lose long-term memory, and some people, through some disease process or anomaly, cannot retain most short-term memory; meaning they cannot remember what they did just a second ago. But both of these types of people still have a consciousness about them that is more than just awareness. It is because of some type of memory or some type of recall. It is what allows them to have emotions; if no other emotion but anger over knowing what they have lost. And just knowing *that* is a type of memory.

They may not remember who the person in front of them is, but they know that there is a person in front of them. They know a car, they may not know their car, but they know a car is a car.

You do not need to know the mechanism of how memory is stored; that is not important. You just have to know that memory is important. It is the seizing of the present. It is what gives the living experience reason. It is why there are living things; to create memories.

For some reason, it was important for Jos to talk about memory and the experience of memories around this time before going on to discuss other things. It was a long time for me to completely understand why getting us all to start thinking about memories and their creation was necessary. Memories were the key to consciousness and the basis of understanding. It was imperative to start to think of the concept and all of the associations that apply to memory. Memory, the creation of memories and the storage of memories were far more important than I had ever considered. It was central to understanding so many aspects of life, in all of its forms. Like I said, I had never considered the concept of memory and its core of importance. But now I do.

One of the things that he associated strongly with memory was the cycles of life. Once when we were at the Church of Understanding there were three women there, three generations, a girl, her mother, and grandmother all at the stove in the corner talking, Jos said to me ...

Cycles of Life

Life is nothing more than just a series of events that one remembers; the rest of the time is just basic living and survival. Your life is marked by "special events." In most cases, certain dates stand out and mark time, like your first memory. You will find that your first memory will actually change from day to day throughout your life. But memories like a birthday party, your first day of school, your first kiss, your graduation, your marriage, your first sexual encounter, every child's birth, a traumatic event, a moment in history shared by many, an extraordinarily pleasurable event, a vacation, the death of a loved one, and etcetera, you get the point. Everything else in life is generally mundane and just comes and goes as a regular or routine day. Much of our lives are spent just surviving with working and eating and sleeping and routine forms of entertainment in between.

Even though most of the mundane is never consciously remembered, it is all stored somewhere. You may have to think about it longer but it is there.

For most animals, however, it is just an *endless series of eating until they are eaten.*

Cycles of life are important to understand. Today that human is just a baby, soon it will be a toddler, soon it will be in school or working, then it will be having children, then it will be grown and watching all the other children go through many of the same things and remembering when it was the baby. All too soon you will be at the end of your life cycle wondering where the time went; and now you cannot get any of it back. That is again why I say that the present is the most important thing in the universe.

You can look at life kind of like a year going past. First you are in the spring of your life, where everything is new and exciting and exhilarating and fun and playful.

Then you move into the summer of your life where some things have grown and matured and are now ready to be used. The body is still relatively new and energetic. Most experiences are new and are now at a time in your life when they are allowed to be experienced.

Then you inevitably move into the autumn of your life. Many things are still as vibrant and as strong, fun and exciting as ever. Some things are even more so than before. You are just now starting to feel the cool breeze of winter coming, but that only sparks the desire to get in those last few days of fun. Most experiences do not carry the same fresh exhilaration as they did in the spring, which for some can be a little disconcerting, but it does not stop them from diving in and attempting to recapture that zing.

Now you enter the winter of your life. By this point in your life, time is no mystery to you. You are very familiar with time and its brevity. You are very aware of the speed that time presents itself. This is generally the point at which you fully mature and come to terms with all the seasons of your life and the entirety of your existence. This is the point of full reflection; in fact, most of your remaining days are filled with reflection and memories. The sum total of your life exists entirely in memories.

As the year turns anew you will become but a memory of the past yourself. But it is within that memory that you exist forever. The winter is not the end; the winter is a time for rejuvenation and a time for preparation for a new and glorious year. The winter of your life is the season to heap the last harvest of the year: your memory.

As Jos finished saying this, a pleasant and soft smile came across his face. It was a gentle smile, like you see in someone amiably drifting off to sleep. It wasn't harsh or sad in any way. It was like he knew that this was how something ended in order to plant a new seed to continue the growth cycle and keep life going. He did not show any signs of a depressing demise but only of a glorious transformation to a whole and absolute unity. It was mysteriously comforting. His eyes were moist with emotion. He knew something he was not sharing just now; I could feel it. But his face was that of a reassuring mother, and you just felt everything was going to be okay.

A few days had passed and everyone had a chance to talk to the others about acquiring the restaurant, full and total. Everyone, as Jos had suspected, decided to join in the adventure. They all knew that it was going to be difficult at times, definitely challenging most of the time, and they feared personally trying. I think that was the biggest concern. They were afraid of straining personal relationships they had attained over the past year. They had come to cherish that camaraderie more than money. They did not want friendship to clash with business because they did not want to see either one harmed.

Sochin, Mariam, and Connie were the most vocal about how the gang had become a family. They didn't want wealth to come between them like it had to so many of their friends and to actual family members of their own.

They knew they had a very real potential to become wealthy, especially if the business continued to gain momentum as it had in the past. It would be a great investment or even a purchase for some enterprising business people. They knew that the restaurant had the potential of being sold for a significant profit; then what? They were concerned how the sudden wealth would affect everyone.

Jos had spoken often about how money changes people. People become quite different sometimes when money, especially large amounts, gets involved. He used to say that when large amounts of wealth become involved, people become absolutely stupid about what is really important.

I was actually quite pleased to see that most of what Jos talked about was being absorbed. The comments and conversations that everyone was having had a strong tone of what Jos had been teaching. The face on Jos as he listened to their concerns also showed his obvious pleasure as well. They kept talking about wealth and how wealth distorts people. It doesn't necessarily make them bad, it just makes them different; it distorts the person that was there before. They did not want to have the need for money to survive, either. I mean, they did not want to have to scratch out a living or beg for help, like others they have known; but they all were perfectly content not being wealthy. To some people that is their measure of success. But the gang, having been with Jos this long, knew what they thought was *important; that was more the wealth of relationships than money. Jos spoke on this often ...*

Wealth

When discussing wealth, it is yet another term that must be defined. Wealth means different things to different people. When you are talking about great wealth, you can be talking about an abundance of money, land, fame, health, or love and friendship. There are those with large amounts of money and poor health. You also have those that really have no money to speak of but great health and lots of real friends. Both sides are considered to be quite wealthy in their respective aspects.

The Religion of Money

I have said before that *religion* is a strong belief in something that cannot be proved. I have also said that the most common religion on this planet is money. It is the one thing that almost every person *believes* in. You cannot prove the value of money. It is just a strong belief system. In a deep depression, money becomes all but useless. Who determines the value of money and how do they come up with that determination?

I once heard it said: "Only when the last tree has died and the last river has been poisoned and the last fish has been caught, will we realize that we cannot eat money."

Economoic Redistribution

People have the means to redistribute the economic power of the world, but you have to do it yourself and do it together. Open and available ownership opportunity for all people will assist in distribution of wealth. But I warn you now that you are very small and you are attempting to fight the very big. There is a lot of power to fight against, and they have been empowered by the masses, the many middle-income investors.

The reason that large amounts of finances are controlled by so few people is because just a few people *control* all the finances. They have control of the actual money. If a business is owned by investors, then they get the lion's share. The working employees typically receive their earnings by time; in other words, hourly pay. In any event, regardless how well the business does, the employees get a set amount for what they do. If the business does really good, the owners and investors make good money; the employee makes the same amount.

When employees own the business, they are in it to make a product that they believe in or a service that they believe in. They do not necessarily have to make a lot of money; they just need enough to live on. The product or service is more important to them than a windfall of money.

The only road to global economic redistribution is with a vastly greater number of people coming together to form completely employee-owned businesses and companies. Only when more individuals come together to form their own "gangs" for creating restaurants, bakeries, clothing stores, construction companies, manufacturing companies, hotels, resorts, transportation companies, energy providers, electronic companies, information technologies, all businesses, the list is endless, will you start to see true economic equality.

I tell you this: when more people own their own businesses, the people, and the area they live and work in, will improve and prosper. When people start to take a real interest in what is going on right outside their doors their interest and their involvement will increase.

What you end up seeing also is that the products and services that these companies provide are better. When everyone owns the company, there is personal pride that is associated with the product or service. There is generally much more unity in the process and it is more efficient and there is less expense involved. There is much more attention to details and to profitability because that directly affects each individual employee.

Big companies compete with cheaper prices against smaller employee-owned businesses because they employ labor at a standard hourly rate for their products and services. Their employees do not share in the fruits of their labor. Their employees do not get their true value. The rich get richer and the poor stay poor.

It is time to start the move away from people owning other people and move into the era when people own themselves. They work together and make companies together and share the wealth of companies, together.

Just as the restaurant has done well, so has the bakery and Desha's textile store. It is all because the people in the business own the business. That is what I wanted to show you all. That even just a few can band together and create a business that will prosper, but only if everyone in the business has an ownership part in the business.

Here Jos suddenly became silent. He looked around at everyone there with deep concern. You could tell that something had just crossed his mind and filled it with trepidation. He slowly began to relay a warning ...

Moneygrubbers

Beware of the moneygrubbers and do not become enticed to become one.

The blemish of humanity is what is known as a "moneygrubber." All they want is money, they do not care about anything or anyone else; just money. Right or wrong is of no interest to them in the least. If they can cheat someone for just a few extra shillings, they will because all they care about is money.

Moneygrubbers are *bad* in every sense of the word. They are the blight of society. The only intolerance that should survive today is to the moneygrubber.

A moneygrubber is someone that values money more than living things, at any and every cost. In their minds, one cent is worth grabbing regardless how many people you have to crawl over or harm in the process. All that is important is money, not the living things in between. That is a moneygrubber.

Having a lot of money does not make anyone a bad or evil person. Having money does not make a person a moneygrubber. Money in and of itself is not evil or bad; it is how it is obtained and how it is used that becomes good or bad. If a person provides a valuable service that benefits others, they should be paid accordingly and fairly. If a person works hard, and for a long time, and is very good at what they do, then they should be compensated fairly and should take pride in their accomplishments.

If someone charges more than what is fair or appropriate just because *they can*, they are a moneygrubber.

To do any business, whether it is making a product or providing a service, and paying or receiving a just and appropriate compensation for it, should be a sense of pride. That is how business should be conducted everywhere all the time.

All of that was easily understood by the gang. With nods to one another and the occasional gentle hand on the shoulder just reaffirmed their own wealth; their friendship.

The gang was all in with the purchase, or I should say the acquisition, of the restaurant. We all sat down with Jack and eventually agreed on a fair purchase price for the business. It was, of course, more than any of us could obtain at this time. Instead, however, of going and getting a loan, putting us in debt with an outside agency, or acquiring an investor, Jack agreed to a deal where he would "front the loan." That way he was not an investor, therefore retaining any ownership interest in the business. He would just become a debt that had to be paid, which was better for him because if anything went wrong, he would have to be paid first before anything left was divided among the owners. In essence, he sold us the business and just carried the note with interest, of course, which he was very generous about.

Even though, now, being owners of the business there was a feeling of more stress and responsibility on all of us. We actually became even more proficient at business. The bakery was absolutely soaring and Desha's little adventure with the Cover Your Heart Designs store was adding to all the success. Lorne at the Church of Understanding now had a couple of other men there helping him to keep the place up, clean and safe. Bufasa and Renn were their names and they received the same compensation that Lorne did. Even Toro and his assorted members were not posing any problem at this time. In fact, many of his crew were now becoming regulars at the church, learning new and different skills. That is, when they were not out doing their "normal" business.

RELATIONSHIP

As some time passed, Natashia and Billy let it be known that they were "with" each other, that they were a couple. Everyone else had known this for many months, but now they were being much more forward about it. It wasn't that long after the official acquisition of the restaurant that they let everyone know that they were serious about their relationship and that it was heading for marriage.

Both Natashia and Billy had been married before, so they had some obvious concerns. That was one of the reasons that it had taken so long for them to go public about their feelings. They had held back letting anyone know that they were interested in each other, although their affections were probably obvious to us even before them.

I was around often when Natashia and Billy would separately converse with Jos, who was a good person to bring concerns to. He would listen and was very wise. Like I said, Jos just seemed to have "been there" before when you would talk to him about things.

They had a whole host of questions, from whether marriage was a smart thing to do to what they should do about the business to how they should raise children, all the way to extremely personal questions.

No matter how serious or how silly anyone else might think about their various questions, Jos always accepted them unflinchingly. He never seemed like any question posed by anyone was trivial. In fact, I think it pleased him greatly that people were inquisitive to that extent.

I was close enough to hear what Jos said to Billy; completely seriously but with a slight, one-sided grin ...

The Female Is the Superior of the Species

First, Billy, you have to understand that the female is the superior of the species; any species. There are always a few exceptions to the rules but in this case very few.

Yes, the male of the species is generally physically stronger on average. The male of the species is generally the one in "control" or so they think. They are most definitely the more aggressive and explosive of the two. Hence, men and war go together like women and home. Completely in general terms, obviously. There are always exceptions to all rules.

However, just how dominantly is the male of the species influenced by the female? "Behind every great man there is an equally great woman." Have you ever heard that phrase? In the avian world, it is the male that has all the vibrant, vivid coloring to attract the female. It is the male that does a little dance to impress and attract the female; the females just take their pick. In some cultures, the power women have over men is so perceived that they have laws that women must be covered for modesty. So as to not unintentionally entice a man.

In elephants and other species like horses, the female is the matriarch or leader of the group. The males are just the studs. With lions, it is the female that acquires most of the food. Ants and bees along with some other species are ruled by the Queen. And, if you want to talk about which sex is more vicious, the black widow eats her mate after copulation, and even more vicious is the praying mantis that actually starts eating the male *during* copulation. The examples just keep going. So, remember how deceiving life can be. The kindest, the gentlest, and most nurturing of the species also can be the most deceiving and vicious of the species as well. Just another yin and yang.

Historical references on this point go on endlessly. Just look at England and its monarchy; which sex has been the most productive, the most impactful and, quite frankly, which sex has lasted the longest on the throne?

I remember, though, the first time I heard what Jos had to say about marriage, it was a little shocking actually. I was not alone in my feelings either. Many people that heard what Jos had to say about marriage were somewhat stunned until they started to think about it.

Marriage

Even though it was a religious ritual, it is really more of a legal ritual in practice; showing all others that these two people are now bound together by the law. God has an interest in the fact that if you pledge yourself to another and then commit adultery, you will cause the other person grievous psychological harm. You do not need to be married, in the eyes of God, to cause extreme pain to another because of a love interest.

Marriage is a human ritual, not a ritual of God. If two people are in love with one another, it is felt by God and to the extent that it is felt by both the humans involved. If two people are deeply in love and stay faithful and true to each other to the end then God is pleased; whether or not they get married is not of any concern. Why would it be?

People care about what is on parchment. God cares about what is in your heart. Render onto humans that which is human and render onto God that which is God.

Many people want to argue that marriage should be between one man and one woman. What does God care? What God knows is the love between two hearts; the love between two people. It is the laws of man that dictate the rules of who can love who and how much. Laws of humans may dictate who can marry whom; God has no such law.

The true law of God is that two people of the same sex cannot have sex together and produce an offspring; that is the law of God and it is non-negotiable. God, however, has no law against two people of the same sex loving one another.

What is more important is the vow you give to another and maintaining that vow *even without the other knowing it*.

This is what I say to you. When you get married, promise to love and cherish one another in a vow, but that is already a given. It is *more important* for you to vow, and to promise *in your heart*, not to ever *harm* one another, in any way ... ever.

Other than asking about marriage, Billy and Natashia had questions about other aspects of family life. One of their concerns was about having children. They thought because of their age, that if they were going to have a family, they would probably want children soon; or at least start trying soon. When those two would talk to Jos about children, I was surprised with the unusual and clear glow on his face. Jos showed genuine enthusiasm for them and for the prospect of them having children. The reason for my surprise was his talks about human overpopulation.

Many times, Jos spoke of his distress on human population growth and how it was the base of so many global concerns. Almost all trepidations of the future for the species and the planet stem from the mass expansion of the human population; but it is a topic that no person seems to want to address. Everything from exhaustion of natural resources, pollution, famine, pestilence, violence, and extinction of other species can be directly related to the exponential growth of the human population.

Presently, science and manufacturing has been able to keep up with the growth, but humans are increasing surprisingly fast. This was an obvious and profound concern of Jos. But how do you tell humans to stop having babies. Even if you told them, do you think it would happen? That is what any living species is designed to do; procreate. Jos said many times ...

Over Population and the Unwanted Pregnancy

Overpopulation of the human species is a very real fact. Almost everyone understands that. When you consider the cost, not only financial but personal and emotional of unwanted births on other human beings, especially the babies themselves, you can understand the need for some control. It is so touchy as a subject that no one is willing to bring it up, let alone offer a solution. How do you tell someone *not* to have babies?

The problem is not too many people wanting babies. The problem comes from too many unwanted or unplanned babies, as well as people living longer due to advances in technology. As far as advanced technologies, humans are at a state in medicine that they survive a lot longer, and that they are able to save babies far earlier in premature births than they have ever been able to do in the past. When in the past, many children did not survive past five years old now most not only survive past five years but go on to make it well into child-bearing years themselves.

Centuries ago it was necessary for people to have several children so a few would have the chance to reproduce themselves. Now in this day and age, most pregnancies are fruitful and most of the children survive to reproductive years. Even those that die in young adulthood tend to reproduce before their demise.

Only a hundred years ago, the global population was about one and a half billion humans; today, just a hundred years later, the human global population is reaching seven billion.

So, how does someone start to broach the subject of population control? One way is to understand that elective *sterilization* is virtually impossible today. When a tube is tied, it does not render the man or woman truly sterile.

Procedures in this time are so well perfected that as long as you have an ovary and a testicle and a uterus you can have a baby. Procedures have also been so perfected that if two people wished, they can probably have the original tube tying procedure reversed and conceive "naturally." The point is, if the tubes are tied then you have to have a conscious attempt to conceive. You have to *want* to have a baby, it is not going to happen "accidentally."

It would behoove any government to offer, without cost to the individual, the *elective* procedure of a tubal ligation to any man or woman that *wanted* it free of charge and to offer a monetary sum to put away for when they *wanted* to have children. A monetary sum equal to the cost of the procedure to conceive. The monetary sum would be given to the individual to be used as desired.

That would be a much smarter way to have children; when two people are *ready*. That would truly be planning parenthood. This initial investment by the government would be well satisfied in the future if that government assists with untoward pregnancies already. It would be better for governments that do not already assist with unwanted births and allows its citizens to die due to starvation or disease in over populated areas.

It sounds like a dramatic and offensive offer; but it is not. Many people today are already being responsible about this, they are just not being recognized nor commended for it, especially not compensated for it. The simple fact is, if the human species does not get a hold of the growing population problem in some way then the whole of the species will suffer, as well as the planet as a living entity.

This is a solution that is available and workable today without violating the individual. They have to *want* it.

Jos paused for a moment. He was distressed about something he was thinking about.

Consider the child that was conceived by accident, brought into the world unwanted and made to live in poverty: is that a violation? And if that is a violation, to whom and how many are violated? And if you want to tackle the "problem" of abortion, it is not to do it in the middle of an unwanted pregnancy but *before* it even starts. People seem to always want to find the answer *after* the problem starts instead of doing the harder thing of thinking about it and stopping the problem *before* it happens.

Religions all have something to say about sex, when to have it and with whom. Can you think of any stronger control system than to have a say, or attempt to have a say, in an individual's sexual practices?

If humans were to practice real planning of having children and not letting it be just an accident, you would never have the question of abortion. When people go through the process of *wanting* a child, then abortion is never considered.

Abortion

Adam said, "You talk about everything we do being a choice. And you talk about the so-called sanctity of life." He looked at Jos studiously. Everyone that was able to hear the question quietly looked over at Jos too. I think many had been wondering how Jos felt for some time, but never broached the subject. "I mean, are you pro-choice or pro-life?"

Jos started to talk, with everyone fixed on his every word …

Abortion is a hot topic, is it not? For years, it was just a religious question. Now it has become a very political question. Pro-life versus pro-choice; these are the terms that people use when discussing this subject. I am not sure exactly how viewing life as important necessarily precludes someone from being able to make their own choices. If I, or anyone else for that matter, say I am for people to have the right to choose, that makes me a "pro-choice" person. If I consider life to be most important, that puts me in the "pro-life" gang. That is a little too black and white for this kind of subject. I am pro-life *and* pro-choice.

Here is the main question when considering abortion: when does a mass of cells become a life? When is a human body alive? When is it just a mass of chemicals, like a corpse or a fertilized egg, or when does it have the energy of the living spirit in it?

Almost everyone in the group had an opinion on this and voiced it spontaneously and simultaneously. Most of the opinions were at the time the sperm fertilizes the egg, the moment of conception.

For most religious people, life begins at the moment of conception. But I want you to think about that for a moment. That is also what non-religious, or the scientific, or atheists, believe. Only they do not believe that the body has a soul, or spirit, again, however you want to label it. They believe that the moment of conception the new life starts and continues on until it dies and then that is the end. It is just a biological process.

The energy that is the soul, or spirit, is around before the body, then it inhabits the body, and then again when the body dies the soul moves on. There are many times when a fetus will die naturally before it is born. Then, what happens to the soul? What happens to the soul of a person that is never born? You see where I am going here?

The human body is a machine. It is an organic organism that is created, lives, and dies and then the chemical components return to the earth's surplus of supplies. The moment of conception is the beginning of a new life but at that particular time it is nothing more than a mass of chemicals in a biological process. It is originally one cell, then it divides and continues to divide until it creates a body. Until that embryo is ready to function as a living body on its own it is nothing more than a mass of cell growth in the female body. It may survive and it may not; naturally.

Here is an example: If you are building a car and you have a frame and an engine, is it a car? No, because it cannot drive yet without wheels. If you build a car with doors and windows and tires and wheels but no engine, is it a car? No, because it cannot go without an engine. If you put a person in a car that has no engine, then it is worthless. Only when the car has an engine, transmission, electrical system, wheels and suspension is it ready to put a person in it to drive. It is the same for the soul and the body. Until the body is ready to "drive," there is no reason to put a soul in it. It is being manufactured and on the way to becoming a car, but until it is finished there is no reason to have a driver.

Listen, the point here is, if a woman has an abortion before the embryo has any viability to it, she is only ending the *possibility* of a living person. In that context, every egg that she has is the possibility of a living person. The energy, or spirit, of God is always around us. The energy of God is in everything and is eternal; it is here before the body that contains it and it is here after the body's demise. The human body, like all living things, is just a vessel for the energy to be able to experience living and manipulate this world. If that vessel is not ready to contain the energy it is just a mass of matter growing in another human body. The energy of the soul will find another vessel.

Abortion is a very important topic; it is hotly debated and extremely personal. It is one of the things that bring out very powerful emotions in almost everybody. The *one* person that will have to live with the decision long after everyone else has argued and gone home is the mother. The decision is beyond difficult for any woman and it is a decision and a choice that she will have to live with for eternity; not just a lifetime but for *all of eternity*. She, alone, has to exist with the responsibility of her decision.

The question astonishes me in this particular time and age. With what we know now about biology, why is it necessary for abortions at all for any reason other than to save the life of the mother? Is it so hard for people to face the question today about prevention? I am more concerned about being proactive than reactive. Let us put more intelligent thought into preventing the reasons for abortion than whether or not it is right or wrong.

I tell you this about the spirit; it is like the wind. You feel it when you are alive, you hear it all around you, and you smell the scent that it carries. You do not know where it came from or where it is going. Before the wind gets to you it is already blowing, and it continues blowing after it passes you as well.

When it did come to the question of children, I found that Jos was really quite passionate about it in a very positive way. Jos said that he thought children were the "light" of the world. He meant it in the context that children were the bright spot, the joy, the fresh new enthusiasm, and the exuberant energy of the beginning of the future. His delight at the new and young "possibilities" was now quite obvious but he did express concerns. How and why a child is conceived, and how it is raised and treated and cared for, is of concern.

When it came to caring for a child, Jos was very adamant in his thoughts. However, he was also the first one to point out the requirements to be in a gang. As he would say, you cannot sympathize and think you know what it is like to be a parent. Unless you have a real human child, you do not know what it is like to be a parent, period. It is easy to give advice when you have never been a parent yourself.

Parents Are the Key for Child Learning

There is no definitive book written to expertly train someone to be a good parent, but there ought to be. The fact is that it simply cannot be done. There are just too many variables. Many people have written books on child rearing, but none of them can guarantee good outcomes. All of this is because of one simple little fact; all people, and children are people, are different, unique, and completely individual. That is the wonder of life. It is also the terror of life; again, the yin and yang.

Everyone wants to be special. I tell you this: every person is special. There has never been in all the history past, and there never will be in all the future to come, another person with your particular point of view. The information that you obtain and provide is completely unique to you and you alone. You are indeed, one of a kind.

Jos had quietly confided in me that he had no trepidation with Natashia and Billy marrying. They were both very good and caring people and their future was very bright. Jos had remarked several times: "You do not have to be a prophet to prophesize the future; you only have to open your eyes." He knew with just their demonstrated intelligence and kind and caring nature that they would be a good couple. If given the chance, they'd make great parents. He could see the kind of people those two were, and it was easy for him to predict a good future if they remained the way they were. That took no prophet.

It reminded me of when people would talk about the prophets of the Bible and prophets in general. The first prophet, the last prophet, and what all the different prophets had to say at different times. Jos was very quick to remind people those prophets, regardless of whom they were and which religion they were part of, were just other human beings; they were just people. Like all humans, they were just another vessel for the energy of God to inhabit. Jos was swift to point out ...

Prophets

Any alert, aware, intelligent individual can prophesize that if something does not change the world, as we know it, the planet will change it. You do not need a prophet to teach you how to treat other living things.

You do not need a dictate from God to know that if humans do not change the way they are polluting the planet, the planet will change. If humans do not change overpopulation, the planet will change. If the economic chasm building between the rich and poor does not change, the whole structure will topple, and if poverty on the entire planet is not addressed, then pestilence will consume vast regions, especially in an era of rapid global transport.

Now, the conflict is with science and religion, or the acceptance of both. The rapid advancement in knowledge and understanding of science, alongside the slow release in long standing customs and longer held beliefs of religion, creates a compression of emotions.

GOD

He commented that he found it beguiling how a belief in a supreme being and a possible afterlife can be so prevalent, and yet be so different in concept between people.

I remember him saying once ...

The Concept of God

God is the living energy that makes up all things in the universe. This is an impossible concept for some people to comprehend. It is not for humans to know. The concept is too complex and too profound for humans to comprehend and accept completely.

It was late one Saturday night, after the restaurant was closed and all of the original gang was finished and sitting around unwinding. Light conversations were going on all around. Rohm was one of the very quiet, but more curious of the eleven. Most of the time, he would just quietly go on about his work, but he always seemed to have an expression of being deep in thought.

This night, Rohm walked up to Jos and sat down gently. "Jos," he asked, "you have talked a lot about God. Everything that you have said about God doesn't make it any easier to understand who you think God is. I am still very confused."

It was a point, when all the conversations that were going on were at a lull. Everyone heard the question and they turned their attention to Jos. Jos looked at Rohm for a long time, expressionless, just trying to decide how to proceed. Then he looked down, almost in a defeated resolve. Really mumbling, "How can I put this?" He looked up and spoke ...

This is what I will tell you. The reason I have not elaborated on God so far is, that it is really pushing against what is accepted and everything that has been taught before about God. That makes it very difficult to tell you about God. Most people feel they already know the concept of God. When most people speak of God, they talk in terms of *who* God is. God is not a who. God is more of a what.

Do you want to know *what* God is?

Everyone nodded. Jos looked around at all of them, realizing the enormity of the request.

One of the best ways to define what something is, would be to first determine what it is not. First and foremost, God is not human. God is God. Many people always give human attributes to all other things, other animals, machines, and even gods. This practice has been going on since, at least, the beginning of written history. It is a normal tendency for humans to give human attributes to other things in order to be able to relate better to them.

Dogs do not perceive the world as humans do. They do not have the capacity to do so, just as humans really do not have the capacity to perceive the world as sharks or bats do. Humans certainly do not have the capacity to perceive the world as God does.

As this tendency to humanize everything is so prevalent, and so necessary for comprehension, it is normal and expected for people to assign human attributes and consciousness to God. But any logical thought on the subject would make obvious the utter fallacy of such a conclusion. Humans are human; God is God. Humans are the pieces and God is the whole.

That is what makes attempting to explain the seemingly unexplainable so difficult. Most feel it has already been explained. But, when you ask someone who or what God is they cannot give you an answer. Sometimes they say, God is love; but that is an emotion. Or they say, God is the creator; but that is an action. I am pushing an idea upstream from the accepted belief.

Jos explained that the best way for him to most clearly demonstrate what God is, would be to give a visual demonstration. He asked us all to follow him into the kitchen, over by the sinks. One of the sinks was full of water where two plates were soaking at the bottom. Jos grabbed several transparent plastic cups of different colors. Standing in front of the sink he asked us all to look at the water. He had Mariam stand on one side of him and Rohm stand on the other. He looked around to make sure that everyone could see inside the sink.

He took several, different colored, transparent cups and put them down into the water. Jos grabbed a clear, colorless cup. Holding the cup upside down, where the opening was in the water, he pulled the cup up partially out of the water. The cup was full of water. The water in the cup was well above the water level. He had Mariam take a red cup and do the same thing; bring the cup up out of the water just before the opening cleared the surface.

He did not let her bring the cup up any farther, because once the opening was out of the water, the cup would lose the suction and all the water would fall back into the pool in the sink. Then, all she would be holding is an empty cup.

He had Rohm do the same thing with a blue cup. Now, with the three of them holding these cups up out of the water, just far enough to keep suction and the cup full of water, Jos explained ...

Can you see the pool of water in the sink? Do you see the water up in the cups? You can clearly see that all the water is the same thing. The water in the sink is all the same thing from one end to the other, including up in the cups.

Now all the material that you see, like the cups and the plates in the bottom, are just chemicals. Atoms of chemicals; matter that you can see. The cups are made up of millions of different atoms. That represents the matter of the universe. What you can see.

The water is the energy of the universe. It is all the thoughts, and feelings, and ideas, and emotions, and, most of all, the memories of everything from the present to all of the past. The water represents the consciousness of everything, from all time. To make the concept easier to understand I am going to call all the material, the body of God, and all the water, the consciousness and awareness of God. The energy of God.

Everyone was looking intently at the water and the cups.

Now as the cups move around in the water you see them create ripples in the water that move over and touch the other cups. The cups can even move around and bump into each other, having a more direct influence on their action. Those cups represent living things, like humans, all moving around gaining a living experience from the particular point of view from that particular cup. The red cup cannot understand what it is like to be in the blue cup, just as the blue cup cannot understand what it is like to be in the red cup. But the water can easily understand what it is like to be in both the red and blue cups. Because, the water is in both cups and is continuous.

The water in the red cup cannot understand the other cups, because it is trapped in the red cup. That is, until the red cup comes out of the water. Then, all the water in the red cup falls back into the pool of water in the sink. Then, the cup is just an empty shell without water in it. It is just a mass of chemicals. The water that falls back into the pool is the "spirit" or "consciousness" of God that was trapped in the cup. Now it can understand what all the water knows wherever the water is.

The water is the energy of the universe; or the consciousness of God.

Now this is not a prophetic philosophy of some mystical supreme being. Science has shown that the energy of the universe is continuous and runs through all things. It has been proven that everything in the universe is connected by the same energy, whether it is here or across the cosmos. As all of the prophets have said, "God is within you and all about you."

Now when the cup is empty, it gets thrown back into the pile of empty cups. The chemicals in that pile get recombined and recycled to make other things that are comprised of matter, like other living things. It makes other cups and plates.

Jos now stopped and looked around at everyone there. They were all mostly just staring into the water. The concept was easier to understand now, but still very profound. Jos knew this. He knew this was a concept that would have to be considered. It was a concept that would have to be put to the test in various ways. He just added at this point ...

If you can understand this concept of God, then you can start to understand the myriad of seemingly mystical questions. You can even start to understand the concept of the afterlife and what it really consists of and what it is like.

Just then, Jos silently walked back out into the dining room alone and left everyone to digest what he had just said, in their own way. Slowly, everyone broke their stare at the water and quietly walked out also. An expression of concentration was on all of their faces.

Everyone was back out in the dining room and had a moment to think. It was very quiet.

In the big scheme of things, the human being is just a short-lived, information gathering, sensory device. It is around for a very short time and experiences the universe in a very unique and individual way, each and every one.

The spirit of humans is the energy of God constrained within the human body. It is restricted to the limitations of the human body and, as such, is confined to the limits of understanding until it is released.

Now with that understanding, you can now say humans are God. God is human, for a time.

Rohm was staring at Jos. You could see in his face he was desperately trying to grasp the concept, but it was difficult. "I do understand what you are saying. But you are right, it is hard to completely comprehend the concept."

Jos was nodding ...

It is all but impossible for anyone to look at themselves as only a collection of many things all together that produces a thought, or a feeling, and thus a memory. There is no one thing that makes up any portion of a human being. The single entity that is you is not any one thing by itself but a collection of many things together.

One of the most powerful things ever known to mankind is an idea. Once you get that embedded into a consciousness it is hard to change it. The old concept of God is something that has been taught since the beginning of human history. It has been taught to you from the very beginning of your life, and is part of daily life. Whether you believe in God or not, it is part of everyday life for every person, because of all the other people on the planet.

Jos looked around at each person there.

It is easier today than at any other time in history for humans to start to grasp what God really is. You have to put thought into it, that is not tainted by preconceived notions or antiquated beliefs. You are in a unique time in human history, take advantage of it. Take advantage of your own intelligence.

I recognized that Jos was repetitive about many things he would talk about, especially God and the afterlife. I thought about that and then I understood. He had a monumental task of busting down a massive, archaic wall of beliefs that had been standing for thousands of years. Well encrusted concepts that had been taught and handed down for generations. It was a Herculean endeavor, but he just kept chipping away at it to eventually create a crack that would allow some new light to pass through.

Going to Church

One day, Jos was talking about how happy he was to see the participation going on at the Church of Understanding. He remarked that this was a much better place to go on weekends, with much better things to do than established religious meeting houses.

Reese asked, "So, are you saying that people should not go to the regular churches?"

I am not saying that at all; absolutely not. There are many reasons why it is good to go to church or a synagogue or a temple or a mosque or any other house of worship. There is communion there. Being with other people is always good. Sharing feelings of goodness and assisting others to feel good is always a good thing. It is just like the Church of Understanding; people get together and share the "good word" with others, and help others, and care for others.

Again, it is not the idea but the action and reason that are important. A church is only a building, it is not a "holy" place where God resides. The only "holy" place that God resides is within you; within all living things.

Reese nodded, understanding. "That is why you call the Church of Understanding that, isn't it? You could have just called it the House of Understanding. You look at it like a real church, don't you"?

Jos gazed at Reese and commented that communion is communion. What better communion than where you actually commune?

It was a dismal, rainy day when I was coming out of the restaurant from doing my morning duties and I met up with Jos, who was coming from the bakery after talking with Natashia. We were both heading up the street to the Church of Understanding. Jos had the customary grin on his face, like he had heard some really good news. I asked him about it. He had not heard anything particularly unusual, it was just the way he approached every day. He asked me the usual, "How are you doing," and, "What is going on in the restaurant?" We just had normal polite banter and comments on the way.

When we stepped through the door, there was already a beehive of activity going on in the place. There were periodic high-pitched whirls of electric machinery in use. There was a dull rumble of many subdued conversations going on at the same time; that would moderately increase when a machine spun up. Some of the people that had stayed overnight were gathering themselves, some with carts, and were starting to head out. Lorne was not in sight but Bufasa and Renn, two of the people that had started helping Lorne out with his duties around the building for a free place to stay, were on the second-floor landing.

They were looking over the railing and observing the activity going on and noting who was where and doing what. Neither were quite as big as Lorne, but both still had a look that was not to be messed with.

Jos had noted and commented to me about several of Toro's gang laughing and talking with one of the older guys that came by frequently to show some woodworking skills. His name was Sebastian and he was an older gentleman, had been an electrician for most of his career and had always enjoyed woodworking. Subsequently, he was very good at it and knowledgeable. The younger guys really got along with him very well and as a result were starting to get quite familiar with wood and woodworking tools also. At first, they made a pile of little boxes. Jos stated one time that he was not ever going to ask what they expected people to put in those boxes. I agreed that was probably a reasonable decision. After a while, though, those little boxes became more and more elaborate and the guys were getting a pretty good price for them that they used to get better and more expensive wood. It surprised me, though it did not Jos, that they were, one, interested in woodworking, two, attentive enough to be patient enough to build little boxes, and three, honest enough to use the money for the "house." I would express my amazement of the boys, and when I did, Jos would just look at me and say something to the effect of, "Oh, ye of little faith."

I noticed some of the other guys from that gang watching and learning from another older gentleman some little construction tricks that he was doing around the building; just fixing this and that around the place. He was just another one of the older, retired guys from around the neighborhood. It was obvious that the gentleman enjoyed showing and teaching and was also surprised at the attention of the younger guys. But that was the whole purpose of the Church of Understanding; to teach, to learn, and to commune with others. The guy was using drywall and plasterboard to enclose a space under the stairs for storage; and to show and teach how to do it. Jos went over to just say some greetings and see how things were going.

I sat down at an unused table with a pencil and paper to put down some ideas for improvements to this building. With my head down and deep in thought, I heard a distinctive voice ask me if I knew where Jos was. I looked up to see Mariam with a solemn look on her face. Not a completely unusual look for her, she was always more of a serious person, but not generally when she first greets someone. I looked around at the last place I had seen him and noticed him walking back to the table where we were. I gazed at Mariam and with the back of my pencil pointed at the approaching Jos. When he noticed Mariam standing there, his face lit up and his smile intensified. It did not change the expression on Mariam's face though. It was obvious that she had a concern of some kind. My attention was now squarely on Mariam and the issue that would have her so serious at this time of day. Jos arrived and greeted Mariam kindly with the knowledge that something was troubling her mind.

"I am concerned about Jordan. I know he likes to drink. I know that he is unreliable because of that." She paused for a moment trying to decide if she should go on or if she was just sounding foolish.

"It is just that I have not seen him for quite a while now," she continued. "He has been gone even longer than normal, several days. I don't know, maybe I have just gotten to where I expect him to show up by now needing some food and some fresh clothes. Maybe my concern is a little unfounded, but with his lifestyle I can't help feeling a little concerned. I just hate to think about him lying passed out in some filthy hole somewhere with no one checking to see if he is still breathing or what." She shrugged a little and cocked her head to a side, like she just accepted that she was being foolish. "I just think about the guy from time to time."

Jos stepped up to her and put his arm around her shoulder. Caring about someone else was what Jos was all about. To see someone else caring, too, impressed him. Jos promised to alleviate her concerns and do what he could to find out Jordan's disposition. But Jordan was under no obligation to make his condition or whereabouts known, even to those that cared about him. That was his choice. But, if the truth be known, Jos had already been wondering about Jordan. The last few nights that he was out under the guise of taking a little walk he had been making inquiries and looking.

About that time, Lorne walked back into the building carrying a few paper bags. Jos motioned for him to come over, which he did. Jos talked to him and asked if he could charge him with the task of finding Jordan. Lorne readily accepted, expressing his concern for him as well. It seemed that everyone had taken an interest in Jordan's welfare. Jordan was one of those people that never seemed to be harmful to anyone but himself. He was quiet, seemed kind of lonesome, he kept to himself, and the fact of the matter was that you couldn't help wanting more for the man. Jordan never had a mean word to say about anything and always seemed appreciative for what he got. But Jordan was an alcoholic; he had an addiction that was his and his alone. Addiction is a real demon possession. It was his demon, and until he wanted help exorcising it, there was nothing anyone else could do about it. It is the tragedy of all well-meaning people that not everyone can be helped, nor does everyone want help. But that does not stop the good from trying and at least thinking about it.

"If he were my son I would at least want someone to care enough to see if he is still alive," Mariam explained. Mariam was a good motherly soul. You were not going to find a more caring person. Jos knew that she spent many days and nights agonizing over Jordan and his affliction with alcohol, ever since the first day he asked her to help him in the restaurant. Jos was more than acutely aware of the deep motherly concern Mariam had for Jordan from that first day. He was not in any way remorseful for bringing the two together and influencing Mariam's emotions either. People are supposed to care about others. However, Jos acknowledged, there are some that are more empathetic than others; and Mariam was definitely one of those. Because of that Jos had spent many hours talking to Mariam about her concerns about Jordan and her general frustration with destructive addictions.

I heard Jos many times talk about habits and addictions ...

Addictions Start

Drug addiction is very personal. It is like love. You cannot tell someone not to fall in love with another person.

What happens when you try to tell someone not to fall in love with someone else? They do not listen to you; you just alienate them from you. They are going to love them anyway. They will cling to their love even harder. Drug addiction is very much the same thing; it acts very much the same way. You cannot make someone leave an addiction if they do not want to. In fact, the more you pull, the harder you push them to it.

This is another of the yin and yang of having the human body for any amount of time. There are physical substances that have a profound effect on it and can cause intense and undeniable cravings, but it is also the only way to experience living. It is mandatory to inhabit the human machine to have a living experience and to manipulate the present, and therefore the future. But the human body is very susceptible to various chemical compounds and conditions.

"But don't you say to be tolerant of other people?" Connie interjected as she walked up. *"It is you that is constantly reiterating not to impose your own values on other people."*

I am not saying to alienate Jordan. I am not saying that he is wrong or a bad person. I am not saying to pass judgment on him using your own values. I am certainly not saying to be intolerant of him.

By saying that Jordan has an addiction, I am not being intolerant of him or passing judgment on him. It is merely stating a fact. It is the same as saying that he has a disease, which it is. That is not judging him or demeaning him. It is merely stating a fact. The only thing that will be different with me about him is, that I will be cautious not to aggravate or exacerbate his addiction. I would do the same thing if he was diabetic. I would not try to aggravate or exacerbate his condition.

One of the tell-tale signs of any addiction is when someone starts *wanting* to be alone. Being alone is really unnatural for humans. When someone starts wanting to be alone more and more often for longer and longer periods, it should be a sign that something is going on. Generally, it is a sign of some kind of addiction. Now, that may not necessarily be bad, but it should definitely raise a flag.

Mariam would frequently ask Jos, "How can somebody become addicted to drugs? I mean, why would anybody become addicted to something that has such a devastating effect to their lives?" They had many talks about this subject.

People always ask how someone can become addicted to drugs. Nobody starts out to become addicted to a drug. They start out because they enjoy the effects. For the longest time, they think they can quit anytime they want; they just do not want to, they enjoy it. They think they have control of the use; when and where. The addiction sneaks up on them long before they have any clue that they have become addicted.

If the addiction did not feel good to start with, it would never become an addiction.

Emotions of Light and Dark

I have spoken before of emotions, and that none of them are either good or bad but how they are acted on. But now I do want to talk about light and dark emotions.

Take, for example, the emotion of love. It can be a good emotion, most people probably think of it that way, or it can be a bad emotion when the love of something causes destruction. That is what I mean about how it is acted on. However, love is a light emotion in the sense that it generally brings joy and brightness when it is around; at least initially. Hate, again depending on how it is acted on, can be bad or good. But for all intents and purposes, hate is a very dark emotion.

Here is what I am trying to say: when someone comes into a room with other people and they are overflowing with love, they brighten the room. They are easy to be around. But when someone comes into a room of people and is reeking of hate, they bring the whole atmosphere in the room dark and foreboding. Do you understand what I mean now?

It is not so much what anyone feels but what they radiate when they feel it. There are light and dark emotions that people can feel when another is close to them. Have you ever noticed that someone is troubled even when they are acting cheerful? You can feel light and dark emotions on people and around them; they permeate a room with it. That is the energy that I talk about that is all around us all the time, like radio waves rippling through the air.

Addictions tend to bring with them dark emotions and therefore drain energy from others. You see this with Jordan. That is why you see so many of you trying desperately to infuse light emotions to him. That is also why he comes around and you see him in a lighter mood when he is here. He is infused with positive energy. His mind and body feed off of that like an emaciated body in a desert.

Mariam asked, "Do you really think that's why he comes around?"

Reese said, "I think he comes around for the free food. Well, not free. I mean, the meal he gets for a little work. Not to mention his clothes cleaned and a place to clean himself. I think he comes around for the benefits he gets, which in his situation is pretty good. That's the way I see it."

Jos started nodding in agreement.

"I have to agree with Reese," Adam said. "I don't see him coming around for the 'good feeling' he gets. I see him coming for the benefits."

Jos was still just nodding. Looking at Adam but clearly speaking to everyone ...

That may very well be true. There are some very distinctive benefits coming here when he does to do some work and get cleaned up and a belly full of needed and fresh food. But do you not see his demeanor when he is here? You saw him on his first day and you have seen him ever since that day. Have you not seen a change in his personality, in his reactions, and in his comfort and, more importantly, his energy? He has come to know us better than he originally did, but do you think that is the only reason he is much more open to us now? Have any of you listened to what he has to say about his life? Do you think that he would be that open with you, even as long as he has known you, if he did not feel a positive energy?

That gave the whole gang pause to think. Which you could clearly see they were doing, especially with what Jos had given them to think about. I know I did. Reese even confirmed a story that Jordan had told him that was what any person would consider to be, very personal; a slight glance into his very guarded closet.

"I guess it is just the way anyone would look at it," Adam speculated. "When you put it that way, I guess I can see it. We probably are refreshing to be around, considering what he is generally around day after day, if he is around anybody at all."

Jos was steadily looking at all of us ...

Perspective, and therefore perception, is a very individual thing.

Brainwashing

Emotions like hope and regret are light and dark. People can use these emotions to influence other people. There have been many cunning people in history that understood the importance of light and dark emotions, and they used them expertly to help control people. People today are very versed in how to use light and dark emotions for various reasons: to sell a product or service, to get elected to office, or to swindle money from others. People use light and dark emotions to control others by drawing them in or pushing them away. One of the main ways that people use brainwashing is to promote ideas and inspire beliefs. None stronger than religious ideas and beliefs and yes, the main religion I am talking about now is the number one religion all around the world: the religion of money. Brainwashing is easy. You just tell somebody something they want to hear and then keep hammering the message in constantly.

Later on in the day, Lorne reported to Jos. They found Jordan a few blocks away doing some menial work for one of the local machine shops. He was not any more disheveled than usual but his skin was somewhat darker, indicating that he has spent more time than usual in direct sunlight.

Mariam and Jordan talked. Jordan expressed his desire to get clean from constant alcohol use and start his own business as a handy-man. Mariam could barely contain her enthusiasm and then directed him to talk with Jos on such matters.

Jordan agreed, and also wanted to talk to Jos more about religions and what they were all about. Would they help him or could they even help him? He wanted to talk to him about the right way to look at things.

It wasn't long before Jordan and Jos met up in a corner of the Church of Understanding next to a drilling machine that was not currently being used. Jos could tell that Jordan was excited about a new future by the speed he was talking and how he was jumping from subject to subject. From my point of view, all I could see was the smiling face of Jos nodding up and down; more to just keep Jordan in sight than in agreement.

The first questions had to do with getting a business going. "Do you think I could start a business?" he kept asking. "Do you think I could run a business? I mean successfully?"

Jordan barely took a breath between questions. He had questions about how to charge for his work, how to buy supplies, where he was going to keep his supplies, how was he going to transport his supplies, legalities, licenses, and the questions just kept coming rapid fire. He had so many questions, he never gave Jos a chance to answer any before asking more.

When he finally took a breath, Jos was able to step in with some answers. First, he addressed whether or not Jordan could run a business. He told him, more in a form of a question, that he had already been running a type of business by himself. It just was not steady. If he really wanted his own business, he had to commit to it. When he told someone he would work for them, he was making a contract that would have to be fulfilled. When you are just taking handouts and gratuities for work performed that is one thing. When you make a contract, even a verbal one, you have to perform to your word. You have to show up and you have to do the work.

Jos asked Jordan if he was ready to make such a commitment. Jordan confirmed he was, enthusiastically. As far as supplies went, he could ask for some minor donations of either the supplies or negotiate a little prepayment of his work to purchase what he would need. His business was not going to be the type that would have to have a large investment for equipment or soft supplies, it was primarily a service business; Jordan was the equipment. As far as the legalities and the general business basics, he took him over and introduced him to Raul Rasshi.

Raul was an elderly retired businessman. He owned a dry-cleaning business at one time and operated a small neighborhood grocery store for a while. Now he showed up at the Church of Understanding to use the furnace to make little glass trinkets that many people were fascinated with. But Jos also knew that he was really quite smart about business, especially small businesses in this neighborhood. He knew who to talk to and what to do. On top of that, he knew Jordan from seeing him around the neighborhood for so long. Jordan immediately started riveting Raul with questions zealously. I remember the wide-eyed look that Raul gave Jos just before Jos, grinning, turned and walked away.

Later that day, Jordan found Jos back down at the restaurant doing his part at the end of the day. It was a good thing that Jos was almost finished anyway because Jordan all but cornered him to ask more questions. His fervor was inspiring, but at the same time it was also a little unnerving. It was so out of character for Jordan to be this energetic and passionate. But I thought it was maybe because I have just never seen him this enthusiastic before or maybe just never seen him this sober before.

Now he was hammering Jos about religion and faith. Could faith help his addiction, would it be better for his business to be religious? What was God? Was he already too far gone for religion to help and which religion should he take up or which prophet could help him the most with their teachings? He wanted to know what the prophets knew and how he could use that in his daily life. Who do I read, what do I read, and who do I listen to?

Jos then became somewhat stern with Jordan. He took him by the shoulders gently and moved him toward the back, partly for more privacy and partly because Jordan's vigor was becoming a distraction. He calmed him down with a gentle voice. Jordan kept exclaiming, "But you know I know you know. I don't know how you know, but you know. I know that. Tell me what the religious holy men know. Tell me. Can it help? It can't hurt. Tell me what they know."

Jos looked at him calmly. Jordan seemed to have finally lost some energy as he started to calm down and took a seat. Jos sat beside him and calmly spoke ...

I can tell you some of what I know. I can tell you some of what they knew. But, more importantly, I will tell you what they did not know.

What the Prophets Did Not Know

The reason that the religious people, even five hundred years ago, prophesized so many different things about God and the future of humans is because they did not know the true history of the earth. They saw the way the earth was then and, without knowing the true history of it, they made up stories for how things came to be and how things were going to be. They had no knowledge of how things really were. It was to be expected that they would make stories of how things came to be. Mythology is all about explaining how things came to be and who or what made them. That is the fifth drive of the human psyche, the quest for understanding.

As time went along, different people came up with new ideas and explanations as to how things worked. After a while, certain beliefs were written down as facts and people believed them, especially when these stories were around and read for hundreds of years. The stories made sense of things that no one else could explain. Before long the gods had merged into one God and different explanations for the origin of life became prevalent. Then, as more knowledge was obtained, the explanations started to reflect the new-found knowledge and, of course, new religions emerged.

Today, with the vast amount of knowledge that is being obtained through science about the origin of the earth, the universe, and life, long-held beliefs are being challenged. Most long-standing beliefs are not being released or abandoned; they are being modified to conform to this new knowledge. It took hundreds of years of undisputable facts just to convince people that the sun did not revolve around the earth. Now it is without question.

Jordan grew quiet, intently listening to Jos for the first time, it seemed. He was engrossed as Jos went on ...

What the Energy of God Wants

Once you understand what God is, it is easy, using logic, to understand what God wants. God is a grand consciousness, living and wanting to experience life. The only way to understand and experience life is through living things. All living things.

Now you understand the "meaning" of life.

When Jordan asked him about how to beat his alcoholism, Jos was just as candid ...

Pray and understand the true nature of prayer. Understand how it really works; who you are really praying to and why. Use the resources that are ready and willing to help you that are around you every day. Understand the true nature and use of communion.

Jordan asked, "Can I abolish the regrets I already have?" His eyes were fixed on Jos, almost pleading. Deep in his gaze was fear and remorse.
Putting his hand reassuringly on Jordan's shoulder ...

Yes. Like everything else there are two sides to every person. No one person is one thing by itself. Every person has good and bad, light and dark. The sum total of who you are will be determined when you can no longer manipulate the results. Remember this: your self is a plank that sits upon a fulcrum. On one end of the plank is holiness, on the other side is evil. Every moment you have on earth your hand is on the fulcrum and it is in constant motion by your actions. If you want to remove regret, you have to move the fulcrum.

You could see Jordan's demeanor lighten up with the possibility of hope. "Do you have any advice about my want for alcohol?" Again, the pleading eyes were back. "You have told me many things. Good things to be sure. And you have given me many things to think about. But you really haven't given me any real advice on how to quit drinking." He now stared intently into the eyes of Jos. Almost in a whisper he asked, "Can you cure me? Can you put your hands on me?"

You could see the sorrow in the eyes of Jos. He could see the desperation in Jordan's eyes and Jos could hear more than pleading in his voice; it was begging, a beseeching desolation. It was the sound of real pain and despair. You could see every fiber of Jos wanting to grab him and do just that; hold him, cure him, and take away the addiction. This was the first time that I actually felt sorry for Jos.

I could put my arms around you, shout and make a fuss, profess that the Lord has heard you in your hour of need, lay you down, and scream, "Praise God!" And you would probably feel a lot better. You would actually feel a weight lifted off of you. You would, in all honesty, feel like the addiction has been taken from you and you are new and fresh and clean and can start over without any repercussions. That is a form of brainwashing. But that would only last until the real drug really did wear off, then that cold emptiness would return. Probably with more vigor now because you thought that it really had left and now you found that it has not. It is the same principle as when someone says, "This is not going to hurt a bit," just before they give you an injection. It hurts. But when they tell you, "Now, this is going to hurt some," then give you the injection, it does not seem to be that bad. That is because the body will prepare itself for what is about to happen, if it is fully aware of what is about to happen.

There is no way for me to take away the addiction. It is a disease. Like any other disease, it must be treated and only with time will your body heal. In this type of disease, you are the doctor and the patient. I can do many things to help you and I will gladly. Everyone here will be there to help also. You are not alone; and that is some of the best medicine for this disease that you can get. Being alone at any time right now is very dangerous and ill-advised.

I can give you advice. I can give you support. I can give you a person when you need one. What I cannot give you is the desire and the drive to do it. I can give you encouragement when your desire and drive start to wane; and that is going to happen often. But I cannot make you stop; you have to do that. And I will tell you this right now, right from the beginning, and I want you to understand it completely and thoroughly. I want you to believe it unquestionably and never doubt it. Are you ready to hear this? Whether you are successful or not it is not going to change the way I feel about you. If you fall on the way, even just stumble a little, there will be no disappointment in me.

History has shown many times that with even the best, most determined and steadfast individuals, that they have some lapses. They have momentary times when they slide. If you do not, I will be there standing with you. But if you do, I will still be there standing with you. As long as no person is *harmed*, then I will do your bidding, I will be your guard, and I will be your rock. So, at no time should you ever feel the need to try to hide something from me because it just would not make any difference. There is no need to ever feel guilt or shame with me if it has to do with yourself. You cannot hide anything anyway from the only one that is really important; that is, you. You must be true to yourself; that is what I mean, you cannot hide from yourself.

I could see Jordan's posture relax more and more as Jos talked. There was a glint in his eye that this might be possible. He was becoming more positive that he could achieve this endeavor. He looked around at everyone sitting there and saw that they were all smiling and nodding in agreement. Everyone was standing by to help. You could tell that really did mean something to Jordan.

"When should I start?" Jordan asked.

You have to start only when you are ready. You cannot want to if you are not ready. But if you *are* ready, then you have already started. If you have started, then be sure you get some help to go get your things and bring them over to the Church of Understanding and find a place to secure yourself and feel safe. Make sure you have someone with you, though. My advice for now would be to make sure you have someone with you all the time for a few days. They do not need to be "watching" you. They do not even need to know why they are there. You just need to have someone close to you for just a while for you and for you alone; not for them, for you.

When you feel yourself start to become weak for whatever reason your body is aching, or you see someone else drinking and it gives you the urge, or you just get wondering what it felt like and you miss it remember to do this. Remember to reinforce what you want and what you want to achieve; talk to yourself and remind yourself what you are doing. In other words: pray. Praying is talking to God. You are that piece of God. Talking to yourself is talking to God. You will find that after even a short prayer your urge will subside. You will find the power to continue on. You will find the strength of energy that is within us all. That is what prayer is and what it is all about. God is within you and all about you. Talk to the one that can actually make the difference. In this case, talk to you. Ask yourself for the strength and the power that is needed to overcome. You will find it.

"I don't know. I'm pretty scared. This is going to be hard." Jordan paused for a moment. "But I have been wanting to." He looked up defiantly. "And I'm ready. You're right. It has already started. I am going to need a lot of help but I am ready right now."

There was muffled applause among the gang with some light cheering. I think it was kept subdued because no one was sure if it was appropriate at the time. But Jos did smile and sat up straighter in the chair.

Many of the strongest and noblest of men, and women, started with doubts. They started with not only doubts of accomplishment but also concerns for their safety and that of their families as well. The one thing they all had, however, that made them all successful is they knew it was the right thing to do, they were right for doing it, and it needed to be done. They may not have started with much support initially but that grew also as time went on. They gained perseverance by that knowledge, and their belief in themselves and their own determination to do the right thing. They may not have succeeded the first time either but they never gave up trying.

Jordan was looking much more at ease but still a little apprehensive. If the truth be told, the rest of the gang looked the same. Everyone knew that this would be a hard road to follow and a significant feat of accomplishment if it could be done. No one was under any delusion that attempting to quit any addiction was a significant change in a person's life. None were as aware as Jos was, but he showed the most optimism. Jos had often talked about how change was difficult but always possible, as long as you are alive you can change.

Jos talked to Jordan for a long while that night after the restaurant closed. He talked with several in our gang, and then he went down and talked to Lorne and Bufasa and Renn. The three men that were working at the Church of Understanding for a place to stay. He knew that those three would be crucial in any success that Jordan might have. They would be the ones that would see and be with Jordan at his most vulnerable times. During the day when a person can keep busy and many more people were around, the feelings of withdrawal would be much easier to combat. It would be at night, after work, that his demons would have the most power over him. That is the time when communion would be the most important. Because one of the three of the guys at the Church of Understanding would be there all night, they would be the angels that Jordan would need to rely on.

Jos often talked about angels and demons; they were very real. They were just not like they were portrayed in the movies or even in religious texts. But the way Jos put it, most demons were within the self and most angels were outside the self. People would see angels and demons in their own way, but the real ones had to do with within and without. It was all in definition of terms.

Several nights Jos would make special trips up to the building to check clandestinely on the tribulations and trials of Jordan and others. Jordan was not the only one who had come to Jos for assistance with addictions and other problems. In fact, the nightly population within the Church of Understanding was starting to be quite overwhelming. That situation was a concern of Jos. He knew that anytime you put many people together in close proximity, especially troubled individuals, it was a recipe for untoward events.

To that end, Jos had started sometime before looking for assistance from local private and public venues. Jos confided in me and some of the others on occasion the reality of the world. He would describe the huge chasm between supply and demand. In this case, the huge disparity between those that needed help and those able to help; even more specifically the financial burden and lack of available funds. As he put it, you may be able to feed the multitudes with two fish and a loaf of bread but you cannot do it continuously. He said it like this...

At some point, if the Church of Understanding is going to continue here, it will have to become solvent and self-sustaining. It will have to be purchased from those that own it for investment by those that use it for what it is. That can be done but it will take the efforts of everyone involved. I know the human race; if they really want it, nothing can stop them.

Just look at this neighborhood that we are in right now. Remember when we came here a couple of years ago? Remember what shape it was in? The restaurant had very few customers, barely enough to keep the doors open, and even that was not going to last. The space that the bakery is in took us days just to clean it up, let alone all the repairs. Remember the shape of the clothing store, not to mention the building that the Church of Understanding is in?

Now look at all of these places. Look at the entire neighborhood.

Do you remember how many people came around here for drugs and prostitutes, whereas now they are coming for food and clothing and education? Can you see the evolution of just this one area with a little bit of personal investment and belief?

There are those that are *not* completely happy with the changes. Believe me, I have heard from them. But they were not harmed in any way. They just did not like the change. One of the most verbal has been Toro and his gang. What we have done here has hurt their "business." We were lucky enough that they *did* tolerate it and just moved their business to another area, which did create conflicts with other street gangs. This area and the people in it were really lucky not to get caught up in those disputes, which could have easily happened and been very bad.

Interestingly enough, Toro's gang, and even himself, have benefited from the change also. Well, more their families than themselves. But, nevertheless they saw the benefit and surprisingly took advantage of it. Hope and hopelessness are two very powerful emotions.

What Toro's gang members saw growing up in this area was the hopelessness of their situation, and life longevity was just not very long. The people around here never really considered that, so they did what they felt they had to do without regard to consequences. Now they can see hope for a future and especially now with them talking to the older people that have survived many hardships that they never knew before, they have reason to consider consequences and possibilities.

Remember the looks we use to get from all of them? That was the glare of reluctant change and fear of the unknown. They did not know what we were about, and they were not really open to find out. Now they understand what it is all about and they have grown accustomed to it. Most change, especially drastic and profound change, takes a lot of time. That goes with any kind of change, whether it is a neighborhood, a business, a belief, human relationships or even, and especially, the human body itself.

Any change can be made. First you have to determine what the change is, then you have to come up with a plan, and then you have to implement it.

Dreams and Aspirations

You must have dreams and aspirations. It is what keeps you going and trying and learning and doing. But you have to be realistic also.

Young people have dreams and aspirations, and they are so

determined to obtain them that when they get just a little older they become disillusioned and depressed with life. In years past, the information a person had of life was extremely limited. They only saw the opportunities that were available in their village and they aspired for that. When movies, and especially TV, started to show many different opportunities, the aspirations of young people grew vastly wider. Because of that, as the hopes and dreams grew ever larger so too did the disappointment and hopelessness, if the dreams and aspirations were not realized. Disappointment and hopelessness are two very powerful emotions that can wreak havoc on a person's mind. It can cause people to do all sorts of things in desperation. Many times, these emotions can lead to substance abuse or other abuses like anger and violence to others, or to other illegal activities.

This is why it pleases me to see young people try to help their communities and try to obtain a strong and healthy work ethic for themselves. It pleases me to see people come together to accomplish something that will benefit not only them but others as well. It pleases me to see people try to work for themselves instead of working for others; just taking the easier road to hire on with a "boss" for a static regular paycheck. It pleases me to see young people strive for lofty but obtainable goals.

When some of the young people, especially new immigrants, children of people who recently arrived in a new and unfamiliar place, would voice their concerns, Jos would comfort them. It was far easier for young people to go astray in a new place. Jos would tell young people ...

There are incredible hardships and extreme dangers involved with trying to start anew in a new land with a new society, but it was worth it to many people. Even today, that kind of freedom is so cherished that people will take extreme chances and make extreme sacrifices for even the possibility of a better life. These are new times all over the world. People of all kinds are no longer satisfied with what they are being told they have to be, or what they have to do, or what their children must endure because of them. People are no longer content to be stigmatized because of their birthplace. People are recognizing all over the world that they are not where they were born but what they can achieve and become through their own efforts. People want that freedom.

Freedoms

Freedoms are not free. For every good there is a bad. That is the yin and yang that I talk about. If you want unrestricted freedoms, you must have incredible self-control. If you impose on someone else's freedom, expect retaliation. Even something as simple and benign as driving down the street with loud music that imposes on other people's space, expect retaliation. You would not want it done to you, you should not do it to others. *It is a simple rule but rarely recognized and practiced.* This is the respect for others that I talk about. It is the *respect* that is so lacking in today's society all over the world.

A form of slavery, or I should say human ownership, is still apparent in industrialized nations. It is very subtle, but when a company or corporation is sold to another entity, the employees are not consulted, and they have no contribution to the decision; they are just sold along with the other possessions of the company, like property. Now they have to conform to the new owners or go without.

It was during some of these talks about dreams, freedoms, nations, governments, and groups of people that Jos would become sullen. His expression would become dark with thoughts unknown to me. He would say ...

Extremism and Terrorism

Extremists that terrorize do not care about improving anything, they just want to destroy and kill for their own pleasure and glory. The sad thing is that they invoke the name of Yahweh or God or Allah to give them an excuse. Like it is *ok* if their self-serving is done so long as it is in the name of a deity. They do not care in the least for Yahweh or God or Allah, or their own people, they only care about themselves and what they want.

The proof is in the results; in the entire course of history, extremists and terrorists have never accomplished anything positive for their people or their deity. They have only increased distrust among all humans and destroyed valuable principles of all of society.

When Jos talked about extremists and terrorists, you could easily see that he saw no understanding or logic to it. And this was a man that showed understanding and logic to all human activities, regardless how *abnormal or perverted they were. He clearly understood that these are the unpredictable and unsavory nature of humans. It may be easy to see, but it still confounded Jos profoundly.*

Jos had said, whether you are doing something right, or doing something wrong, if you keep doing it and do it long enough you are going to be recognized for it eventually; you will be caught. Generally, you will be noticed sooner for doing something bad. He was always trying to get that through to people. He always tried to get people to understand that what they did mattered.

Band Together

One of the major problems with the world today is that the good people do not band together. They are happy with their lives and they do not hurt anyone else or impose themselves or their attitudes on anyone else. So, they just go along not harming a soul and want to be left alone. But that is the problem; there are so many good people that go completely unnoticed because they want to be left alone. There are far more good people than anyone knows about because they just do not impose themselves on anyone else; they are quiet. If all the good people started to band together openly, visually, verbally with just respect, tolerance, and kindness, other people would see how many there really are. They would not be reserve about coming out and banding together also.

Jos dropped his head and slowly shook it in resignation. He quietly added ...

Prejudice

Prejudices are learned responses. Prejudices are not only bad, they can also be good. A prejudice is merely a preconceived notion of what to expect based on past experience. Generally, a prejudice is developed with a first encounter of something or someone. *First impressions* are very important not only to the individual but also for the group or gang that the other people will associate them with.

Most people think that what they do only reflects upon them as individuals. That is generally not the case and is a great misconception. When someone does something that reflects badly, they are generally looked at by an individual trait and associated with that group of people. If the first encounter you have with a guy with a nose ring is an unpleasant one, then you are going to develop a prejudice about those who wear nose rings. If you have a first encounter with a girl with purple streaks in her hair and it is very pleasant, then you are generally going to produce a fondness for girls with purple streaks in their hair.

To pre-judge something, one must have an experience of some kind with that. It can be told to someone, in other words, the prejudice can be developed by comments from other people or it can be firsthand. The strongest and most lasting is firsthand experience with another, but verbal influence can be very powerful also. It is generally the verbal influence that children grow up with that taints them.

I tell you this: in my life and travels all over the world, I have seen and met many people. I have known good and bad, all with different gang associations. The one thing that I have never seen is someone that I could look at and make an accurate assessment of the *individual* using any of their particular gang associations. I have never seen a gang that everyone associated with it was either good or bad. Individuals are far too diverse to fit into any specific gang entirely. The only exception is *moneygrubbers*.

Unfounded hateful prejudices must be constantly reinforced in order to remain viable and that is generally done by verbal influences from those eager to promote the prejudice; blatant outspokenness, chanting, protests, fights and riots.

Do not get mad at those with the prejudice; get mad at those that promote the prejudice. Get mad at those that cause the prejudice.

For some reason, Jos was interested in all kinds of different theories of life. He was a very real person. What I mean by that is Jos was not interested in many fantasies that people discuss. He was not the type to get involved with "interesting possibilities" that many people talked about. He looked at the world with very clear eyes and with real logic and understanding. He did not consider things that logic just did not substantiate. He was not deceived by what the world could be, or the way the world should be. He was only interested with the way the world really was. He was about reality. The true nature of the world was not a mystery to him. He had a perfectly good understanding of the way the world really was. He understood the true nature of things; how good and how bad everything really was and why.

That is why he would talk about things that fascinated me as to why he would consider them. He would talk about some things that many people would just dismiss like sweeping away a pesky fly. He would consider things that other people would relay, that most other people would not contemplate. There were times when he would talk

*about strange experiences that most people would only consider as
fantasy and conjecture.*

I heard him talk about things like ...

Resurrection and Reincarnation

There are two beliefs out there I would like to address: that of
resurrection and of reincarnation. What I find amusing is those
people that believe in one do not generally believe in the other.
Resurrection is the belief that you will return in your own body.
Reincarnation is the belief that you will return in another body, of
some kind not necessarily in the same species.

My question to you for the belief of resurrection is this: If,
when you die, the chemicals that make up your body are recycled
into other things, which they are, where are the chemicals for your
old body going to come from for you to resurrect into? Your body,
after death, decomposes back into chemicals. Those chemicals get
absorbed by something else. Your body cannot just steal them back.
It is not going to reanimate at some future time. That just does not
make realistic sense, sorry.

On the other hand, reincarnation is the return of "your soul" into
another body. Some people ask where all the new "souls" come from;
as there are far more people now than ever before?

When you understand that God is the accumulated knowledge,
experiences and memories of all living things into one consciousness.
When you understand that God is the total energy of consciousness
of the entire universe. When you understand that God is all things.
Then you understand that the "soul" is just a small part of the energy
of God inhabiting a human vessel for a finite period of time. When
any living thing is born, it is essentially a reincarnation of a *piece* of
God in a new living form.

Remember the demonstration with the cup and the water? God
is the water that is everywhere. Reincarnation is just a new cup,
coming out of the water, bringing a little of the water with it trapped
inside. *Every birth is a reincarnation.*

The reason that some people have "past life experiences" is
because a small bit of a memory from some past life is retained by
that portion of "soul" that inhabits the new living body. It is not a
returning individual soul. It just has some retained memories of past
experiences.

You will notice that most past life experiences are experienced by
children and only for a period of time, then it is generally forgotten.
Just like a dream is only remembered for a period of time then it

is generally forgotten. God is the experiences and knowledge and memories of all past living things. It is not unnatural for there to be some reminisce of previous memories retained in the energy of a new body for a period of time.

One day, when Jos was talking about all living things are made up of many, many things that combine to make one thing, Lajita, the young girl working at Desha's clothing store, was sitting there with her mind wondering as Jos spoke. Her face was frozen in concentration. Then, suddenly she blurted out what she had been thinking about.

"That is why you only help start businesses where everyone is part of the business. Where everyone has an interest in the business. Where everyone working there owns the business." She stared at Jos with wide eyes, waiting for confirmation.

Jos looked at her surprised and delighted. A grin grew on his face. He could feel what she was thinking.

"That is how living things work," she said. "No living thing is only one thing. Everything working together is how living things work. You are not creating businesses; you are creating living things."

Without thinking it possible, but indeed, the smile on the face of Jos increased. His eyes now sparkled but he did not say a thing.

Now everyone else that was in the room was looking back and forth at Lajita and Jos. Slowly, you could see the realization of the thought develop in their own minds. I had thought about it a year ago, when I saw him start up Desha's Cover Your Heart store. It made perfect sense to me then, and I thought I was the last to "get it."

"Living things do not have one thing that controls everything else," she went on to postulate. "They may have one thing that is in charge but even that one thing is made up of many things; the brain. But everything in the living body is only working for a single purpose. Just like the businesses you created. Many things are working together for a single purpose." She popped up out of her seat. "That is why they have been successful even in an unhealthy environment. They are living things and they have a natural survival instinct. Like any other life; they will find a way."

Wonders of the Universe

Lajita, you have just explained the wonders of the universe. You have just realized the center of all truth. Why learned, much older people cannot grasp the simplicity of what you just became enlightened to, I do not know.

Why is it that, it is well-recognized that energy traveling from one place to another, in whatever form, is what creates memories, and dreams, and thoughts? Why is it that no person argues these principles? But when they look up and see the exact same thing happening in a much larger scale above them in space, they cannot see it nor understand it? When people watch the exact same thing happening throughout the cosmos that goes on within a brain, it looks the same, it reacts the same, the principle is the same, it is just in a vastly larger scale, why do they dismiss the idea that it is the same?

Jos stopped for a minute. He looked at everyone sitting there, some with faces of comprehension, some with faces of confusion. After a moment, he softly added ...

This is why Jesus spoke to most people in parables. Some people will get it and some people will not, but that is not the important part. Understanding how everything works or how everything relates to another is not imperative. As I said before, the important part is how you get along with other living things.

If one person tries to accomplish a goal, it can generally be done if they work at achieving it. If five people work on the same goal, it is much better. Imagine, now, if hundreds of thousands are working at the same goal. The question is only, what can humans not do? You have heard the expression, "Two minds are better than one?" Imagine if you allow many other minds to combine with yours, the possibilities of possibilities. Then, just imagine millions of minds, like on the Internet. Now you can start to consider the vastness of knowledge if you had firsthand experience of every living thing that has ever lived throughout time combined.

I want you to just sit there and close your eyes and imagine this. You are a gazelle. You are running across a field. You have your offspring running next to you. You are afraid because you are being chased by lions. You do not go full force, fast as you can, because your offspring could not keep up. But your little child is running as fast as it can to keep up with the herd that is slowly getting farther ahead. Your heart is pumping, you can feel it pumping fast and hard, your breath is almost painful, it is coming so fast and deep. You can feel the earth beneath your feet giving just a little with each step, your hoping not to hit a hole or rut that would trip you up. You are zigzagging a bit to make it harder for the lions but you cannot zigzag much because of your offspring. Then you suddenly notice that your offspring is not right by your side. You look over slightly to spot it, but it is not in sight. You realize that you are alone and you stop. You look back to see the lions stopped. That is when you see the neck of your child in the mouth of a big lion. You can see clearly enough the huge canine tooth of the lion penetrating through the flesh of your child's neck. There is blood around the tooth. You see another lion with teeth gripping the hind leg of your child and pulling hard opposite the other lion at the neck. You see yet another cat biting at the abdomen of your child and ripping it open, internal organs protruding from the wound. You can see the wide, frightened eyes of your child staring at you in terror. It is being eaten while it is still conscious and aware of what is happening. You see this but you are completely helpless to do anything about it because you know, without doubt, that if you tried to do anything you would only become a meal also. You stare for just a moment, but you know you have to move on and join the herd or be left behind on your own, which is a death sentence. There is nothing you can do. You have to abandon your child and leave, but that vision that you just witnessed is now seared into your memory for life, for eternity. The last thing you remember of your child is those wide open, frightened, pleading eyes staring at you, knowing that it was being eaten alive.

This is not a rare occurrence, this scenario plays out at least once a day, somewhere in the world every day. True life is far more horrifying than any of the very worse horror movies. Human imagination cannot possibly fathom the true horror that occurs in real life on a continuous daily basis. This was a gazelle, just one gazelle, this is not all the other animals that have a very similar experience daily. Just think of all the drama going on in the sea constantly. And this does not even include the horrors of humans on a daily basis. This is what God is aware of moment to moment, because God is that gazelle, and the offspring, and the lions, all at once and feels all of the senses of each animal at the same time. God does not get an edited version. God gets the full impact: sights, sounds, smells, tastes, and tactile feelings of each animal all at once.

God understands the horror of the gazelle, watching their offspring getting consumed in front of them, completely helpless to do anything about it. God feels the offspring's terror of being eaten alive and the pain involved. God understands and feels the pleasure of the lion's triumphant kill and satisfying full meal. God is aware and conscious of all of these things all at the same time. God is also aware and conscious of all the other scenarios like this all over the world, all at the same time. Humans cannot possibly understand or appreciate or even comprehend having all that information coming in at once, but that is because they are human, and not God. To be human is to be only one piece of God in one individual body experiencing only one life at a time, but that one piece of God is only one part of the whole that experiences everything at once.

Now to mention the *rest of the universe* would completely blow your mind. But everything everywhere is connected. All other worlds and all other galaxies are all connected because the fabric that was just one thing at the beginning, at the big bang, is still just one thing. It is just a lot bigger.

But alas, take heart, humans are not meant to know and comprehend everything. Not while they are in an individual vessel.

I was soon to understand fully what was meant by that comment.

THE EVENT

I was helping Sebastian with a woodworking project and Jos was over by the steps talking with Lorne when Rohm came bursting through the door of the Church of Understanding. He covered the distance across the entire building almost instantly but not without everyone noticing his ghostly white color. Beads of cold sweat dotted his forehead. He quickly said something to Jos, then in a flurry, he and Jos closely followed by Lorne hurried out of the building. Naturally, I fell in behind them and followed along with a few others whose curiosity overwhelmed them, everyone in complete silence. Once out of the building, Rohm made a direct line to the restaurant. Just as we arrived in the parking lot, two police vehicles swiftly pulled in, lights flashing, having turned their sirens off already. Before we could reach the door where Sochin, Curtis, Ahmed, and Adam were standing, the police officials refused our insistence to enter. The look on the four at the door mirrored that which was on Rohm's face.

Shortly, Connie and Rudy came gradually out of the restaurant with the same ghostly color and defeated expression. The face of Rudy was crushed into a grimace, and there were obvious tear streaks running down both sides of Connie's face, with fresh tears dripping from her jaw. It was undeniable that there was some tragedy unfolding that I was yet aware of, then, in my mind I asked, "Where is Mariam?"

I heard my own voice say, "Where is Mariam?" With that, Connie instantly clasped her face, with tears streaming down. Rudy was unable to stop his reaction either; it was the same as Connie's. Rohm in that moment gasped a huge breath, looked up and slowly let it out, attempting to maintain control. Jos met my eyes and locked, nothing was said, it did not need to be. I instinctively knew that I was going to dread the moment I heard confirmation of what I thought. I refused to

174

believe what I suspected or even to further investigate out of denial. I just stood there in silence.

Moments later a police official stepped out of the restaurant doors and first looked at Connie. Seeing her despondence, he turned to Rudy. He asked him if he would be willing to answer some questions.

Jos stood there, not looking stunned, or even surprised, to my dismay. He seemed like he was just waiting for time to pass, knowing that everything had its own timeline and had its own progression. Two of the officials without uniforms emerged from the restaurant. They talked for a minute then one of them approached Jos. Jos accompanied the official into the restaurant. Earlier, Billy and Natashia had joined the gang, along with more of the neighborhood and patrons of the restaurant. Natashia had been comforting Connie, and Billy had tried to get Rudy, Curtis, Ahmed, Adam, and Rohm to speak. I was standing by Connie, when Billy looked at me and all I could give him was a shrug and a look of bewilderment.

Just before Jos reemerged from the restaurant door, two men walked in with a gurney with sheets folded on top. I remember noticing the red stitching on the end of the sheets. I do not know why, but I even remembered the way the sheets were neatly folded, no particular fashion, I just noticed the way they looked. When Jos came out, he slowly walked to the gang standing there, not looking away, but just looking at everyone without a real expression. Just as we were grouping together, I noticed at a distance behind him, just now coming from the door, Jordan being escorted by one of the police officials with his hands behind his back. He was staring at his unsteady footsteps and nowhere else. It appeared to be the best he could manage in his state, which looked highly intoxicated. Jos had still not said a word.

I remember feeling a great cautious relief, that all this was about Jordan and some crazy damage he caused in the building from some drunken outburst. Mariam may still be in there explaining what had happened and what she did to get him to stop. I had just started to let myself think that there was a great worry about nothing when I suddenly remembered the gurney going in. Just as these thoughts were going around in my head, the gurney reemerged from the building. This time the sheets were not neatly folded on top. They now draped what could only be the deceased body of the only one that was not standing here with us. I lost it. My legs released all strength and I was down on my knees without knowing it.

Jos still had not spoken, continuing to get us all to gather closer when I heard Reese say lowly, but loud enough for us to hear, "I will fucking kill him." That brought an immediate glare of disapproval and distain from Jos directly at Reese. I do not think Reese even noticed Jos' glare continuing to remark, "I mean it, I will fuckin' kill him. If what I am thinking is right, I will come unglued." Just then he looked at Jos. You could tell that it struck Reese, the look he was getting. But his ire was up and working overtime.

"What? Why are you looking at me like that?" Reese responded. "This is bullshit. If what I think happened actually did happen, I am going to go nuts."

In an unusually stern but even and quiet voice, all Jos said was ...

Have great calm and great respect. The vessel for my lovely Mariam is passing by us now.

Honestly, I cannot recall clearly what happened after that moment. I know that Jos was able to calm Reese, which in itself was an incredible feat. I know he was able to get us away from the crowd where it was just the original gang that came to the restaurant just a couple of years ago. I knew that the rest of our extended family that had developed within the neighborhood gave us the respect of privacy, even though they now felt part of the whole gang. They had great understanding now and allowed Jos to talk to us. A clear sign that they, too, had been listening to the teachings of Jos and were learning. I also somehow recollect all of the emotions that I was experiencing all at once. Jos had given us time to process the moment. Clearly, we were all having similar and different emotions at that time. Some of us were having primary emotions of grief, some it was rage, and some it was just pure confusion, and for some the primary emotion was just utter emptiness. But, overall, the feeling of sadness was the thickest atmosphere around us. The only question I can remember was; why?

Over the next few days, as Jos had waited for the inevitable future to present itself over time, I heard and began to know the whole story. Mariam had expressed her concerns about Jordan to Jordan. She presented it to him in the manner of interest in his wellbeing. Jordan had taken this interest as something more than just concern over his wellbeing. He had read far more into her warmth than what was really there. That was the yin and yang with Mariam; her warmth and concern were so genuine that they could easily be mistaken for a personal affection. That was the beauty of Mariam.

At some point in the morning of the incident, Jordan had come to the restaurant in an intoxicated state, but for what reason was still not completely clear. He found Mariam there unusually alone. The sequence of events that followed were not known. I do not think even Jordan remembered exactly what had transpired during those moments. What is known is that at some point, Jordan had sexually assaulted Mariam and ended up strangling her. Whether that was intentional or accidental is also not clearly known; again, not even by Jordan. What was said or done to initiate the event will never be known to us. Only the aftermath is known with any certainty.

Connie and Rudy were the first ones to come in after the event and found Mariam deceased and Jordan passed out beside her. Rohm was met by Rudy on the way to the phone and was told to go get Jos, which he did. It was only after all of us arrived back at the restaurant that information started to become known to anyone else other than Connie and Rudy.

The restaurant was closed that day. Everyone, not only our original gang, but everyone in the area had to process the episode and the aftermath. History cannot be changed, Jos had made that abundantly clear, only the present could be changed. There were many things the present presented us with, not the least of which was the emotional impact that struck everyone insidiously. Then there were the notifications that had to be made to Mariam's family. And lastly, and most imperatively, was the coming to terms with the present and how drastically it had changed. Every moment to moment changes the future and this event had radically changed everyone's future. Her murder had affected many things for countless people, for all eternity. Unfortunately for Jos, he was the one everyone looked to as the center point of understanding.

When people came to a point where they could hear what Jos had to say, he said ...

The Irony of a Good Relationship

The problem, and the pleasure, of a good relationship, is that you become sad when it is over. Everything comes to an end at some time. The more you enjoyed the relationship the sadder you are when it ends. The reason it is so painful to lose Mariam is because it was so glorious to have her with us. She could quickly get into your heart with feelings of joy.

The dark irony is that most people do not appreciate how much they enjoy something until it ends. The important thing to remember is that the pain is only intense because the experience was so valuable. The pain is directly related to the pleasure and value of the time with her.

Mariam taught us to enjoy life, embrace passion, reach for love, just never forget that all pleasure is fleeting and never take it for granted. Build relationships everywhere you can, with as many as you can, but do so with the knowledge that it will come to an end. Then treasure every moment.

Jos looked at everyone straight into their eyes ...

Ask all those who have paid the price with tears if the precious gift was worth the pain, and I am sure the overwhelming response will be ... yes.

Within the whole circle that had surrounded Mariam, there was an overwhelming feeling of anger toward Jordan. At the same time, there was an abundant confusion and essentially disbelief that Jordan could do such a thing with everyone's knowledge of him. The overpowering question was, "How could Jordan do something like this?" Had he fooled everyone into thinking he was nicer than he really was? Was he far more evil than anyone ever expected? Did he intentionally come across as a docile and meek person just to get into a position to take advantage of people? How could everybody be so wrong about a person?

"Did you ever expect something like this from Jordan?" Curtis asked Jos. The tone in his voice was half curious and half accusing. Jos looked at him for a moment, getting a feel for the real underlying question. Did he know that something like this would happen?

If you are asking, did I know that Jordan was going to harm someone, the answer is no. If you are really asking if I thought Jordan was capable of harm, or did I expect he would cause someone harm, the answer is that I do not make any expectations of any human being. I trust all human beings until they give me a reason not to.

Did I think Jordan was *capable* of doing something like this? Yes, but then I know anyone is capable of doing something like this if they have the physical ability to. Did I think that Jordan was *likely* to do something like this? The answer is no. Understand that the future cannot be predicted with any certainty. If I thought that Jordan was likely to do this, then obviously I would have tried to prevent it. I do not think even Jordan thought he was capable or likely to do something like this. I think if you were to ask Jordan right now why he did this I bet he would not be able to give an answer. I am sure he is remorseful.

Am I surprised that he did this? I am not surprised by anything people do. I know the human capacity for both good and evil.

I know that most of you are angry with Jordan. To harm Jordan would harm other people, just as harming Mariam has harmed you. And if you really think about the true person Mariam is, she will be the one harmed if you were to harm Jordan. Her body has ended, but Mariam has not; she now is Jordan.

I rest in the comfort of knowing the fate and future of Mariam.

She will forever be in an afterlife that she created while on earth. Again, it is not a place but a time. Unlike so many, I do not just *believe* in her eternity; I *know* of her eternity, for sure and certain, and it is good.

Protection is required, I agree. Punishment is appropriate with that too, I agree. Anger and revenge are not necessary, on that I know. In the fullness of time, Jordan will not only know but will also feel and understand his effect on Mariam and others, first hand. Mariam now knows and understands the effect she had on him and everyone else in her lifetime. Mariam is now the water that is everywhere. Mariam is in a good place, because she created it while she was with us.

The Sermon

A week had moved on without really even knowing it. So many things had taken place in such a short time that I actually had to stop and think about the amount of time involved.

The Church of Understanding was cleared and cleaned and set up for a memorial for Mariam. I was astonished with how many people attended. Her mother and sister had been summoned and were there; her father was no longer living. Her mother's name was Mary, and Liz was her sister. There were many people sitting there quietly waiting for Jos to give a eulogy or to say some kind words or recall fond memories of Mariam. Many more were standing all around and all the way outside. It really never occurred to me how many people we had come to know in just the last couple of years here. What did not surprise me was the affection they all had for Mariam and how many she had touched.

Jos stood alone in front of the mass of people for a long time contemplating the urn on a stand in front of him. Then he looked up engagingly to the people and spoke...

When someone asks me, "When is the kingdom of God coming?" I say, watch as you may you will not see God come. No one will say, "Here God is," or "There God is." For God is within you.

When people ask me, "What must I do to inherit eternal life?" I answer, love your God with all your heart, with all your soul, with all your power and your entire mind and love your neighbor as you love yourself, for they are all one and the same thing. "And who is your neighbor?" they ask. He whom you show mercy and compassion; whether you know them or not. All people. Pleasing to God are the merciful; for they make everything better.

When someone asks if I am a messenger, I simply reply, I am a good friend. A good friend wants to help other friends. I come not to destroy the laws or the prophets but to explain and to fulfill them. For I say onto you, love your enemy. Bless them who curse you. Forgive those that despise and persecute you. Show compassion to those who you despise. For if you love only those that love you; what reward shall you have? Everyone does that naturally.

I was once told by a moneygrubber that he was only doing his job and that he prayed every day and people still despised him. I told him simply, no man can serve two masters. Either you will hate the one and love the other; or you will cling to one and despise the other. You cannot serve God and the greed of humans; your own pocket or the pocket of your employer. I say to you, be not all caught up in your life, or for the food you eat, the things you have, or for your body image or the clothes you wear; do not worry how you look to others. Is not life greater than food; and your body more than the clothing and beauty? Look at the other animals on earth. They do not worry about petty things and they enjoy a good life. They are forever on guard for their life; and yet they still enjoy life. How much more or less are you than they? Can any one of you, by worrying, add a moment to your years?

I have had people come to me who have nothing and ask how they can help. I tell them, you have by what you have said. Come to me, all of you, who try and try hard, and I will help you. For I have come to serve, not to be served. For whomever among you who would be great must be a servant. To be great you must serve everyone you see; you treat everyone as your employer and as your customer.

When I have been asked how to judge other people, I have answered, you have heard it. Judge not, lest you be judged. For you will be judged by the standards you yourself apply. Why are you so quick to point out the faults of your neighbor, but do not recognize your own? You hypocrites; first recognize your own faults, then it will be much easier for you to understand your neighbor's.

Jos paused for a long time, looking at everyone with a warm smile.

So many people have heard of the Sermon on the Mount by Jesus of Nazareth. Unfortunately, rarely does anybody practice those instructions and principles on a daily basis. But all people really do need to *listen to the words* of what Jesus was saying. This was one of the few times that he talked to many people all at once and was clear and direct with what he was saying. In my life, I have really said nothing different than what he said then. Times have not changed so much from then to today, that the truth of what he said has changed.

Mariam and I had talked often, these are some of the things that I told her. Her favorite passage in the Bible was this Sermon on the Mount. She asked me once why I did not tell everyone the same thing. I told her that it has been said many times; what more could I say? She still asked that I reiterate it sometime, for they were important to her. She also wanted people to know me and what I was teaching.

He paused ...

I have done what I was asked.

With that, Jos slowly walked over to a chair next to Mariam's family and sat down. The room was absolutely silent except for some muffled sobbing.

The rest of the morning, people were talking amongst themselves, telling their own personal stories of Mariam. Almost everyone, at one point or another, made their way to her family and gave their condolences and remarked in many fashions the truly special person that they had known. For the most part I listened, occasionally commented or agreed and sparingly shared some of my personal precious moments, but not nearly all of them. What I did notice was how uncharacteristically quiet Jos was through the whole morning. He said a few words to Mariam's mother and sister and then mostly just sat quietly with them as others came up to speak. He sat in their presence the whole morning, listening with a sporadic nod here and there but without comment.

Later that night, after a day of remembrance, the gang, accompanied by Mariam's mother and sister, ended up in the restaurant. Months ago, Adam had come up with an idea of having an open fireplace in the dining room closer to the "romantic" tables. He thought it would give the place some class and elevate the ambiance. Everyone else agreed with him. Jos had some people from the Church of Understanding install it as an instructional opportunity. It had been a great and remarkably inexpensive addition that everyone appreciated. Now it provided an appropriate vocal point. It gave the restaurant, which had been the scene of despair and horror just a week or so ago, a feeling of warmth and a symbolic spirit of Mariam's last place of life. It produced the feeling of Mariam in our presence. There were long periods where we all sat quietly, enjoying that warmth and comforting sensation.

Curtis was staring into the flame and said, more in passing than an actual question, "Is there life after death?" The question may have taken some by surprise, with Mary and Liz sitting there, but it was not startling or even unexpected. Jos looked across the flame at Curtis and said ...

The afterlife is not a place you go to after you die. Is there an afterlife; yes. It is a rather hard concept for humans to comprehend. It is simply hard to understand because there is not anything to compare it to.

Drawing his attention to Mary and Liz, he quickly explained the example he gave of God. Verbalizing the demonstration of a pool of water representing the energy of God throughout the universe. The accumulation of all memories and consciousness of every living thing, past and present.

Jos was quiet for a moment, looking into the fire himself. He was trying to find the words that people could understand. As he spoke, he looked around at all of us...

To understand the afterlife, you first have to understand God.

God is not a stagnate memory, God is past *and* present. You will not experience the afterlife as just a memory but also a constant, current awareness of everything. That is why I said that to harm Jordan would harm Mariam, because Mariam is Jordan now.

You create the afterlife by how you experience other people and how other people experience you. As you go through life you have a direct effect on everybody and everything and it is those effects that you will be totally aware of for eternity. You will be perfectly aware and can feel the past memories of all things and you will be perfectly aware of the effects that you caused from your life. You will go through, and experience, the future and know just how your existence altered and affected that future.

Mariam's effects are beautiful. She is happy.

Again, Jos paused allowing everyone to reflect. I saw him look at Mary and Liz. I could see that he was trying to assess if they were being comforted or confused.

Mary said, "Mariam told me you had an insight and understanding, more than anyone she had ever known. She would tell me some of the things you would talk about. She really loved you and the person that you are." I saw a tear well up in the eyes of Jos. He stared into the fire.

It was getting late. Natashia and Billy reluctantly left to go to their home. They had a bakery that had to start in a few hours. But everyone else just sat there.

As the days went on and everyone was in a sullen mood just going through daily motions like automatons, Jos would talk to each of us individually. The message was about the same for each person; he just knew how to say it to each of us exactly.

A couple months had passed and the trial of Jordan was coming up. Every time the name of Jordan would come up in the company of Reese, he would become livid. If you were near him at the time, nothing need be said, you could feel the heat, the darkness of hate, and the anger. If Reese even tried to say something tolerant of Jordan, you could still hear in the voice the total rage. I do not know if Reese could control it, nor did I think he even wanted to.

Jos was quite aware of it also. You could tell that it really affected Jos, but I am not sure of the reason that it affected him as it did. I do not know if it was a slight sense of guilt that Jos felt because he had introduced Jordan to the gang, or if it was his feelings toward Jordan, or if it was his unease about the way Reese was feeling. When Reese would let it be known how he felt, Jos would look at him with slits for eyelids and steel for pupils. It was not a judging stare, nor was it a comforting gaze. It was as if he was trying to look through Reese's eyes into his brain. Jos was trying to understand.

Jos, if anybody, knew the futility of feeling guilt. I am sure he did not have evil feelings for Jordan; it would not be in the nature that I understood of Jos. I am sure it was his unease about Reese and the amount of anger that was eating at him. Jos had told me often of the destruction that anger and regret had on the internal person of those that did not have control of it. Jos did not want Reese to be eaten away, nor did he want him to one day have regret for his natural feelings now. Jos understood that it was Reese's affection for Mariam that drove his anger. He also knew that it would be that same affection that would haunt Reese in years to come if he allowed his feelings for Jordan to run wild and uncontrolled.

Jos talked to him about anger ...

Anger

Like hate and love, anger is a strange emotion; also like hate and love, anger must be fed or it will die. Most people look at anger, like hate, in that it is a "dark" emotion. Again, like all other emotions, it is neither bad nor good until it is, and how it is, acted on. But anger, like hate, will eat away the inside of a person; that is why it is so dark.

For some people, problems create stress and pile enough stress on top of other stress and to trigger an episode of anger is easy. This can lead to violent and unwanted actions; actions that are irreversible.

Reese looked at Jos sheepishly. An odd look for someone so big and stern. "There are times when I just cannot control it. I mean, it just gets away from me sometimes. It comes on so fast, I'm angry before I know it, and then I do something before I know it. You're right; I wish that I hadn't done it afterward. But like I said, it happens so fast sometimes that it is just like it is out of my control until it is over."

Jos questioned Reese to confirm he was talking about trying to get control of his anger. So, Jos talked to him ...

There are many reasons for anger and for someone getting angry. Most times, it is because they have felt wronged in some way. One of the most powerful is when a loved one is killed; when the loved one was a victim of a crime or, even more commonly in today's world, the innocent casualty of a battle or fight that they were not even part of. Like an innocent victim of a drive-by shooting or a war conflict. They were an innocent person simply in the wrong place at the wrong time.

Allow the anger to move through you, do not feed it. That is the best reaction to the emotion of anger; that is the most positive thing you can make from a very dark emotion. This is the time of testing your resolve. Anger and hate will eat you and ruin your own life with regret.

Reese said, "There are times when the regret eats at me more than the anger did."

Jos agreed with him. He put his understanding hand on Reese's shoulder, gave him a look of acknowledgement and nodded. Jos reiterated to everyone to avoid regrets at all costs. He explained it as a stink that would cling to you for far longer than any other emotion.

Knowing the reason for anger and resulting regrets, Jos explained
...

Ends

People hate endings. But that is a life experience. Going from one thing to another; constantly moving down the timeline into the future.

Do not despair, all endings are only beginnings. Time changes all things, and all things change with time. It is inevitable. I am not saying that any of this will get easier with time. But look at it another way; no beginning can ever happen without an end to something. No nutrient that enters your body can create any new tissue without first destroying the substance that the nutrient came from. Everything is in a constant state of change, that simply means that all things are in a constant state of either beginning or ending.

Everyone always sees death as an end and it is in one sense. But at the same time, if death is an end in one sense, it is also a beginning in another sense. That is the inescapable yin and yang of all things.

The Afterlife

Probably, because of the incident, many people were asking Jos about the hereafter. They wanted to know what it was about and also if things would become just. Some wanted to know if "justice" would prevail?

The first thing you have to come to terms with is the universe. You have to understand the vastness of the universe. You have to understand what is God to understand what is the afterlife.

God is not just about Earth or even the Milky Way galaxy, God is about the entire universe. Any human that thinks that God is just about Earth, then they have no concept of the true nature of God. Once you come to the realization that everything in the entire universe is connected in some way to everything else then you are on your way to understanding God and the afterlife.

Here is something to explore in your own mind. The theory of the "Big Bang" is the moment of the birth of God. It is the moment of creation. It is not the creator; it is creation itself. From that moment, everything was connected and remains that way even with the vast expansion. It was the birth of a living entity.

The human consciousness is a mystery created by matter and energy. God is a consciousness and a mystery created by matter and energy. Life is nothing more than going through a series of experiences and storing them into memory. Life is the instantaneous instant of now.

The afterlife is very much like a continuous dream, except it is not a contrived dream sequence, it is the actual memories of individuals. Your afterlife is all the experiences and the memories of every living thing that has ever been all at the same moment. Everything that has ever happened is in the conscious *memory* of God. You are now fully aware and conscious of your effect on others because you can feel them, because you *are* them. Remember, you are now the water that is in everything. Everything is connected, that means you with all other things.

Only for a short time, a time to experience living, are you separated from other living things. You are trapped in the cup.

Here is the yin and yang of God. When you are in a physical body of mass and matter, you have the ability to control other three-dimensional objects of mass, but you do not have access to the full consciousness of everything. On the other hand, when you have the full consciousness of everything you no longer have the ability to manipulate anything with atomic mass. That is the inevitable consequence and tradeoff.

Suffice to say that you make your own afterlife by how you affect other people in this life. That is your afterlife. Consider this; if you are good to others you will feel and know that from their point of view, conversely if you are not nice to others you will feel and understand that also, from their point of view.

Jos stopped for a minute to let everyone digest what he had just said. It was obvious that the concept was obtainable to everyone, but nevertheless, still very profound and complex to fully understand.

Trying to describe the afterlife is such a difficult thing to do because the concept is so profound and so completely different than what you have been told. You do not go to a heaven or a hell. It is not that simple.

When you separate from your physical body you are energy that really just blends back into the energy of everything else. It is a force that completely incorporates the entire universe.

In the afterlife, you can receive information by energy from all past experiences and all current experiences; you can receive but you cannot transmit. God is a receiver and recorder not a transmitter. God is a singular, continuous consciousness of everything all at once all the time, not the consciousness of many separate people combined into one. Even though the experiences of every individual are being obtained separately, they are happening all at once with God.

Can you prove an afterlife? Can you prove a past life experience? Can you prove a near death experience? No, none of these things can be proved with any certainty. Can you prove a memory? Can you prove a dream? Can you prove a thought? Can you prove a feeling or an emotion? No, none of these things can be proved either. But, I can assure you that they happen, and are real.

You cannot influence the past, but you have a direct influence on the present, during your lifetime, and an indirect influence on all subsequent time in the future. That is why I say the most important thing in the universe is the present.

Not only will you know exactly how it felt to be the other people you touched in life, but you will also be fully aware of the further influence those actions have on all other people living now, and in the future, on into eternity. That is why you are told to love your neighbor as yourself.

Do you understand now that, you reap what you sow? From the Bible: Galatians 6: 7-8. "Do not be deceived, God is not mocked; for whatever a man sows, this he will also reap."

This is what I say to you: *What you do to others, you do to yourself.* Always think of that and you will look differently at what you do.

Now does that not make more sense of how what you do in life relates to your experience in the afterlife? If you think that all things will become just in the afterlife, you are correct. Does that not make more sense as to how all things become just?

Now I have told you how all this works. Look at it any way you care to. You have to make your own decisions and come to your own conclusions. I am not going to try and convince you of any ideology. I know what I know and I am bound to share what I know. This I have done.

I have spent my whole life listening and contemplating and have really never thought about the entire question like I have in the last couple of years. But what I have learned, more than anything, is that the question of God and the afterlife is just not that important. What is important is the lesson that I have learned about life in general, and how I correlate and connect to all other living things. What is important is my relationship with all other people and how I interact with everything as a whole. What is my place, and how does what I do affect everything else? That is what is important. And I know that Jos was pivotal in that understanding.

Occasionally, I would call my parents and discuss with them the things I was learning, and what I was doing. They were as crushed as I was when I told them about Mariam. It was as if they knew her as well as I did. It was strange, but when I would talk to them, that world seemed so far away and in another lifetime. My life was now here.

THE HOUSE

Months after the traumatic events that happened to Mariam and Jordan the gang, and even the residents of the area, refused to allow the neighborhood to slip back into despair. Even though the incident caused great turmoil throughout the lives of so many people, they were determined to keep the momentum of positive progression going.

One day, two of the girls from the neighborhood and Reese approached Jos for some guidance and advice. They had been talking it over and had found a relatively large house. A turn-of-the-century small mansion, just on the border of this relatively low-income neighborhood and the nicer area closer to commerce and tourist attractions.

Because of its location, just inside a poverty-stricken neighborhood, the building was abandoned and left in major disrepair, like so many others. No one in the immediate vicinity could afford the cost to purchase, repair, and maintain the building. It was not worth it to any outside investors to come in and risk any money of their own. So, the grand old building was left to falter and be used by many for sordid criminal activities. At this point, it was not even worth it for the city to destroy it.

Reese and the two girls, I should say young ladies, as they were in their mid to late twenties, had seen this building and had seen the hopeful possibilities that it possessed. Again, with the teachings and examples of Jos, the three of them could see where it would, and could, be a benefit to whoever currently owned the property, the neighborhood, and the city as a whole to obtain the rights to the place and restore it to a former glory.

As usual, Jos was able to obtain the information on the current owner of the property and their requested price. And, as usual, it was more than Jos thought to be fair. Jos always thought about the buying and selling of something as if he were the buyer and the seller. He always tried to come to some agreement with himself as to what he thought something was fairly worth for both sides before he even went to someone else to start a negotiation.

He took many things into account when making his determination. In this case, he looked at the structure and the estimated worth of the property in comparison to the other properties in the vicinity. He then looked at the estimated cost to repair and restore the property to basic function; not to the highest standards that could be bestowed on it, but just what a normal, reasonable restoration would cost. Then he looked at the potential benefit to the area it would produce and the potential benefit it would be to the seller to relinquish the responsibility of the property. This is what Jos brought to the bargaining table. Though he did have interest in the benefit that so many would obtain from the transaction, Jos had no personal vested interest in the outcome, which actually put him in a very beneficial place when negotiating.

With all parties involved coming to an admirable decision, a purchase price was agreed to. It was more than Reese and the two girls had available between them. However, with a little get together with the other businesses that Jos was involved with, it was easily agreed and the needed funds for the purchase and restoration were obtained. In short, everyone in the neighborhood that was able to help suddenly became a part owner in the business and, in essence, had a vested interest to make the business succeed.

The purchase took place immediately and just as immediately, people from the neighborhood came over and started cleaning and clearing the old building. On this particular project, Jos wanted to stay as far back in the shadows as he could to allow everyone the opportunity to express themselves and function as a team. Reese and the two ladies, Crystal and Keisha, were going to be the principle owners and directors of this project. The proposed idea for the old mini mansion was to turn it into a bed and breakfast with Old-World charm and, as Reese pleasingly said, Old-World attention to detail and care. If it was not obvious before, Reese had his opinions of modern so-called professional attention to clientele that he had been exposed to. Just one of the reasons he was so outspoken at the restaurant when it came to taking care of the patrons, he always wanted to see them treated well and that attitude was contagious. I was sure it was one of the reasons that the restaurant did so well so quickly. He was now going to bring that ethic to this endeavor. Reese, in all his fury, was not bossy or outwardly insistent. Reese was one that led by example. He certainly was not immune to voicing his opinion if he thought you were not keeping up with him, but he was in no way condemning or curse about the way he did it. It was just matter-of-fact. His focus was on the patron and nothing else, and that was quite obvious. Because of that, he did not acquire any resentment, he only commanded respect; a respect that was always given freely and genuinely.

A few guys from Toro's gang decided many months ago to develop a small restoration and remodeling company, and had actually been able to do very good work. A result of which was they were obtaining many requests for their work. In fact, the requests were becoming so numerous that they needed more and better equipment. Because their work and their reputation was not going unnoticed, there were a few people willing to supply them with needed equipment and supplies for a small percentage of the business for a limited time.

It was obvious to Jos that the gang was still involved with minor criminal activities but much more as a side line to their now legitimate business. Jos expressed his condemnation of this and pushed his discouragement of the activities, because of the risk it posed to the greater and more admirable legitimate business they had produced. He would explain to them that they could take this adventure safely into their old age and have something to be proud of and could sustain them and their families for years. On the other hand, any illegal activity jeopardized their livelihood, their progress, their families, and even their lives and certainly their longevity. But Jos also recognized that some habits are hard to break and take time to change. He could see the change happening so he knew he just had to bide his time and allow their change to happen their way to their schedule. Much to the surprise of Jos and everyone else, despite the fact that Toro, himself, did not actually take any interest nor want any part of the business, the guys making up the company decided to call the company "Toro Restoration."

Back at the old mini mansion with everyone busy cleaning and organizing, Reese got in touch with the guys from Toro Restoration. They were more than receptive to the idea of becoming a part of the old house, and because of the respect for Reese when he talked to the guys from the gang, they agreed among themselves that they were going to give Reese priority. Not only were they going to give him priority, they wanted to make the old house a demonstration of what they had learned and what they could do. They wanted to show their very best and why they were the best at what they did. It became a pride thing for them. Pride is also a very powerful emotion and one that is prevalent among gangs of any kind. With many gangs, pride is the pinnacle emotion.

When all the cleaning and clearing was finished, it became apparent that the old building was in worse shape than anyone had figured. But again, the potential could be seen. Generally, the potential is only seen by a few enthusiastic individuals, but this was a different case. Everyone that had come by to lend a hand was able to see the potential and was eager to bring it to fruition. I think that was because of what Reese and Crystal and Keisha had decided to name the old bed and breakfast. They decided to name it; the "Mariam House."

I could not be stopped giving every free moment of my time to helping in any way I could. I was at the house every day. Many of the people I saw on a regular basis at the Church of Understanding, I was now seeing over here just as regularly. The one person I did not see as often as I would have expected was Jos. In fact, it was only occasionally that I would see him come by to pitch in on the work but rarely to confer with Reese or the girls. His obvious intention was to allow this project to flourish without him. I think he knew, with the apparent motivation of everyone involved, that this was one time he could step back and see if what he taught us was really going to be put to use. I also think that he was cautious to show his pride at the accomplishments of everyone.

The work that Toro Restoration did was far superior than anyone could ever have imagined. The work was extensive, exacting, exquisitely intricate and plush, and well beyond their apparent experience level. But every phase and procedure was examined and inspected by the men of the Church for accuracy and legality. Every permit and inspector required was obtained. As far as the inspectors were concerned, all were suitably impressed. Toro Restoration proved their value, and with that their pride soared along with their requests. They were at the top of the game of restorations and remodeling, and to prove that all you had to do is walk into the Mariam House. It was the most classic Victorian-style mansion in any part of the city and it was perfection.

As soon as it was ready, the Mariam House opened with six gorgeous and lavish rooms; each with its own bathroom, small but complete. Within a week, reservations were being made and it was fully booked. Along with the included breakfast in the morning, the girls would also have a hardy lunch available for a reasonable but additional price. They also made a home-cooked meal ready at dinner time. Now, the dinner was not what you would find in most restaurants. The dinners were what you would find being served to a large family at the end of a hard day. These were full meals made in one pot or on a giant platter and served "family-style" with everyone passing around the various dishes.

The dining room had been designed and constructed with an elaborately large dining table that could comfortably seat more than sixteen guests at a time. More often than not, however, they would have to seat twice an evening because the top quality of the meal was rapidly reported throughout the area. Soon, the Mariam House had reservations for both rooms and meals at capacity almost every night.

In fact, the dinner meal quickly became the go-to place to show off your favorite girl or boy, or your fine new clothes and trinkets.

The bed and breakfast had become an instant hit and phenomenally successful almost overnight. It was definitely a full-time job for both Crystal and Keisha with preparing meals and cleaning rooms, but their rewards far surpassed anything they could have gotten doing the same work for someone else on an hourly basis. Reese spent his time managing the books and supplies and making sure that the girls only had to concern themselves with the hour to hour operation. It did affect his time at the restaurant, obviously, but he would still spend some time there as well. He truly enjoyed what he did daily.

The mansion was two-stories with a partial basement that contained the washing and drying machines along with ironing utilities. The six bedrooms were on the second floor, while the kitchen and dining room were on the ground floor along with two other smaller bedrooms that shared a bathroom.

Crystal and Keisha shared one of the bedrooms, and Reese took up occupancy in the other. The personal relationship between the girls, and the relationship between them and Reese, was never obvious to me as they were always completely professional and concentrated on their business every time I saw them. Crystal and Keisha were both attractive in their own way and Reese was certainly what most women would consider a hunk, but what the relationship between any of them at this time was a complete mystery to me. Nor was it of any concern.

There was a reasonably sized living room with a small library, books donated by the neighbors, and off to a side a television. There was a fireplace and sitting area centered in the room. On the other end of the room was the more popular "card" table that, on most nights, was the center of various activities and entertainment for the guests.

All in all, the Mariam House was a surprising success, with complete strangers, and out-of-towners, filling the occupancies, which was unexpected by me. But the word had gotten out quickly about the service and the convenience, with the good price and exceptional personal attention offered. It quickly became known as "the best kept secret" of the town. People, without knowing the significance of the name, were pining to get there for the pampering that, rumor had it, was all the rage.

With the introduction of the Mariam House into the neighborhood, I really started to notice the change that had been subtly coming over everything since we started here. Things had been changing all the time but just so slowly that I had really not noticed before. The area had evolved. There was less obvious drug use. The people that were all around had less looks of despair and hopelessness and brighter, more vibrant appearances and actions. The small businesses that were here before and were just barely hanging on were now much more profitable, and even the buildings themselves looked more alive and healthy. Part of that I have to give credit to the Church of Understanding that either used some of the businesses as teaching opportunities, or the neighborhood just became the benefit of some people wanting to practice different ideas.

The Church of Understanding had been another huge factor in the change of the neighborhood and, by extension, the entire area. It had brought many people together that would have ordinarily never have been introduced to each other; different ages, different backgrounds, different beliefs, and just different styles. The people in the neighborhood that wanted to be left alone would have never mingled. The diverse drug and alcohol addicts were not the type to make friends, or be accepted into the general public. This place had drawn them all in for one reason or another, once there they all mixed.

At times in the past, before we came here, all the different factions of people in the neighborhood were violent, keeping other factions off and away from their general areas. The area and the neighborhood were really very fragmented when we first arrived. I had not really paid attention to that in the beginning.

In fact, the garage that I had left my car at originally seemed at the time to be in a completely different town, when in truth, it was only two streets over and a little down the block. When we first got started with the restaurant, I had almost completely forgotten about my car. I went and retrieved it two weeks later, just in time. The man at the garage was surprisingly understanding. I was happy about that, because in my life at that time that car was about my only valued possession. Having left my old life completely behind to start anew.

Since that time, and because of the help that man needed and his type of business, auto repair, he benefited from the guys at the Church of Understanding also. A few of the neighborhood guys asked to use his shop and tools for fair and equal reimbursement of assistance with his work, or upgrades to his business, or just pure protection and peace of mind when he went home for the night. The garage had been the frequent victim of vandalism from the neighborhood kids. After he allowed the guys access to his establishment, the vandalism surprisingly stopped and he was able to actually do some jobs that he was not able to do before, because it just took two people to accomplish. Now he had the readily available help. He even paid some of the boys that knew how, after being taught, to repair carburetors and rebuild engines. Eventually, he developed a partnership with two of the guys who wanted to restore cars. Now they were all talking about expanding and collaborating in a restoration and sales business.

I also noticed that because of the people becoming more familiar with each other, the politics of the area started to change as well. There was more control retained by the citizens of the area as to what was and was not allowed around their homes and businesses. They had developed more of a voice that most all agreed with. With that, they started to accumulate the numbers that make differences in politics. With their voice and the bond that they started to develop with more and more people in the area, they really started to have quite an influence on those that governed and policed them. That was something that most of them had never been accustomed to before in their lives. Most of them never really felt like their single voice had much power. Now they learned that, in most cases, there were many more like them who felt the same way about things and together their voices were much louder. It was just another example of what Jos tried so hard to show people. Jos often told people ...

It is simply amazing what can be accomplished when many people come together and work for a common goal without regard to threat, differences, or *a single great orator's broadcasted opinion.* When one voice talks over many other people and all that can be heard is the one voice, that should be an indication that something is very wrong. It is when one voice is dictating policy without the input of each and every other voice, that more people are going to suffer.

The Mariam House is a shining example of how when people care for something it will do well. If people care for something without regard to how they can specifically benefit personally, then many can benefit and the advantage will spread and will eventually affect everyone. All of the businesses in the area benefitted greatly with the addition of the Mariam House.

Months had gone by when I finally sat down to take stock of everything I had witnessed over the last three years. Yes, three years had gone by with me listening to Jos and sharing my life with the gang. Only now, the gang was so much bigger. Jos was right, time is so fleeting that it is hard to comprehend how important and precious it truly is. It seems like just yesterday I was standing on the side of the road with a broken car.

The Church of Understanding was always in action; a school during the day, not to mention a place where many and a variety of products were produced and a place for the less than fortunate could get a safe and comfortable place at night. Even though it was an old worn-down, dilapidated warehouse and manufacturing building from decades past, calling it a church was very fitting. It stood out proudly in the center of this area and was the focal point of good to everyone around. It was truly, a house of God. I had never seen nor imagined any place that could have such a dramatic impact on so many lives. It was a real church, temple, communion hall, or anything else you might want to call it. Whatever you wanted to call it, the Church of Understanding was exactly that.

I sat sipping a drink with the sun warming my shoulders, thinking about all the different people I had met and all the different ways that I looked at them now. The variety of people I know now and my feelings for them were much bigger than I would have ever believed. I looked at, and felt about, people in a whole new way and it made me feel good about myself and the things around me. I was calmer and angered less easily. I had different priorities than when I first met Jos. I had a much different mindset than I had then. I think I had a truer understanding of the things around me and why people did the things they did. I know I have much more tolerance for others than I use to. I have noticed that my concerns for other people were much deeper also than they use to be. I used to be concerned about people because it was normal and human and I had empathy for others like most people do. But now the concern was different; the concern was deeper, the concern about them was more personal. I noticed, as I took a long sip, that it was even hard for me to completely understand why I felt so differently about people. There were still times when I would get absolutely frustrated with someone, and there were times when I came close to losing my composure. Most of the time, though, I could take a breath, and try to put just a little understanding in, and things really would get better.

Oddly, I found myself in thought about people on this planet that I had not even met. I thought about all the different kinds of people in the world. There are just so many various and distinct people.

Mostly, I thought about Jos. How he saw the world. Then wondered just how he did see the world. For such an apparently simple man, he was very complex. Just another example of the yin and yang that Jos was so quick to bring up. He had a very simple way of looking at the world; even some of the more complex and seemingly intricate problems he looked at very logically and simplistically. Like the chicken and the egg, a question that had confounded scholars throughout history, was a very simple answer for him. You start with simple first then complex; you started with one cell before millions of cells. It was completely simple for him. He looked at the extremely multifaceted humans with the same simplicity. What was utterly confusing to most people about other people, Jos found totally understandable and even natural.

Sitting here I remembered some of the odd things he would talk about just out of the air that would help to make sense of strange *things that just came up occasionally. I remember him talking about such different things as the Paparazzi to the Apocalypse. Just other things he wanted to talk about, such as ...*

What Is Life?

The Bible says that God made man in His own *image*. That is truer than anybody every really thought. The problem people have with this, is they think about the "image" of what humans look like ... on the outside. When it was said that God made man in His own image, the image is the inside, not the outside. When you look inside the human mind, the physical brain, in very small scale to where you can visualize the neurons and neuro-connections, you can see the image that resembles God. Only the image of God is much more enormous. Compare the image of the neuron network of a living brain alongside the image of the universe and you can easily see the similarity; it is not coincidental.

There is an uncanny comparison photograph circulating around of a brain cell by Mark Miller and the universe by the Virgo consortium that demonstrates this particular phenomenon. You can see it on the internet for yourself, and that is what I want you to do; investigate knowledge for yourself. I do not want you to just listen to some person's opinion and take it as fact. Come to your own conclusions.

How can people look at a microscope slide of a human brain and see the structure of a consciousness, but they cannot look up into the universe, see exactly the same thing, and not see the structure of a consciousness?

One day Jos came into the restaurant and put up signs that said the restaurant was going to be closed for a night. He put it up two weeks before, to give everyone ample notice that the restaurant was going to take a needed day off. Everyone was excited and curious at the same time. Jos informed us that it was, as he explained, a needed day off together, nothing more and nothing less. Everyone seemed rejuvenated just at the idea that we were all going to be able to have one night together by ourselves. Everyone always had one or two days a week off to do what they wanted, even though many days we would just end up at the restaurant anyway.

Most of the original gang along with many new gang members, like Lorne, Syria, Saliha, Desha and Lajita, joined us that night. We had the second seating at the Mariam House and after a fine dinner, had the dining area to ourselves. Many of the gang, including Billy and Ahmed and even Adam, could not help but get up and assist Reese and Crystal in cleaning up. Reese and Crystal insisted that it was not necessary, but gave up knowing that they were going to anyway and they were not to be stopped. It just made the atmosphere that much more family and warm.

After we all finished congratulating Reese and the girls on their astonishing accomplishment with the Mariam House, we spent some time reminiscing about Mariam. The mood was soft and nostalgic. More than a few tears moistened the eyes of many at different times. Long periods of reflection would prevail at times. We were all enjoying the relaxation and after a few more sips of wine, conversations would go off in other directions.

There was a particularly long silence after many different topics and everyone started to gaze at Jos. I knew he felt amusement at being the source people would look to for continuing a conversation. With everyone in a reclined and comfortable state, Jos repositioned straight up in the chair, and with his usual contemplating smile said...

Throughout history people have been looking to the stars and seeing God and created stories in relation to celestial events and beliefs that they could relate to and share with others. But they always had to put them in human terms in order to reference and understand the unexplainable.

Like any evolutionary path, the stronger kills off the weaker, and the dominant party survives. The same with religions. When you get to the family of Abraham and his descendants, you see this. Many of the stories are the same as many others in history, but that family tree became the dominant religious belief system that is prevalent in the world today. Mostly because it was recorded and passed along.

It was Muhammad who said, "Verily your deeds will be brought back to you, as if you yourself were the creator of your own punishment" and "God is not merciful to him who is not kind to mankind," and probably most revealing, "Do you love your creator? Love your fellow-beings first."

Jos became very solemn. He looked around slowly and intensely at each one of us. What he was about to say was meant for each one of us individually, as if he was talking to each one alone.

This is the whole reason I have come among you. The whole world has fallen into the abyss of either blindly listening to others that can spin the best tale, or those that educate themselves for the purpose of getting ahead by silently abusing others, being the ones that can tell the tale you want to hear. You have to be ever cautious of the leaders, those that tell the tale, whether it is a business person, a political person, a religious person, or the paid assistant to all of them, a media person.

The whole reason for my existence is simple: it is to shine a light at you to understand that you do not need any other person to tell you what is important or to do your thinking for you. I am here to tell you a simple message: stop worrying about prophets and messiahs and deities and extraterrestrials and miracles and magic and rituals and old archaic customs. Only concern yourself with human beings. Stop all the hate.

Humans have a lot of problems plaguing them today: poverty, addiction, overpopulation, injustice, pollution, crime, health epidemics, and hunger. If people were to put aside their greed and their ability to be unfair to one another just because they can, then all of these issues can be overcome. All of them. If people were to start caring more for one another instead of just themselves amazing things can be accomplished. And if that were to happen, not only would it be better for everyone, it would be better for everything. Even people who think they have it pretty good right now would have it better if everyone had it better too. Remember, it is better to be half way up a large mountain than it is to be on top of a small hill.

Everyone looked around at the others and sort of nodded. They understood what he was saying. They had seen it in practice with this very neighborhood in just the last three years.

Jos sat back in his chair and took a sip of a beverage. Looking up into the air for a moment a smile drew across his face.

What I Am About

That is what I am trying to tell you. Band together with good people and stop listening to the conniving people that know how to get you to do what they want. Think for yourself and stop letting these people get ahead. This world is not fair ... everybody knows that. But it can be a lot fairer if everyone stops feeding the *bad* people. That is what I am about. Stop listening to all the lies that people say about some magical fictitious God just so they can take advantage of you and others in the process with your help. That is not what a real God wants. God wants all people to thrive and prosper because that is what feels good, but they cannot if you have a small few running the show. God wants to enjoy the living experience in all of its different forms.

Stop taking the "easy road" that all these con artists are telling you about. You should do the right thing regardless what *they* want. Do what you know is right no matter how hard it is, because it is the right thing to do, and it is truth and it affects everything.

If something they say sounds goofy, then it is goofy. I do not care how many people believe it. I do not care how long people have believed it. It does not make it right or even logical. Just think about things with all of your intelligence and all of your discretion and all of your skepticism. Do not just listen to others, no matter how much you "like" them. Think for yourself. Make your own decisions. Many people are just trying to get you to do what they want. Do not be deceived.

Then the always inquisitive Curtis asked, "Jos, you're pretty knowledgeable, tell us, how can we be better?"

Jos lit up like he had finally just been asked the question he had been waiting for ...

How Can We Be Better?

That is the question of all questions. That is the question that should be asked before the questions of; where did we come from, what is life about, what is God, is there an afterlife, how should we pray, why is the sky blue, what makes fire and all other questions. The question of all questions: how can we be better?

I said once, if aliens were to come to this planet they would probably ask, "Is this the best you can do?"

Remember what the Buddha said: "All life is suffering." There will be some good moments but eventually you will come back to suffering. Sooner or later you will become sick and you will die. I say this to you: it depends on how you look at whether it is a blessing or a burden. It is your decision to consider your own point of view. Yes; you will get sick and you will die. Life is a series of suffering, but what is important is what you learn during the process. Life is the experience of living. If there are no trials and tribulations, then there is very little learning. Life is the experience of learning; that is living.

For people to become better is almost like rebooting a computer. First, you have to denounce almost everything. That includes the religion of money. You have to denounce greed. Stop idolizing money, stop worshipping money, stop bowing to money. It is a tool, it is only a tool. Look at money that way and you will be much happier. It is a tool to help you, to help your family and to help others. Acquire what you can of it for the more of the tool you have the more help you can provide. But do not hoard it only for yourself. Tools will rust if not used well. Money can be very useful to make a better world for others. It only depends on how it is acquired and how it is used.

Next denounce any religion that has you wasting time on worship, praise, and rituals. If you truly understand God, then you would understand that is not what is required. God is the fabric of everything, well then, worship everything, praise everything, and have a ritual of helping everything. That is what is requested and required. Any religion that you subscribe to should be for the betterment of *all* people. That is the religion of the one true God. That should be the religion that draws you. That religion should not be *observed* weekly but *practiced* moment to moment. Know this: you can be religious and believe in God without having to belong to any established religion. You can practice any religion without having to proclaim that you are one of the gang members. Established religions are institutions with a leader, a hierarchy, rules, regulations, and punishments, and have procurement practices for funding to further their own cause. Unless you are prepared to except all the good *and bad* that the gang states and does then divorce yourself from proclaiming alliance to it. Why do you feel the need to proclaim your association to any particular religious sect, including atheism? I would advocate the religion of independence. You do not have to reveal your personal belief to any other person. It is only required to be accepted by the others.

Understand sex and what it is, without the snicker. Sex is a very important part of life. The creation of life is generally initiated with sex, sometimes accidentally. When you create another life, you become the creator. Do not become a God without some thought. It should never be done lightly and especially not accidentally. Sex is normal and is not going to be denied. Take actions that can have you act with reason and responsibility. Remember that a principle action is to never harm another person. That includes a new life.

Abstain the working for others when you can. The big corporations will fight any attempt at that, but it is what will keep people strong and in the process, a nation strong. Band together to own businesses together. It is the only true way to have economic freedom.

Denounce old customs and old cultures of the past. Yes, it is where you come from. Yes, it is a symbol of your identity. It is also the past. You can live in the past or you can proceed to the future. The past is colorful and nostalgic and enormously informative and entertaining, but for human life to move forward and progress it has to embrace the future. Denounce the prejudices and problems of the past and move into the future with new thoughts, and creating new customs and building a new culture. A culture of reason, understanding, knowledge, respect, and tolerance would be a nice culture to live in for everyone.

Denounce ignorance. Denounce it in yourself. Do not try to denounce it in others, because that only promotes distain and anger. Strive for understanding in all things for yourself.

Denounce hate and anger. Those are the two most stifling emotions to the growth of any healthy entity. Denounce hate you feel in you, and denounce the hate that others express. Do not follow the gang that hates. Do not get sucked in to the hate that others promote. There is too much hate in the world now for various reasons. It affects all living things. You are a living thing, so are the people you love. Humans have to release the hate or it will annihilate them and I mean the whole species.

Most importantly of all, understand that humans are one species, one gang. They must work together or they will harm themselves. Everything affects everything. There are many things that do not recognize any prejudices with humans. Just one of which is the virus. Viruses like Ebola do not care if you are young or old, male or female, the tone of your skin, who you want to sleep with, or what you want to pray to or what you believe. It does not care if you even are religious, what country you are in, whether you are rich or poor, or even good or evil. It does not even care if you are a moneygrubber. Many things do not recognize any human prejudices, they will attack and kill you just the same. Viruses are changing astonishingly quick and with so many people so close together now it is becoming increasingly easy and likely to have something far more dangerous than a nuclear holocaust. Humans are your gang.

Humans must care for everyone in the gang.

Jos stopped. He looked at Curtis with smiling eyes.

That was a very good question.

Jos frequently talked about time. Time was an extremely important subject for him. He kept explaining it was because time was the only constant and it defined the living experience. It defined life, but it did not define God or the afterlife.

Matter belongs in a linear timeline, whereas energy, on the other hand, does not belong to a linear timeline. In that energy, you will find God.

I Know What I Know

I asked Jos, "How do you know the things you tell us? I mean, how do you know them for sure? Every teacher in history had conviction. They knew, and they knew what they knew with such surety that no one was going to steer them different. I understand that you are convinced and have a strong conviction, but my question still stands. How do you know what you know, and how do you know that it is the real truth of things? How can you be so sure you are right? How can you have such conviction? What makes you different from any of the prophets of history?"

With his eyes piercing up just under his eyebrows looking straight at me, Jos said ...

I know what I know. I understand that is hard for you to accept and to know with certainty that I am right about what I know. You do not know what I know or how I know it. In your eyes, I could be crazy.

You will not hear me say, "Trust me. You have to have faith in me. You have to have faith that I am telling you the truth." You will not hear me say that. The only thing I ask is that you listen to what I say with an open mind. The irony of that is it is the same thing that many con-artists say.

Check the things I tell you with the evidence or when there really is no evidence, check the things I tell you with your heart. See if what I say makes sense. Do not just "trust" me. Question what I say. That is what I want you to do with everyone who tells you anything. Question it with either evidence that you can rely on or with your own heart. Like I said before, you know the truth. Does it feel right? When you think about it, does it seem right to you? Do not just trust in what I say. Think about what I say. Sometimes it is hard to comprehend what I am saying. It is not easy to explain in *words* what it is that I know. I know that.

Those that have had past life experiences have a terribly difficult time trying to get other people to understand that they know of the past life. They have a hard time telling other people what they know without having the other people think they are crazy or making something up. People that do not believe in past life experiences will never be convinced. But those that have had and remember past life experiences know what they know. It is the same with people who have had near death experiences. They know what they know, but it is all but impossible to convince another.

When I say that the energy of God, or whatever label you put on it, the energy that permeates throughout the universe, is in you and you are part of it, that is really a simplistic way to put it. It makes it sound like it is a separate part in you and it goes back to God afterword. It is not separate. It is all one fabric all of the time. Your body has some of it in order to relay information about living.

While you are in your body, you have essentially no knowledge of the entire fabric, but you are relaying information all the time. That is why some people have knowledge of past life experiences. They are not the other person in a new body. They are the same energy and they just have some remnants of previous memory, some residual memory of life before. It is all the same fabric or energy, they have just retained some leftovers that they should not have. You should not have knowledge of the entire energy. If you did, you would live entirely differently and lose the reason of living a new life.

I am supposed to share my knowledge, like everyone else. So, I tell you the best I can, what I can, in a way that you can understand it. I know my true beginning. I know and remember where I came from. That is why I can only just say; I know what I know.

With that I understood. When I think about it and look at the science and look at the history and look at the belief that is in the heart, I understand what he was trying to say. I understand the truth about what is important and what is not. He made things clear; all the things I have heard and all the things that I have seen and all of the things that I have felt and believed. He made me feel more secure with what I knew and what feels right. The things that he knew, he tried to teach without trying to convince you to see things his way. He just had a way to make me open my eyes without someone else's point of view, but from my own point of view; my own perspective. He let me have my own understanding of everything around me. He did not tell me something that I did not already know, he just made me see it more clearly and with a better understanding. Now I knew that he did know, what he knew.

In the last three years, I had seen an entire neighborhood...no... more than that, an entire area transformed. It was all done by allowing the people that lived in the area to own their own businesses and at the same time own their own lives. They worked for themselves and were responsible to themselves. They were not restricted by someone else's clock, rules, or opinions.

That was where Jos was trying to get this neighborhood back to considering. He wanted it to become more self-sustaining and self-supporting. In the last three years, I watched a real miracle happen right before my eyes. People of the modern age regained the peace and prosperity of self-worth, not dictated by other people for their own desires. I had seen people become free.

Of all the miracles that I have heard of, that was the one true miracle that I saw. The miracle that came from many people working together. That is how true miracles are performed. That is how God works in mysterious ways; through living people. A hope realized is a true miracle.

There were many times when I questioned if Jos was a religious person. I knew he talked of God but more in a scientific way than a spiritual way. But he talked of so many things; he talked of very worldly things and discussed many different subjects. He did talk of religion but not in any way I had ever heard any other religious person talk. He also talked about human behavior and human nature, and the world itself, and time. He talked of all things. When he would talk about them, it made them all seem very important. Like everything was connected; all the different subjects related to the other.

God the Creator

God does not intervene. God is not a creator. Human beings are the creator. All other living things are also the creator. They are what make things happen. *They* are what intervenes with life. They are the part of God that creates and intervenes. So, when I say that God does not intervene or create, I am correct. When I say that God works through human beings and other living things, I am correct. God did not create the universe, because God did not create itself; God is the creation. God is a living thing made up of many, many things, just like every other living thing.

Current established religions try to make you think that there is a one, all powerful God that makes decisions and intervenes for "right" and "wrong" to make things just. That is just a great way to exert control over other people, well disguised as not coming from anything else but one religious prophet that "talked" to the God. They, not God, now become the all-powerful. They, not God, now become the creators, and the interveners. So, if you are a living thing then you are the creator for, and intervener of, the entity of God.

Natashia looked at Jos with inquisitive eyes. She was studying him for a moment. Her head cocked to a side. "Who are you?" she finally blurted out. "I mean, really, who are you? How do you know all the things you know? Who are you?"

Who do you think I am?

Natashia was silent, just looking at Jos. Everyone was quiet. Then, suddenly, Rohm spoke up, "I think you are a new age prophet." Then Ahmed agreed, "Yes, a new prophet." Then it was deathly quiet again. Rudy spoke, almost in a whisper, "I think you are the Messiah; or maybe, the second coming." Now the whole room was so quiet as to be deafening. I'd never heard such a deep declaration and the possibility this might be true frightened me.

Jos smiled. He looked down for just a moment, slightly shaking his head, then back up.

After everything I have done, after everything I have told you, after everything I have tried to do and teach, this is the answer to that question?

Jos bowed his head and shook it remorsefully, then whispered to himself ...

Mercy onto the weary; what do I have to say?

He looked up and stared at each one of us with a piercing stare ...

All of my time with you I have tried to tell you that no one person is more important than another. That has been my message to you the whole time I have been with you. You should not look at any other person as more special than you. You should not recognize people as celebrities. You should never look at another individual as someone more important than you; especially in the eyes of God. That includes Moses, Buddha, Jesus, or Muhammad. They were all just "sons" of God.

They were all just the same part of God that you are. Each one of them had no more and no less energy of God than you do. Each one of them had the same love of God you have. We are all just children, just part of God. No person, or any other animal, has more of God than any other living thing. Every living thing is a "child," or sensor, of God. Every living thing is part of the same source. It is all the same fabric with many different threads going in all different directions, but all still the same fabric.

No person on this planet is any more special than you are. You can give all the praise you want to others. You can make anyone you want into a celebrity. You can idolize any person you want to. But you should not do that. That has been going on for far too long. In the mind of God, there is no one that is more important or more special or more different. Each and every person gives God the same amount of information; the same amount of life experience. Therefore, each and every living thing contributes the same amount.

I am not special. I am not a prophet. I am not a Messiah. I am not the great messenger. What I have told you was the truth; the truth that you already knew; the message that has been told to you and everyone else since the beginning, since people could communicate with others. Just like all the religions say; a truth that is imprinted on your heart. A message of truth that you do not really even need to be told; you know what is right and what is wrong. You can feel it. It is within you. I am not special in that regard. I am no different than you.

I am just *another son.*

I Have Done What I Have Come to Do

I have not come to denounce the good of religion but to enhance it. I have only come to enlighten. There are three time zones that are relevant to me. The time before I existed, the time I exist, and the time after my existence. I cannot change the past, which is history; I can and should learn from it, but I cannot change it. The time that I exist is the only time that I have any control over and at any given time it is ever so brief. The time after my existence I have no control over, but I have an enormous influence on. So, the most critical time for me is *now*, and that *now* is instantaneous. It is so fleeting, the moment, the now. We do not live day to day but moment to moment. That is why I say that the most important thing is the present.

I have done what I have come to do. I can do no more. Now, all I can do is show examples of what I have said; "practice what I have preached" so to speak. Whatever happens to me from here on is for time only to say. My time, my vessel, like everyone else's, is limited. All I can do is the same that anyone can do and that is sharing what I know. When it is time to blend back into full consciousness, it will be good. As all of you will know. Understand that what you leave behind will be felt by all, and that you will know what you are.

Natashia was concerned. "Some of the things you have said, some of the things that you tell people to do. There are people out there that are not happy with what you say." Her eyes were pleading with Jos. "Do you not see there are people out there that will kill you for what you tell people to do? There are religious extremists around here that believe strongly in their religion. There are people in this neighborhood that think you try to undermine what they do. It could be some pusher that thinks you hurt their business, or worse, think you try to get them arrested. It could be some political person that thinks you get people against them. What you say is good, I understand what you are telling people to do. But there are some people that, if they hear what you say, will kill you. I mean, really kill you." Her head was down now and she was slowly shaking it, almost in tears. "I mean, you are not really making friends with some people with power. There are really mean people around here."

I know what you are saying. It does not matter now. I have told you and the others what I know and what is important. Whatever happens to me now or in the future is of no importance. Anybody can stop me, but they cannot stop what I have already done. They can kill me, but they cannot change the past.

This brief time on earth is not that important to me. Jesus was only on earth for thirty-three years, and he only got to teach for three of those years, and look how much was influenced. That is why I said the most precious thing in the universe is knowledge and sharing that knowledge to whomever you can is the meaning of life. It is your responsibility to share it with whoever you can, whenever you can, for as long as you can. I do not mean your beliefs, I mean your experience and knowledge of how to make the world and living easier for everyone. That is what I have been doing to the best of my ability.

When my end comes, I will say, "This is the end. I go now to live with my life." I will have to live with the deeds that I have done and the influences that I have created. My past cannot be erased, whether I end tonight or whether I live another thirty years, my past cannot be erased or changed. I will have to live with my life for the rest of eternity, and my influences will continue on with the linear passage of time.

I tell you this: be ever respectful of time. For time...alone...is the sole ruler of kings and gods.

Once you pass on you will understand just how worthless money is, and how priceless doing the right thing will become. A moment in a loving embrace, that will be cherished forever, is worth much more than money.

Remember what is important is the present, and the most precious thing is knowledge, and the sharing of that knowledge with others is the true meaning of life. There is always a yin and yang to everything, and the happiest place is that which has the best balance. And, most importantly, live your lives with the understanding that *what you do to others, you do to yourself.*

It was the morning of a day like any other day that many people from the neighborhood, and the extended gang that I knew, were standing around outside of the Church of Understanding attending a type of yard sale for the things that had been made by the people from the neighborhood.

Out of the mist of the crowd came a person for no apparent reason, without any expression on his face. It was the face of anyone; the face of the one that Jos had spoken of, the face that had no reason to want people to flourish. The one with no past and no future, the one that did not know of the moment; the one that held time captive and choked it. Wherever the person came from, whoever had sent him, would never be known to us. He suddenly brought up a gun, pointed it at Jos and fired. Then instantly, he turned the gun to his own body, fired, and fell himself to the ground.

I watched as the body of Jos collapsed to the ground with no expression of pain or surprise. The vessel of the man I had known and followed for three years melted down to the earth without control. His face was empty. At that moment, I felt everything in me, all my energy flow out and follow him down.

Jos had said that time was a perception. That time would continuously move forward but it could seem to slow or speed depending on your point of view. That was a moment that sped incredibly fast at the same time seemed to stop forever. Nothing could be done. It was over. Was it meant to be? Yes. Why? Because it happened. It was an end. The most important thing in the universe was the present. That is what he had said. This present, this moment, this was the most important thing in my universe at this time. Now that it had happened, it was as if it all happened at once. When I first met Jos, everything he said to me, the moment this stranger emerged from the crowd, the moment Jos hit the ground. Everything, all at once. The past, everything in the past, time, all together and all encompassing. Now I understood what he was talking about. "Heaven is not a place; it is a time." This was Hell.

In that instant, Natashia and Connie were completely inconsolable. Ahmed and Reese were beyond angry. Adam, Billy, Sochin, and Rohm, like everyone else stood in stunned silence, staring and not believing. I dropped down next to Jos. As I looked down at him, watching the pool of blood growing, I could not move. My mind was racing. There was no question that this was final, that there was nothing that could be done. The utter finality was obvious. I took his hand into mine. His body was lifeless, yet I was not terribly grief-stricken at that moment.

Jos had known that this was coming. Like he said, "You do not have to be a prophet to know the future." The end is inevitable. All things end. Yet, somehow, probably because I knew Jos and had listened to him and had understood him, I knew that this was not the end of him.

I felt quietly comforted and calm. This was a decent man. This soul will have an exceptional afterlife. This man had built lasting memories and only had good influences on others. The awareness that he has right now is pleasant. How do I know that? Because, like he said, I could feel it throughout my entire being. I could feel it.

I grieved, but only for myself, for I would not see Jos again. I would not be able to look at him and smile, with him just knowing exactly what the smile was about. I would not hear him laugh again in this three-dimensional world. Most of all, I would no longer have his physical companionship with me nor have available his advice. I did truly like ... no, love ... this man. I learned more from this man than any other person I had met. I grieved for me; not him. When he was in a room you could feel his presence. I would miss that. But that was why I felt strangely calm right then. I still felt him. He had not been gone for long. I knew that was just his lifeless body lying in front of me. I knew that my life had now changed forever. But I still felt strangely calm and comforted knowing that he was here; within me and all about me.

THE REFLECTION

That is my story, the story of a time on this planet when I walked and talked to a simple man for a short time. He didn't say anything new. In fact, he actually said the same thing that has been said over and over again. However, what he said only evolved to modern times.

I personally think that he had an insight that most people just don't have. He seemed to be connected to the very essence of life and consciousness.

People are all just part of the whole. People make up the whole. Without people, the whole is not complete. People, along with all other living things, are made up from the same source. It all makes sense now. Why everything is so similar and yet so different. Everything has the same energy, just in different vessels and that is just for a different experience for each one. That is how a God can learn far more in less time than anything by itself. In the end, everything that is learned by one is known by all.

I could tell you about how Jos performed miracles, I could tell you how Jos healed the sick. I could tell you how he made life better for each and every person that ever met him. I could tell you that every person that met him became more aware about the whole world around them and about themselves also, which they did. I could easily tell you that Jos practiced treating every person he met like he was actually treating himself. I could tell you many things about Jos but sadly none of them would do any justice to just one hour in his presence.

I can tell you that over the course of the last three years Jos showed that anything worthwhile was not easy. His constant motto was: "Nothing is ever easy." Exercising patience, understanding, tolerance, and respect for all other people and all things is not easy, but it is very meaningful, as well as necessary for the health of the species and the planet. Understanding what God is, what God is not, and what God is about is not easy, but that is enlightening and again necessary.

I wish I could tell you that the world will be a better place. I know that it was a better place when Jos was here. I wish I could tell you that people would hear more about Jos and what he had to say and what he was all about. I wish I could tell you that. I will be able to if everybody that met Jos told others what they had learned and felt when they were with him. I wish I could tell you that the majority of people will recognize that the human species is really their major gang and that their loyalty needs to consider that gang first. I wish I could put into words what was put into me. The only thing I know I can tell you is that Jos is within you and all about you. Everything in the universe is one and connected.

I know that changing is the hardest thing anybody can do. I know that all Jos ever tried to do was make a better place and time for everyone he ever met. I know that if you did everything knowing that what you do to others you do to yourself, you would automatically treat everybody better. Some people are very hard to like and are even hard to be civil to, but I know that it gets easier each time you try.

I have thought about this for the last three days as I have grieved. Now, however, I feel obligated to save his memory, to preserve his message, and to pass it along.

Just who am I to tell this man's story? There were so many who heard him, so many who walked with him, and so many who knew him. Anyone could write this story. Many could write this story much better than I. So, why am I the one who thinks I must write his story and tell you what I saw, what I heard and what I felt? What gives me the right to be the messenger, the writer of such a good man? Who am I to pass along the message that this man was telling everyone? To resurrect him in a sense.

Who am I to tell you the things that you might already know, the "Truth" as he put it? I am the exact same as you, no different in essence. The same energy. I am just in my own vessel. I am you and you are me; the same energy from the same source. I am what I am. Who am I? I … Am God.

AFTERWORD

I am the author of this book. I am not the narrator in this book. This is essentially a work of fiction based on extensive readings, study, and conversations I have had. I present this work as fiction because it allows me to write with more dramatic effect and also because I'm permitted to present conclusions in a more engaging way.

To list all of the influences that inspired this book would create a whole other book. The list is endless. The inspirations for the character of Jos are a combination of many, like the prophets of history, Buddha, Moses, Jesus, Muhammad, as well as others like, Albert Einstein, Carl Sagan, Abraham Lincoln, Mahatma Gandhi, Martin Luther King Jr., the list is virtually endless as I cannot possibly remember the names of all those whose words I have listened to and credit. Not the least of which was my own father; my creator.

The conclusions in this book are based on science and real facts and beliefs from many different disciplines. Such as: history, religions, biology, psychology, archeology, physics, quantum mechanics, cosmology and many more. It has been a lifetime of obtaining all knowledge available without prejudicial bias to any. But alas, all combined is from only a single point of view. As if any person were to write this book, it would only be from that particular point of view.

Any particular point of view is always subject to debate and denial. This includes all the different religious texts. Anyone can see whatever they want to see.

But this I know, and this is why I wrote this book. This cannot be debated. *We must all live with all other humans on this one single planet.* That is universal and undeniable.

We can live in harmony or in conflict; the latter will inevitably lead to the destruction of the entire species.

Kurtis Bell

www.ingramcontent.com/pod-product-compliance
Lightning Source LLC
Chambersburg PA
CBHW031244120726
47905CB00002B/709